Published by Heathview Publishing

Paperback ISBN-13: 978-1-7396768-0-3
eBook ISBN-13: 978-1-7396768-1-0

Printed in the United Kingdom

Cover design and layout by www.spiffingcovers.com

THE LAST CORNER SHOP

PETER TANTON

CONTENTS

CHAPTER 1

Eddie Rogers ruminated on the trials and tribulations of his 'new' life – it had certainly been eventful. He was of course blissfully unaware that it was the two-year anniversary today, ironic really as he commenced most mornings with a ritual of reflection and self-indulgence. He surveyed the ramshackle storage shed stacked high with pre-packed bright yellow plastic bags of coal, hessian sacks of potatoes, cardboard boxes of locally grown cabbages and Brussel sprouts still housed on their stalks; there should also have been a stock of fruit but the delivery wasn't due until later that afternoon as he had forgotten to phone the order through in time. Two old battered chest freezers hummed in stereo at the end of the room, noisily doing their job. A flickering strip light precariously hung from the wooden flat roof, it was a real Heath Robinson construction in continual use, even in broad daylight, as the storage shed was windowless.

Eddie blew on his fingers to get some life back into them; it was bitterly cold, with a stifling musky smell that he could actually taste in the back of his throat. He reached into the neatly stacked plastic wall of pre-packed coal bags and retrieved his vodka bottle – always fourth row down, three bags across to reduce the risk of discovery and aid the speed of recovery. It was a half-bottle, freshly opened that morning at half past six when Eddie was tasked by Marilyn with setting up the fruit and veg at the front of their village corner shop. He often thought that most people that knew them would, quite fairly, describe Marilyn to be his long-suffering wife. They had been married for over 25 years, although Eddie would be the first to admit that he didn't like to be pushed on the exact date, just grateful that as he had now turned 50 it made the year of marriage calculation easier as he could still, surprisingly, remember that he had just turned 25 when they got married. Numbers were never Eddie's strongpoint, as he demonstrated by incorrectly charging and wrong changing their patrons on pretty much a daily basis, the new electronic till fulfilling the role of both nemesis and scapegoat. Though surely it was not beyond the wit of this man to subtract 25 years from 1989 – bingo! They got married in 1954, or was it 1964?

Eddie shuddered as he took a large swig of vodka. His convulsion wasn't from the taste of the vodka, which though initially unpleasant on the palate had sadly become a familiar friend, no, it was from the rueful memory of his first day putting out the fruit and veg. He had been using the flatbed barrow, precariously laden with fruit and veg which he had cautiously manoeuvred from the storage shed at the side of the shop, past the front door of their adjoining private accommodation to ten feet or so outside the shop front – where the fruit and veg would sit proudly on display. Before he could unload the cargo, he needed to bring the old empty green plastic milk bottle crates from the shed to rest the boxes of fruit and veg on – after, of course, draping the crates in the green plastic faux grass. The frontage of the shop was about 20-feet wide with a ten-foot slight incline to the pavement and the adjoining lay-by which housed, at a squeeze, four customer vehicles. As Eddie hurried back to the shed to collect the first of the 'display' crates, the brakeless fully laden trolley started on a journey of its own as it descended, slowly at first, down the incline, picking up speed and momentum as it landed like a medieval battering ram at the gates of a castle under siege and straight into the driver side door of the only taxi in the village. Eddie heard the impact and knew instinctively what had happened, he immediately moved at lightning speed… to the coal bags and reached for his bottle, he needed a quick livener before returning to the scene of trolley-induced bedlam. As he emerged from the shed, Marilyn was already trying to pull the trolley embedded in the now mangled driver-side rear door. But the sheer weight of the trolley and her feet sliding in an upturned box of overripe peaches led to her short but stocky frame catapulting forward into Cloth-Eared Jack, the hard-of-hearing owner of the village taxi, who was standing in a state of open-mouthed shock-induced paralysis, taking him out with an unplanned two-footed tackle that Vinnie Jones would have blushed at. His slight Asian frame went somersaulting through the air and he landed on his back as his recently purchased – now airborne – packets of SuperKings and four pasties found a cushioned landing on his chest, along with his thick-lensed black NHS glasses. The pasties were a mid-morning snack for his short corpulent wife. His birth name was Javas but he had been given the nickname *Jack Spratt* soon after appearing before the Heathview public for the first time with his now virtually housebound wife Dot; its use became so commonplace that he now simply introduced himself as 'Jack' to his paying customers. As Eddie surveyed the scene of carnage before him, their neighbour Mr Bowford, a retired military logistics officer, emerged from the shop doorway clutching a pint of milk to his chest. 'Well I'll put to sea in a rowing boat! That's one way of making an introduction to your customers I suppose – thank you for shopping at The Corner Stores! I've left the money by the till,' he had gleefully chirped.

Eddie pushed the vodka bottle back into its sanctuary and proceeded to lift the sack of potatoes that he had used as an excuse to visit the shed for a much needed 'top-up'. It was just after 8 am and all of the local secondary school kids would soon be coming in for their morning supplies, the most common request being a pack of polos and ten Benson and Hedges. He liked to let Marilyn deal with all that; he would fulfil his duty by standing guard on the door, only letting two in and two out – they had learned quickly from the deliberate chaos created when a ferocious unrestricted hoard of youths descended on the shop and tore into its contents like a plague of spotty locusts. The teenage infestation left the confectionery shelves stripped bare but with little money in the till to show for it, but what really amazed Eddie was that they would steal absolutely anything.

Although the shop floor space was tiny, only 20-foot wide and

30 or so feet long, they stocked hundreds of items. It was a vast array of produce, from everyday groceries, confectionery and tobacco to the more obscure items such as shoelaces, video tapes, sewing kits, ladies' tights, pens, envelopes and stationery, pipe cleaners (inherited from the previous owners), dusters, cards for all occasions, and even Happy Shopper aftershave (which they had been reliably informed could also be safely used to clean brass). Most of the basic stock was an 'own brand' called Happy Shopper, produced by the cash and carry group to provide a cheaper option that could allow the smaller shop to compete with the emerging supermarket titans. It was presented in garish orange packaging with a logo of a cartoon face with a beaming smile – Eddie often said that the accompanying orange promotional posters made the shop look like the inside of an Amsterdam brothel.

In those first few naïve days of trading, the spotty locusts had depleted their ancient stock of pipe cleaners and they even took the rubber door stop that was propping the shop door open – if it was a physical object, it was fair game to be taken. They even had to resort to chaining the plastic Sooty (a charitable coin repository for the blind) to the counter after they caught one of the Brown brothers from the village's rough estate trying to put it into his school bag. He had said it was an honest mistake as he was only going to give it to his dad who was blind drunk most nights. Eddie was relieved that hadn't gone missing as they wouldn't have been awarded the privilege of housing another after such carelessness, and he had become quite adept at angling a butter knife into Sooty's greased slot after the shop had shut, to help get his own 'beer' money – he used the Brown lad's own logic about his father to square the guilt.

Eddie made a fairly good doorman for the spotty locusts. On the pro side, he was a couple of inches shy of six foot and had a wiry frame, albeit with a seemingly contradictory emerging 'beer' gut (neatly hidden by a body warmer), and, importantly, he always felt quite courageous with half a bottle of vodka pumping through his veins. On the con side, he wore glasses, a woollen hat to cover his greying and thinning hair, and had a face glowing like the tip of a Swan Vestas match through the constant fuel of alcohol. He had also noted that some of the spotty locusts had started calling him 'Central Line', not to his face but just within earshot for him to hear. He found out this was a nickname coined by one bright spark in reference to the vein destruction in his cheeks and nose through his sustained ingestion of the falling-down water. That evening when he looked closely in the bathroom mirror he had to reluctantly concede his face did look like the tube map of the London Underground. Eddie begrudgingly acknowledged that it was a nice touch of detail to highlight the Central Line, which was identified by the colour red on the tube map, instead of just deferring to the obvious and calling him 'Underground', although recently he had also noticed some of the veins becoming more purple in colour, akin to the shade represented on the Metropolitan Line. Metro-central would be a better name he had thought and chuckled to himself, then felt a pang of anxiety at the changing vein colour and what it represented in terms of declining health. 'Best not think of that,' he had quietly murmured then quickly polished off half a bottle of mouthwash and flicked the bathroom light off.

Eddie laboured with the potatoes as he dragged them from the shed without the assistance of the flatbed trolley battering ram. As he pulled the sack onto the frontage of the shop he saw Mr Bowford emerging from his detached thatched corner cottage on the opposite side of the road, clutching a newspaper. Eddie grimaced, not at the physical strain but the thought of having to engage in conversation with old man Bowford, with his inane repetitive conversation and so-called jokes. Every morning, Brigadier Bowford, as Eddie liked to call him, would pluck a bottle of milk from the crate positioned outside the shop next to the front door and before entering the shop hold it aloft and shout from the doorway, 'A pint of your finest cow juice, Landlord!' Marilyn would always force a laugh, Eddie just smiled as he imagined obliterating the bottle of cow juice on the back of Brigadier Bowford's head, saying, 'Have this pint on me, compliments of the house.' Mr Bowford would then enter the shop and invariably look up at the shelf behind the confectionery counter at the postage stamps and say, 'How much are your stamps now?'

'It's 19p for a first-class stamp Mr Bowford, the same as yesterday.'

'Did you know the post office had to recall the last commemorative issue of postage stamps? It was a commemorative series on estate agents. Trouble is people didn't know which side to spit on.' The same joke was recycled every few days with different professions inserted. Even Marilyn couldn't go through the motions of raising a smile 'Do you want any stamps or not Mr Bowford?'

'No, not today thank you, just the cow juice for Mrs Bowford's cornflakes. Did you know the second-class postage stamp was introduced in 1968? Do you know how I remember that? It was the day after my 60th birthday or was it the day before? Anyway, I'm 80 years young you know.'

Marilyn would chirpily respond, 'Really, you are looking well for your age. That's 25p for the milk please Mr Bowford. Anything else we can do for you?'

Eddie, on the other hand, would always, without exception, say, 'Yes, I know, you are just short of five years over your life expectancy, and counting – that's 25p.'

On the good days, old man Bowford would immediately retreat back across the road with Mrs Bowford's cornflake cow juice, but on other occasions he would stay for a 'nice' chat, regaling Eddie with tales of his army days. Of course, this was always at the same time that the plague of spotty locusts was descending, and they seemed remarkably well equipped to ignore his 'in my day…' rebukes at their boorish behaviour. Eddie envied them.

Today, Mr Bowford made a beeline to Eddie, waving the paper frantically with a beaming smile on his face.

'Have you seen this?' Eddie saw it was the local *Evening Gazette*, presumably last night's edition.

'They are building a new Salter's superstore in the village, not quarter of a mile from here. All approved by the town planners apparently. Nothing like a bit of healthy competition eh Edward?' He grinned, thrusting the paper into Eddie's hand. Two thoughts went through Eddie's head as he read the article, the first was his usual reaction of impacting a bottle of 'cow juice' against Brigadier Bowford's paper-thin skull at high velocity, the second and more appealing was to return promptly to the shed and 'rearrange' the coal bags. The recession was slowly draining the life blood from most small retail businesses as their customers fought to make ends meet; the only part of the economy that seemed to be flourishing were the supermarket giants with their cut-price offers and heavily marketed own brands. They were also breeding a new type of devil child, the superstore with everything under one roof – food, clothes, electrical items, even those new-fangled CDs. The supermarket monster's tentacles were reaching ever further, constricting round the throat of the small local independent retailer. Eddie knew that they were struggling as it was, he didn't know the actual extent of their plight (nor did he want to know) as Marilyn dealt with that side of the business – but he had heard her quietly sighing in the evenings when she was doing the books and trying to work out which suppliers took priority. Until now, Eddie had always felt that they would be OK, that it takes time to settle into a new business, but this news made him feel uneasy and a tsunami of anxiety washed over him. He could feel the shed remedy urgently calling.

'Thanks for that Mr Bowford, do you actually want anything?' Eddie offered the paper back.

'Oh please, you keep it and show your good lady wife, we've finished with it. We normally only use it to put on the wet kitchen floor when Mrs Bowford has washed it on a Thursday morning, just in case I forget to take my shoes off and traipse in unpleasantness. Ah, yes can you take for a pint of cow juice landlord… and how much are your stamps?'

CHAPTER 2

Heathview was a large village situated in Essex, boasting an estimated population of around 8,000, which demonstrated continued growth on the last published census eight years ago in 1981. Heathview's hamlet status was a distant memory as its Parish Council members had led a determined and relentless campaign to bring business, jobs and affluence to the once rustic village, and the accommodation and infrastructure to support it. The main employer, the re-named Heathview Manufacturing, had been wooed to the village in the 1960s from its city base with preferential land deals for its factory and warehousing. It was a well-respected joinery manufacturer that relocated snuggly on the outskirts of the 'old' village, which due to the residential expansion soon became the centre of the 'new' village. Heathview was situated 50 miles north of London and provided the promise of work and rural life to those living in the polluted and crime-ridden streets of London. The Parish Council ensured that planning permission was granted where developers could provide affordable housing and suitable infrastructure for prospective employees. The new estates soon began to emerge, but in startling haphazard fashion and with seemingly no overall thought or reference to an end vision.

The regional research and marketing report that Jerry Bailey Johnson – Salter's Supermarkets PLC Head of UK Business Development – had commissioned was unconcerned with the aesthetics of the village, it was purely driven by the statistical data of population and economic growth potential, and, importantly, their market competitors. Heathview had been highlighted as a gold hotspot on the regional report, which meant it was a prime location, with the nearest superstore over ten miles away, only one small central independent mini market and two corner shops situated at either end of the village. But it had remained virgin territory for the rapidly expanding supermarket chains as the Parish Council door had been firmly closed on approving any applications for consideration by the town planners – that was until Jerry Bailey Johnson had wedged her size nines firmly in the closing door.

*

Marilyn was in the kitchen adjoining the shop and could hear a commotion. It sounded like Mr Bowford. Eddie should be able to deal with him by now she reasoned, although he's bound to have asked about the stamps again and she knew how aggravating that could be to the most tolerant of people – and Eddie most certainly didn't fall into that category where shop work was concerned.

Eddie had never aspired to running his own business, certainly not in the village where they had lived for the past 25 years. He had always been a heavy goods vehicle driver since leaving the army after his national service, where he had earned his licence, but that was no longer an option after he had been 'let go' by the Grimwood Brothers Haulage Company just over two years ago. The new transport manager, Ian Edwards, had victimised him from the start; in fact, Eddie was surprised that he had lasted a full six months under the Teutonic-like regime of Edwards who took a very dim view of heavy goods vehicle drivers who liked the odd fermented beverage before climbing into the cab. On those moments of early morning reflection, Eddie did now reluctantly concede that perhaps he hadn't helped himself, but surely giving him the brewery run was a deliberate act of entrapment by Edwards, who by his own admission was a plain-speaking Yorkshireman who liked to manage with an iron fist in an iron glove. The drivers felt the winds of change when they returned to work after the first weekend of his appointment to find that all their vehicles had been fitted with tachographs, to track their activity and driving hours. Edwards had gruffly announced while staring at Eddie, that it was his duty to both the company and other road users to monitor their activities, and anyone who didn't like it could leave now as this was merely the start of his efficiency transformation. It wasn't long before Grimwood Brothers Haulage made Eddie an offer he couldn't refuse after he was found asleep in the cab of his lorry after imbibing some free samples provided to him during the brewery run. He had been rumbled by Edwards accompanied by his brother-in-law, an off-duty police officer, who just happened to be passing the lay-by not five miles from the brewery that Eddie had indiscreetly parked in to sample the hop-based gifts. They paid him three months money and got him to sign a confidentiality agreement – and reluctantly agreed to provide him with a less than glowing reference. With a potential disciplinary looming over him, Eddie had decided that discretion was the better part of valour and decided to take the deal on offer. Marilyn hadn't been happy at all – in fact she hadn't been happy for a long time.

Marilyn knew that she would have to get out there and help when the plague of spotty locusts, as Eddie called them, started to descend on the shop in half an hour or so for their 'Mum's or Dad's fags' and daily ingestion of their diabetes-inducing sugar fix (be it in solid, fizzy liquid form, or more commonly both). She had just taken a phone call from Granny Smith, an elderly housebound customer who always rung her order through before her home help arrived. She prided herself on still being independent and a lifelong early riser.

'Hello dear, it's me. How are you all today, dear?'

'Hello Granny Smith, we're all fine thanks. How are you?'

'I'm wonderful dear, sitting with my pot of tea and my little Elvis at my feet.'

'I hope Elvis is keeping out of trouble! What can we get you today, Granny Smith?'

Granny Smith always laughed at that, which was why Marilyn always said it. Elvis was a 15-year-old cocker spaniel, cataracts in both eyes and, like his owner, virtually housebound too. He could still just about lift himself up to go out of the bungalow and into the garden to perform his 'ablutions' as Granny Smith so quaintly called it. But occasionally his 'ablutions' were performed on the kitchen floor or lounge carpet, much to the ire of Shirley, Granny Smith's home help.

'Can I have two bags of coal dear, I'm running low and it feels so cold out, and could I have one of your delicious pasties, a couple of nice oranges and a bar of fruit and nut… you know the size dear. Thank you.'

'No problem, Granny Smith. Now, have you got enough food for Elvis? I don't remember us delivering any for a while. I was thinking about that last night when I was doing our cash and carry order.'

'Oh thank you dear for reminding me, can you bring him four tins? I had to give him a bacon sandwich with ketchup last night, and I only had brown bread!'

Marilyn briefly wondered how Elvis's 'ablutions' had worked out after last night's supper – unfortunately Granny Smith's eyesight, like Elvis's, wasn't what it used to be, and often the output from Elvis's 'ablutions' could be inadvertently trodden into other areas of the house. Marilyn thought on the balance of probabilities – the brown bread being the tipping point – Shirley wouldn't be in a good mood when she came in later and did her two hours in the shop after her stint with Granny Smith.

'OK, Granny Smith, I'll add it on to your account and I'll get Danny to drop it round this afternoon if you have enough coal until then?'

'Oh thank you so much dear, is he not doing his proper job today then?'

'Not really, he's on day release for his college course this morning but will be back at lunchtime, Granny Smith.'

Marilyn hadn't asked Danny whether he was going to help out with deliveries this afternoon – he just always did. Danny was their 21-year-old son and had moved with them to The Corner Stores and, despite being a trainee accountant at Heathview Manufacturing, he helped serve in the shop and delivered groceries to their elderly customers, and heavy or bulky items to those younger and able-bodied who couldn't afford their own transport. She knew that he had to be careful when he was on college day release as he would skip the afternoon lectures to help out, but had to be cognisant of the jealous prying eyes of the relatives of his less fortunate factory-based brethren. Consequently, in transit during his covert delivery operation, he would often wear a grey wig recovered from a charity shop, his father's spare glasses and a woollen hat to pass as his doppelganger from a distance.

Marilyn really didn't like Eddie driving much past midday as she knew that he liked to pop into the pub on his way back from pick-ups from local suppliers for a 'couple of scoops', and she reasoned that it was only a matter of time before the police laid in wait for him as she had no doubt that his previous indiscretions were widely known – that was an inevitable consequence of village life. When Eddie had lost his job in such socially shameful circumstances, she had noticed the knowing looks, and experienced the room go quiet when she entered. Friends that they had known in the village for the past 25 years kept their distance, he lost his job through an indiscretion, he wasn't even charged with any offence, yet they were socially shunned with the same intent as if he were a kiddy fiddler or an estate agent. He had seemed a broken man with no direction. She had seen through her work at the solicitors that a proposed sale of The Corner Stores had fallen through, and the shop was back on the market, and she had heard the solicitor dealing with the case saying that the owners were becoming more and more desperate and were open to silly offers. It was on her 45th birthday she made the decision that they would buy The Corner Stores, selling their own house and using the inheritance they had saved from their respective parents. They would work side by side and she would help him rediscover his self-respect and dignity. She made the decision as she lay quietly sobbing in bed that evening after he had fallen asleep, her tears were for the gift tag on her present from him, it simply said *'To my darling Marilyn, my love always, Useless Eddie xxx'*.

The Corner Stores was situated on the corner of Hawtrey

Way on the Wisdom Estate which was the first and largest estate of the village, with the secondary modern (now comprehensive) school constructed within its midst in the late 1960s. It was a mishmash of semi-detached houses and bungalows interspersed with blocks of terrace housing – the only commonality was the theme of English comic actors of the 50s and 60s which extended to every road name, now lost on the spotty locust generation. The Bowford's chocolate-box thatched cottage was there long before the estate developers had been a twinkle in their grandfathers' eyes, and stood across the road from the shop on the opposing corner of Hawtrey Way as a testament to a bygone era, alien in its surroundings. The road meeting the junction of Hawtrey Way housed a recreation park that consisted of a vast expanse of grass with a small children's play area, home to a few ancient and perilous rides that often had frantic parents carrying their blood-soaked and bruised offspring to the shop, where a finger had been jammed in a ride called the Witch's Hat, or an infant's fragile head had bounced on the hard concrete after a six-foot fall off the monkey bars. Within a relatively short time of acquiring the shop, Marilyn had recognised that they needed a bountiful supply of Happy Shopper plasters, antiseptic and pain killers; and on more than one occasion with most serious incidents had to call an ambulance on behalf of a distraught parent or gleeful friend of the afflicted. The ambulance crew were always very good. They administered the first aid fairly swiftly – then they tended to pile into the fresh pies, pasties or sweet pastries and usually a few cans of fizzy pop with gusto before grabbing up a handful of take-away confectionery as their mastication was inevitably rudely interrupted by another 'emergency' call. On a busy summer day, the shop could look like a World War One field hospital with Marilyn dispensing dressings, sterilisation treatment, pain relief and sustenance – the antiquated park equipment proved a rather good source of custom.

Marilyn had given up her role as office administrator at the village solicitors, a position she had held for nearly 15 years, and at times she really missed it. Only on reflection did she realise that it was a comfortable stress-free existence that had provided her with a great insight into village life. She had come to know a large proportion of the ever-increasing population through the job and also from being a mum. However, the enjoyment and comfort waned somewhat when Eddie lost his job. He would arrive unexpectedly at the office asking her for money – as 'any self-respecting man needed money in his pocket' – but it was his appearance and condition that caused her maximum embarrassment. Eddie's face would invariably be flush from a 'couple of scoops', and as he approached the office on one occasion, she was alerted to his impending arrival by overhearing one of the clerks whispering, 'Roll out the popcorn, here comes Captain Scarlet.' He would also be dressed in bizarre combinations of clothing. She dreaded a warm day as he would wear a pair of white tennis shorts that were so small they looked like hot pants from the 1970s, and to complete the ensemble he wore a pair of grey socks, a blue sweatshirt and trainers. But the crowning glory was a wide-brim Australian hat that he had acquired one lunchtime at the pub. To add to its authenticity he had folded and pinned one side of the hat and had a military captain's metal insignia pinned to the front – seemingly to pay homage to the Australian troops in World War Two; perplexing as he had no affiliation or connection to the country. So Captain Scarlet became his whispered office moniker among the junior office staff. Marilyn found it hard to admit the truth, that for the first time in her life she was ashamed of her husband and dreaded the sight of him approaching the office. It became a source of conflict between them, and during one such argument a couple of days before her birthday Eddie had belligerently said, 'Anyone would think you were ashamed of me.' Marilyn's silence provided the answer.

Marilyn picked up the list she had written while on the phone to Granny Smith and walked over to the tired beige kitchen unit and replaced the phone headset in the cradle to charge. She was still getting used to the extraordinary concept of a phone with no cord that allowed them to take calls in the shop if they so pleased – just pull out the extendable wire aerial and you are good to go! The only minor annoyance was the limited battery life, so quite often it would remain in the kitchen charging in its cradle. This cutting-edge technology was mighty expensive but seemed necessary with Eddie often absent without leave; it was difficult to go 'out the back' to the kitchen and leave the shop unattended – she would have to break the shopkeepers' sacrosanct rule of never locking the front door during opening times. She fired up the kettle and took two spoons of coffee out of the catering-sized tin of Happy Shopper coffee, and as she opened the fridge to get the milk she heard the sound of scurrying claws across the tired linoleum floor and Ronnie and Reggie the two long-haired dachshunds sat looking expectantly up at their owner. 'OK boys, just a small piece of ham each,' and Marilyn carefully cut a piece of ham from the joint that was due to be taken out and put on the deli counter. She watched 'the boys' as they woofed down the ham without taking their eyes off the remaining joint.

They hadn't originally planned on calling them Ronnie and Reggie. Their names had changed from Jake and Elwood, their original puppy names, to provide a more appropriate reflection of their true temperament. Their new names were bestowed upon them after Eddie had witnessed them a couple of months earlier, still at a tender age, brutalise a rat they found lurking around the storage shed. They worked with a deft and vicious precision, like a psychotic canine tag team, on a large rodent that wasn't that much smaller than their own puppy frame. After Eddie had managed to get them to relinquish the tail, he threw the remnants of the rat into old Stanley's adjoining garden and took a nice refreshing slug of vodka before running back into the shop to tell Marilyn with glee about Ronnie and Reggie's exploits and their new calling as proper working dogs. In fact he got so excited, he had served two customers with ham, cheese and bacon from the deli counter before he realised he hadn't washed his hands.

Marilyn grabbed the two mugs of coffee with one hand and instructed the boys to 'stay', as she carefully opened the laminate wood-effect kitchen door and entered the shop behind the till, placing the coffee mugs on the counter. She could see Eddie was still setting up the fruit and veg on the frontage of the shop; she beckoned him to come in as he looked up after dumping a box of cabbages onto the artificial-grass-festooned crate display. Eddie puffed out his cheeks and then blew on his fingers. Marilyn thought, 'It looks like he could do with a nice drink, he looks bitter cold and that wind has made his face very red, a nice cup of coffee will do the trick.' Eddie pushed the heavy wooden-framed door open and pushed the new rubber doorstop underneath to keep it propped open.

'Oh Eddie, don't leave it open, it's too cold today, and you know the kids will be here creating merry hell shortly and we need to have it closed so we can let in two at a time.'

Eddie kicked the doorstop and released the door shut. His very favourite part of the day, the descent of the spotty locusts. 'That sounds like a good working title for either a horror movie or a sex education lesson on venereal disease,' he pondered, 'and in half an hour's time I'll probably have material for either plot.'

Marilyn stood on her tip toes so she could see the tops of the fruit and vegetables on the frontage of the shop without moving from behind the till.

'Oh Eddie, you still haven't put the fruit out yet. There's only Bramley apples and some conference pears, and you haven't pulled out the awning, the vegetables could get wet if it rains… you will have to do it after the kids' rush now.'

Eddie picked up his coffee, clasping it in his hands to help get a bit of feeling back into the tops of his fingers. He was wearing fingerless gloves, which actually seemed rather pointless as he gazed at his blue fingers returning to a normal hue with the coffee warmth, but they were slightly better than gloveless hands. Holding the long ice-cold metal crank to unwind the bright orange Happy Shopper awning was a far from appealing prospect.

'Errr, slight problem on that front. I forgot to phone the fruit order through in time, it won't be here until this afternoon. Sorry love.'

'Oh Eddie! Granny Smith wanted a couple of nice oranges, we will have to wait now for the afternoon delivery and I don't expect we have a time slot.'

'Just stick her in a couple of Terry's Chocolate Oranges and say that's what you thought she meant by 'nice' oranges – she will be chuffed to bits with that, and we can stick it on her tab, god bless her.'

Eddie nodded toward the top of shelving behind which all the boxes of chocolate were housed, along with the more expensive chocolate items such as Matchmakers or Terry's Chocolate Orange – a security measure to keep them out of reach from the mandibles of the spotty locusts.

'I think there are some up there that we inherited as stock when we bought the place. Although they look as though they have probably been through some serious environmental stress testing, especially with that heat wave last summer.'

'Just ring them back and ask them when the delivery is likely to be here. When I was on the phone to Granny Smith was it Mr Bowford I heard in here? I could hear raised voices… well, a single raised voice to be precise.'

'Yes, Brigadier Bowford was in here. I tell you what, I would love to insert cow juice and stamps right where the sun don't shine – I'd liquidise the stamps and use a funnel and a bottle brush for the job. He spends less than two quid a week, and brazenly boasts about travelling to the out-of-town supermarket to get all his shopping as it's so much cheaper – the tight-fisted boring bastard – and I bet they don't have to stand there and listen to him prattle on about cow juice and spitting on stamps.'

'He's an old man in his twilight years Eddie, show some compassion.'

'I'll show him compassion when his wife brings him home in an urn! He's well past his sell-by date, and if that lot get their way he won't even have to drive out of the village to screw us over.'

Eddie thrust the newspaper into Marilyn's hand.

'…and I'll tell you what, when he brought that paper in, he was absolutely delighted. I don't think he could have been happier if he had come up on the pools.'

Marilyn read the article and Eddie fell silent as he saw her face change; he suddenly realised he hadn't witnessed that look before. It took him a split second to realise what it was – panic.

CHAPTER 3

Jerry Bailey Johnson, or JBJ as she preferred to be called, had cut her teeth in the retail business in her own country, where the superstores housed everything imaginable from shot glasses to shot guns, where there were no obstacles that couldn't be overcome by the application of good honest negotiation, sound business practice and of course the delivery of plenty of greenbacks to the right movers and shakers, also known as politicians. If that model could work in the good old US of A, well hell it could work in the UK!

The board at Salter's Supermarket PLC had brought her in at great expense to ensure they remained ahead of the curve in what seemed to now be an accelerated race to the top. From a suitable organisational distance, they watched their empire start to rapidly expand; and they loved the results! They very skilfully put a governance framework in place to ensure they were protected from approving or even knowing of the methods employed – and what impressed them most was that JBJ had recommended this approach at her interview. JBJ was a tall, slim imposing woman in her early thirties, although she looked older, with platinum blonde hair (dyed from her natural mouse brown) pulled back tightly in a short ponytail. Her facial features, though liberally attended to with expensive make-up, were not pretty, and could be generously described as distinguished – she had a large nose, prominent chin, thin lips and eyes to match. Colin Salter, the chairman and one of the family shareholders that made up the majority holding required to exercise control of the company, referred to her as 'that geezer bird' – but never in earshot. It was not a reference to her somewhat masculine appearance, but deference to her blunt and forthright approach to business and her ability to seemingly move every obstacle that fell in their way. In Colin Salter's mind, 'geezer bird' was a term of endearment, a compliment; he possessed just about enough insight to realise that JBJ might not see it that way. He was the third generation in his great-grandfather's business and although he had been afforded an excellent private education and all the trappings that came with the Salter name, he still liked to think of himself as a self-made man of the people. At lunch after the board meeting where he had first called her 'that geezer bird', Colin Salter was desperately trying to think who JBJ reminded him of. Ah yes, he had it! 'Rick Parfitt in a frock, you know the guitarist in Status Quo!' he roared at his fawning entourage. He felt truly regal as he rolled his brandy glass and sucked on his King of Denmark Cigar. Yes Rick Parfitt in a frock! 'My goodness,' he thought, 'that actually got a great, and for once genuine, laugh.' He would have to think of some more equally relevant quips – good old JBJ!

*

Marilyn re-read the article. Not only had the planning permission been supported by the Parish Council, the proposed timescale for the build was astounding. It seemed that as the site was on vacant land that the superstore would be up and running in less than four months. The site that was mentioned was probably less than a five-minute walk from The Corner Stores.

'Eddie, it says it will open from seven in the morning until ten thirty at night, six days a week, with Sunday opening to be determined – we open seven until six thirty and that's enough.'

Eddie noticed a slight tremor in her voice, which very quickly changed to that of a screeching banshee.

'Hells bells, have you seen this quote? "Parish Councillor Beaton gave a ringing endorsement to the proposal, saying the village welcomes Salter's superstore with open arms, the extended hours will convenience those of us that have full-time jobs and still want to do our shopping locally out of working hours." The backstabbing little shit, excuse my French.'

Councillor Gary Beaton lived on the Wisdom Estate with Janice, his wife, in one of the few detached properties. He had put his own stamp of style on the property. At the entrance to the driveway he had installed imposing wrought iron gates operated with an electric remote control, housed between two mock Roman pillars, each adorned with a faux marble horse's head. The interior was styled by Janice, his wife and beard, in rather garish 1970's décor. Above the fireplace in the lounge hung the obligatory Blue Lady print and in the far corner he had built a red brick bar complete with optics, which was his own personal touch, carefully selecting the garish red bricks to match the leather settee and armchairs. He frequented The Corner Stores with some regularity, always saying, '…us small businessmen needed to stick together, and that's not reference to your missus' height, Eddie.' He owned a small family building firm, and was forever saying to Eddie and Marilyn how they were struggling in the recession. He had also made it crystal clear to anyone that would care to listen that his sole reason for standing as councillor was to open up more opportunity for development and expansion of the village.

'That's about right,' said Eddie. 'Bloody Brown Envelope Beaton leading the charge.'

Before they had opportunity for further reflection and recriminations, the first wave of spotty locusts started to approach the shop. Marilyn tossed the paper behind the counter and instructed Eddie to assume his position on the door and enforce the 'two in, two out' policy. The children had already discerned that Marilyn was not to be messed with; although she was small in stature her encyclopaedic knowledge of their parents and wider family made her a formidable adversary. However, they had also quickly established, through trial and error, that her cognitive process that allowed her to correctly estimate the age of the older girls and boys appeared to be somewhat temperamental. They had learned that if their nominated cigarette champion hid his or her school bag in the bushes at the side of the shop and ensured that their coat masked any school ties or blazers, then the chances of success in purchasing the day's cigarettes were high. The performance was equally as important, confidence was the key. The tried and tested technique was to pluck a pack of Polo mints from the confectionery display and place them on the counter next to the till and nonchalantly say 'Just these please, oh and ten Bensons as well please'. It was important to make it sound as though the cigarette purchase was an afterthought; as it was a steady hand as you handed the money over. Then holding steady, ensuring that you didn't then bolt to the door without receiving your change – a novice first timer schoolboy error. Once procured, the champion would sell their bounty in the form of individual cigarettes for an unhealthy profit. The nominated cigarette champions would often spend time at home practising and honing their skills, teenage boys making the timbre of their voice as low as it could go, while the teenage girls worked on venom and aggression in their delivery. The younger children had to try to get their cigarettes after school with a carefully forged note from a poorly parent, or even better a housebound invalid grandparent (which allowed potential repeat purchases) – this was more challenging as a call could be made to the alleged nicotine-starved relative now that Marilyn had the cordless phone in the shop. What they didn't appreciate was that Marilyn always pretty much knew their age, but as a smoker herself who started at the tender age of 14 she thought those that, in her view, were responsible enough should be allowed to make that choice – and they provided a nice profit with the 'child surcharge' she added on each transaction. Central Line, on the other hand, would pretty much serve anyone cigarettes – no charade required.

The spotty locusts proceeded to diligently strip the confectionery shelves and the fizzy drink Corona stand, while also procuring the odd packet of fags. After 20 minutes, the rush was over, and Eddie returned to the dank storage shed to bring out the rest of the veg, and to have a quick leveller from the coal bags after the stress of dealing with the acne-ridden infestation. As he took a heavy hit from the vodka bottle, the severity of the situation dawned on him. They could lose everything – and where would he get another job, especially one that had booze on tap?

Marilyn was replenishing the confectionery shelves when Cloth-Eared Jack shuffled in waving the newspaper like Neville Chamberlain with his iconic 'Peace in Our Time' paper. His taxi sat in the lay-by with no evidence of the damage sustained in the trolley attack. Jack had used Wyatt Motors, a small independent garage situated in the centre of the village, to do the work and provide him with inflated invoices for the insurance claim. The proprietor Bruce 'Jesse' Wyatt also kindly shaved 50,000 miles off the vehicle's true road life by winding the clock back for no extra charge, and produced a new logbook complete with fictional MOT history to support the vehicle's new lease of life, all for a mere £30. Jack also claimed for two weeks' loss of earnings even though he was only off the road for a day. He had made a nice little earner from that incident, with no effect on his own insurance premiums. He had only recently been contacted by a no-win no-fee solicitor encouraging him to make a personal injury claim. They had advised him that although it was two years ago it was still in the statute of limitation – he hadn't mentioned that to the Rogers yet. He looked wistfully out of the shop window as he saw Eddie bringing the veg boxes out individually – the flatbed trolley now sat idle in the backyard, next to the storage shed, consigned to serve the rest of its useful life as a canine sunbed on wheels, where Ronnie and Reggie would lay prostrate on the faded wooden bed for the hour in the day when the winter sun warmed the trolley – 'A monument to stupidity,' was Marilyn's wry observation.

'Forty of my fags, and 'er pasties. I suppose you've seen this? It's absolutely bloody outrageous we should do something about it. All my bloody customers are livid, absolutely bloody livid and the other traders are too. I have four customers that I take to town every week to do their shopping – so it's going to hit my bloody back pocket, Mrs Rogers, I don't mind telling you.'

Marilyn proceeded to shovel the four colossal fresh pasties into a brown paper bag, wondering how they would impact on Dot's ever-expanding waistline. Although Dot was only about four-foot-six-inches tall the last time she had been in the shop,

Marilyn had observed she was not far off that in width. She had taken to wearing brown elasticated trousers with bright yellow or orange tight-fitting polo neck jumpers. Eddie had rather unkindly christened her 'The Space-hopper'.

'We've just got some nice fresh Chelsea buns in – do you want a couple for Dot?'

Jack fiddled with his hearing aid.

'Better stick four of them in there Mrs Rogers, you know once she gets the taste… better to be safe than sorry.'

'No problem, four large Chelsea buns it is – packet of butter to go with them?'

Jack gave a resigned nod. The bread, pasties, pies and buns were freshly baked each day by Bowles the Bakers from the next village and delivered at 7 am each morning by young Jenny, who had a style all of her own. She wore Dr Marten boots and had long flowing hair that really could be any colour under the rainbow, but it was her entrancing blue eyes and melting smile that left an enduring impression on those who met her. It hadn't escaped Marilyn's notice that Danny would volunteer to accept the bread order before he set off for work, even though it meant him getting up half an hour earlier than he needed to, enthusiastically remonstrating, 'You've got enough to do, Mum.'

'What do you suggest we do about the superstore then, Jack?'

'A bloody petition in here and all the local shops for a start, and then a placard protest on the site, then a full-blown bloody boycott when it opens… well at least during your opening hours, outside of that if I might need something urgently for Dot in the evening like a family pack of Revels, you wouldn't begrudge her that would you Mrs Rogers?'

'I'll mention it to Eddie. Forty Superkings was it?'

'Better make it sixty, I'm feeling stressed out about those bloody fares.'

'That's £8.30 Jack, do you want it on your tab?'

'Yes please Mrs Rogers, one of my customers suggested the local traders could call it SOS.'

Marilyn looked perplexed.

'SOS – Save Our Shops – that's what we should call the bloody campaign, Mrs Rogers.'

Jack was right, something had to be done. They couldn't just sit back and do nothing, 'bloody campaign' that could be quite apt, thought Marilyn.

*

Granny Smith sat watching the television, with Elvis assuming his customary position at her feet. The lounge in her tiny two-bedroom bungalow had a coal fire and her favourite chair was positioned next to it. There was an old settee opposite with the television positioned at its side, perched on an old dark wood leaf-drop table. At one end of the room there was an ornately carved heavy dark-oak sideboard which was far too large for the room, giving the impression that in times past it must have resided in much grander surroundings. It was festooned with family pictures of those past and present and ornaments and mementos of long-ago holidays in seaside towns. Its centre piece was an old dark wood clock that belonged to her father; on the rare occasions when the television was off, its ticking filled the room, a salutary reminder of passing time. The opposite side of the room had a large window which overlooked a postage-stamp garden, a bird table was positioned a few feet from the window, and Granny Smith would sit for hours watching the different varieties of wild birds visit. Although Granny Smith loved all birds her favourites weren't the superstar blue tits or the mischievous, albeit common and plain, sparrows – no, it was the robin that patrolled the garden with a confidence that belied his size. But at this time she wasn't paying attention to her feathered friends, she was enthralled with a new daily programme called *This Morning* on ITV presented by a lovely young couple called Richard and Judy. She watched it religiously. Judy was such a lovely young girl, and Richard was nice too in his own way– a bit of a dish actually – although Granny Smith also rather guiltily thought that sometimes he could be a bit of a berk. Granny Smith's daughter lived in Newcastle so she didn't get the opportunity to visit too often, but she always stayed for a week in the summer and called at least once a week come what may. Last summer she had treated Granny Smith to a colour TV with a remote control, the remote was certainly a godsend now with her ever-decreasing mobility.

Granny Smith's walking frame was in front of her. It was an unwelcomed intruder, a constant reminder of her ailing health and mobility. She had fallen several times and it took a stay in hospital before she finally acceded to use the damn thing as a condition of discharge. She was 79, and told all that would listen that she wanted to reach 80. Although daily her body became frailer, in her own mind she still thought of herself as she was 50 years ago. She was unfailingly astonished when she looked in the mirror and saw a wizened grey-haired stranger staring back at her.

She had tied an old kitchen apron to the front of her nemesis so that she could use the pockets as storage for her remote control. But its original remit had widened and it now also contained her reading glasses, address book (with useful telephone numbers), the remnants of her (once) large bar of Cadbury's fruit and nut, and her tobacco tin and lighter. She would also store her oranges in there for a healthy snack, but she was all out until Danny dropped the delivery off this afternoon. He was such a thoughtful young man; he would always tend the coal fire for her and make her a cup of tea, it always brightened her day up. She could hear Shirley beavering away in the kitchen, washing up the breakfast things no doubt.

Shirley had helped Granny Smith get dressed and washed. It was difficult for Granny Smith to manoeuvre the walking frame in the small bathroom, and it always had to be moved out into the hallway to enable Granny Smith to get to the sink for a full body wash. It was trying to perform this rather tricky manoeuvre on her own that had led to Granny Smith's stay in hospital, and Shirley's subsequent engagement as her helping hand. Shirley always emptied the commode from the bedroom once Granny Smith was settled in the lounge; she knew how undignified the lovely old lady felt having to use it. She would also take the opportunity to inspect the bed, as she had noticed recently that it was not only Elvis having continence issues, his mistress was too. When that happened she would strip the bed and discreetly put the sheets in the washing machine with the nightclothes. She was paid by Granny Smith for an hour each morning, but when there was an unexpected accident in the bed it would take much longer as she had to wait for the machine cycle to finish and then put them in the tumble dryer, then airing cupboard – at best the visit would be an hour and a half. But Shirley didn't mind, she loved all her little jobs. She was 55 years old and on her own – her husband had died after a long illness and she survived now on his army pension and her various part-time jobs. Money was tight for Shirley but as the mortgage had been paid off with his life insurance she could just about manage.

Her late husband had once described Shirley as his Glaswegian diamond in the rough. To her it was a compliment that she treasured for life; a diamond was a rare commodity, both beautiful and precious. She was a heavy-set woman with tightly permed hair and a sallow tobacco-worn face. Unbeknownst to Shirley, Eddie had picked up on an observation made by Trevor and Leslie, the couple that lived in a bungalow next to Mr Bowford, on Shirley's rather heavy-set features and somewhat cumbersome movement. He overheard Trevor say to Leslie, 'Blimey, she moves with all the grace of Lurch.' Marilyn didn't approve of Eddie's new nickname for Shirley – so he kept it for special occasions... when Trevor and Leslie were in earshot.

Shirley had a spare two-hour block (although often the additional time spent at Granny Smiths meant that it was reduced to an hour) before she helped Marilyn in the shop, then she would pop to the bungalow next to the shop to make a late lunch and tea for old Stanley – that wasn't her favourite part of the day, he was a cantankerous old bastard with a heart that had been replaced with a swinging brick.

While the wash-cycle was going, she would get a meal out of the freezer and pop it in the microwave for Granny Smith's lunch and make her a sandwich for her tea as the microwave hummed softly in the background. She would then add a few slices of beetroot to the plate before wrapping it in cling film and placing a wrapped chocolate biscuit alongside (normally a Penguin, but sometimes a Taxi or Blue Riband) before the 'ping' of the microwave would inevitably make her jump and stir her from her own reflections. Shirley marvelled at the time efficiency of the microwave and vowed that one day she would buy one for herself, when her boat came in. She would then put the kettle on and make them both a nice brew and sit with Granny Smith watching daytime TV until the washing finished. They did share one common hobby – they both had a real passion for smoking. Granny Smith enjoyed rolling her own and was never without a pouch of Golden Virginia tobacco, Shirley was a fan of the ready-rolled Superkings – their price being the main attraction. When they were having a cuppa, Shirley would roll a couple of cigarettes for them both using Granny Smith's tobacco. On the rare occasion when Eddie made an early delivery he would comment on the lung-choking fug in the lounge, where shards of light from the window struggled to provide any illumination through the billowing smoke. Shirley smiled to herself when she remembered what he said when he came in to find them both puffing away to their hearts content – 'Bloody Hell, it's Puffing Billy and Fag Ash Lil.'

Today Shirley was furiously mopping the tiny kitchen floor after Elvis had performed his 'ablutions' several times during the night. She also had his blanket in the washing machine along with Granny Smith's bedding, while his wicker bed aired in the garden. The paper on the kitchen work surface caught her eye, it had an article on Heathview inside. She put the mop down and picked up last night's paper. She fumbled with her glasses which hung on a chain around her neck. 'You are going to want to see this hen…'

CHAPTER 4

Beaton & Son Ltd had been awarded the contract for the groundworks, and with the site fenced off and out of the sight of prying eyes, work had already commenced, several weeks before planning permission was granted. The job was immediately subcontracted out by Beaton & Son Ltd to the large construction company used by Salter's on all their UK projects, but at a reduced fee with the significant balance of £175,000 being retained in the coffers of Beaton & Son Ltd. The construction company had also agreed to employ Councillor Beaton and his merry men when the project was further underway, and this would extend to ongoing site maintenance for the next five years – which he would openly publish in his councillor's public declarations of interest. He had decided that his best strategy would be to make a really big play of it and sanctimoniously announce at the next Parish Council meeting that in order to ensure probity and transparency that he would sit out of any future discussions on the development (not that there would be any now permission had been granted). If he was challenged on a conflict of interest, he would throw out the righteous line that he was keeping the jobs within the village, and if things turned nasty he would simply take the moral high ground and resign his position as councillor, rather than see employment and money move out of the village economy. Jerry Bailey Johnson had outlined the approach and prepared the script for him; she had been through this many times before. But the scenario of resigning wasn't appealing to Beaton, after the countless meetings he had endured listening to the endless trite and drivel spouted by his fellow councillors and the moronic villagers in attendance, relating to such life-critical matters as littering, dog fouling and child-maiming park play equipment. In his own mind he was owed these small perks for his invaluable expertise and precious time that he had already wasted on a seemingly endless stream of banal trivialities, and now it was finally starting to pay off.

Councillor Beaton saw Heathview as a giant monopoly board and was already working on a land acquisition that had potential to be his own Bond Street, and with Salter's cash behind him he was soon going to be in a position to make his move. There was one old buffoon that he had been working on for some considerable time. He owned a lot of land on the other side of the Wisdom Estate, and he lived, dressed and smelt like a tramp. Judging by the state of his ramshackle bungalow, with its front garden blighted with tyres, car parts, old washing machines and cookers, Beaton reckoned the wretch could do with a few quid. He seemed to make the bulk of his money from his illicit home brew made from the apple orchards in the vast expanse of land he owned surrounding the bungalow, supplemented by fixing up and selling on old appliances. He certainly didn't have any business nous or financial common sense, after all the halfwit did all of his shopping at The Corner Stores! However, Beaton did concede that although Tramp Juice Ron, as he was known, must have been at least 60, he still cut quite an imposing physical figure – he was tall, thick set with a severely weather-beaten face that looked as though it could be used to make a tanned leather handbag, feral grey hair and unkempt whiskers to match – so he had to be extremely careful how he handled the situation. He didn't want those gnarled club hammer hands raining blows on him as had been known to happen to more than one misfortunate who had crossed his path. The only thing that stood in Beaton's way was his own peccadillos, which he knew had held his business empire back for all these years – he loved more than the occasional line of showbiz sherbet and of course his other interest…

*

Eddie languidly turned the metal hand crank to wind in the orange awning. He was nearing the end of a tiring and eventful day and he still had the veg to put away. The fruit delivery was safely stowed away in the storage shed; it had only arrived an hour ago so there was little sense in writing the price cards and putting it on display – at least that's what Eddie told himself. Marilyn was in blissful ignorance of its arrival. He really didn't relish carrying the 20 kg sacks of red and white potatoes to the shed, in all honesty his hand-eye-feet co-ordination was somewhat compromised. After he had taken the unsold coal bags back to their night-time home, he had taken the opportunity to polish off the afternoon's half bottle of vodka. He looked into the shop and saw Tramp Juice Ron leaning against the chest freezer on the far wall. He was silently facing Marilyn who was standing behind the till, arms tightly folded against her chest, making it patently obvious to anyone with a modicum of common sense that she was waiting to close and cash up. Ron was in the process of making a rollie, he had the fag paper drooping and flapping from his lip, while his gnarled hands fumbled in his tobacco pouch. He was extremely comfortable in silence. Eddie and Marilyn suffered this ritual virtually every day when they were in the process of closing. At 5.50 pm Ron, and his accompanying putrid aroma, would amble in the shop and perch against the freezer and survey the shop for his potential tea, while he made a rollie to aid his contemplation. He would invariably purchase tobacco, green papers and a 'box o' scratchers' as he liked to refer to a packet of matches. Today there were two cold beef and onion pies and two iced buns left on the top shelf of the bakery counter which was situated in the aisle at the centre of the shop, arm's length from Ron's freezer perch. He didn't move to examine the daily leftovers, he just waited until he caught Marilyn's eye and nodded in their direction.

'Do you want both pies and both buns, Ron?' said Marilyn, pleased that they still had an obvious and easy choice. If the pasties, pies, pastries and cakes delivered by young Jenny from Bowles the Bakers from the next village had all been purchased, Ron would have to conduct a further survey of the shop from his freezer perch.

Firstly, the deli counter on the door side of the shop (he lifted himself on tip toes for that), then scanning the remaining shelves in the shop (he didn't bother with the carousel at the bottom of the shop as that required moving from his fixed position), and finally if all else failed he would have to move to examine the contents of his freezer perch. This exercise was carried out without urgency and scant regard to the Rogers' 12-hour day and their own need for sustenance.

'That'll do for m'tea m'dear, and the baccy, greens and a box o' scratchers, gel'

'Do you want me to put anything by for your tea tomorrow, Ron?'

'Na, y'are alright m'dear, don't knows what ah fancy till t'mar evenen.'

After experiencing Ron's time-consuming shop survey on more than one occasion, Marilyn now ordered either two pies or pasties and a couple of pastries or cakes and stowed them away under the till counter, only putting them on display five minutes before Ron's expected time of arrival. Very occasionally, a late shopper would scupper the plan by swooping in and taking one or both of the cakes in the five-minute window, but Marilyn would hurriedly open a McVities ginger cake and place it in the vacant space. Ron liked a 'nice bit ah ginger' if it was from a 'proper bakery mind'.

'Shall I put it on your book Ron, settle up on Friday?'

Tramp Juice Ron nodded as he gently shaped the rollie with his giant thumb and forefinger. He put it to his mouth and reached for his 'scratchers'. The scowl on Marilyn's face reminded him he needed to move outside before sparking up. He pushed himself off the freezer perch and his shovel hand effortlessly scooped the distended brown paper bag containing his tea from the counter, as he moved towards the door he paused and turned back to Marilyn.

'Saw about the shaap op'nen down the road – bad business that, bad for the village. Summits not right about that, mark my words gel.'

Tramp Juice Ron still had the unlit rollie hanging from his lip bouncing jauntily with each word he spoke. As soon as he was outside, his spare hand pulled a match from his pocket which ignited with a violent scrape against the side of his whiskered face. He lit the rollie and flicked the match into the lay-by. He turned to see Eddie emerge from the storage shed with a face glowing like a belisha beacon, lurching forward with an ungainly gait.

'Alright boy?'

'Not three bad Ronald, my good man,' slurred Eddie. He then proceeded to vigorously tap the side of his broken-veined nose.

'Sold all of that apple juice Ron, any chance you can drop some more off tomorrow morning?'

Eddie was selling Tramp Juice Ron's illicit 'home brew' cider from the storage shed, and delivering to some of the elderly customers as a nice side order to their shopping. Tramp Juice Ron had cultivated this arrangement with many of the local business owners. His home brewery was contained in a hidden underground cellar which extended from the front room to the full length of the front garden, serviced by the orchards at the rear of the property and with the help of his boy Scotty he was pumping the stuff out on an industrial scale. Much to Eddie's annoyance, a legal covenant prevented The Corner Stores from selling alcohol, which on the one hand impeded their ability to evenly compete with their rivals but on the other had probably already extended Eddie's life expectancy by five years.

Ron's cider, or Tramp Juice as he liked to call it, wasn't Eddie's first port of call when he needed a tipple. It had a distinctive and somewhat unpleasant taste (pre and after) but was renowned as an extremely potent brew; the latter quality certainly ticked the main box in Eddie's key requirements of an alcoholic beverage. However, although it could not be disputed that Ron's Tramp Juice would deliver immediate serious and extremely pleasing impairment to the prefrontal cortex, Eddie found the fruit-based concoction didn't always have a beneficial effect on his digestive system, more specifically his bowels. The first time he had experienced this extreme reaction he had to perform what he later called 'the sour apple quick step' or 'crab apple cha-cha' – a veritable sprint from the storage shed, through the yard, into the back door and straight into the ground-floor toilet. But this physical act was far from straightforward, as sprinting – or any form of walking for that matter – was severely impeded by a less than functional prefrontal cortex, which he had reasoned was a perfectly natural reaction after consuming a four-pint jug of Ron's Tramp Juice in less than half an hour. Instead he initially navigated the route by carefully placing one foot in front of the other, while at the same time squeezing his buttocks to hold the dam fast against the building torrent. As the pressure became more intense halfway across the yard, the gentle cha-cha suddenly turned into a frantic quick step with limbs threshing like St Vitus as he clawed at the back door, pushing himself through and throwing himself, with a sprinter's-like dip at the finish of the 100 metres Olympic final, into the ground-floor toilet housed at the back of the shop's living accommodation. As he fell, he felt his bowels release with ferocious force. Eddie lay fully clothed as his rectum erupted, pebble dashing his underpants and seeping through to his legs. He howled with despair and cursed his confounded luck of having such a weak digestive system. Ronnie and Reggie came sprinting from the yard to investigate the kerfuffle but stopped short outside the toilet door when the foul aroma hit them. They sniffed the noxious air with a perfunctory twitch of the nose, immediately turned tail and sprinted back to their trolley sunbed in the yard. Sometime later, as Eddie surreptitiously bundled his soiled trousers, pants and socks into the washing machine, he vowed only to drink four pints of Ron's Tramp Juice in 30 minutes in an absolute emergency.

On the plus side, Eddie had also added another musical artist to his lexicon of stool conditions that he liked to share with Marilyn after a visit to the lavatory. When his faeces were solid (as a rock) he would throw open the kitchen door and enter the shop and loudly proclaim, 'Good news, I'm pleased to announce that I've just had an Ashford and Simpson.' Any customers in the shop would look up quizzically and then continue with their shopping, but he would often get a sly kick in the shins from Marilyn if he was in range. His other terminology up until now, was reflective of a bowel movement that started off well with solid stools but ended up disappointingly with a liberal 'crop spraying' of the lavatory pan. On the return to the shop after such a visit he would announce 'Ladies and gentleman, I've just had a Dave Clark Five', in reference to their 60's hit 'Bits and Pieces'. Now, after his recent accident, if his faecal matter was projected with violent force from his rear orifice in pure liquid form, he would be able to share his bad news with the shop '…I've just had an Eddie Van Halen', in reference to Van Halen's solo guitar instrumental track 'Eruption'. Before he used it for the first time in in the shop, he would have to find a subtle way of letting Marilyn know about Eddie Van Halen as she wouldn't be familiar with his work. Marilyn failed to see the funny side of his public bowel updates as she rightly pointed out that it wasn't the sort of announcement customers would appreciate from someone who was going to potentially be serving them cold meats or cheese off the deli counter.

'How much you wanting, boy?'

'Same as last week Ron? Forty pints? And I'll give you four packs of baccy and a dozen green fag papers in fair exchange.'

'Alright, throw in a bag of coal an' I'll send the boy round 'morrow first thing to drop off and pick up.'

Tramp Juice Ron spat on his hand and held it out for Eddie to shake on the deal. Eddie winced looking at the filthy hand and grime-encased fingernails.

'Ok Ron, better not shake in case Marilyn sees, she wouldn't approve… Mum's the word and all that.'

Tramp Juice Ron didn't speak, he just left his mammoth hand outstretched. Eddie felt his own hand small and insignificant as it was held in a vice-like grip as he shook Ron's gorilla-sized hand.

Eddie picked up the metal crank again and finished the job he had started, winding in the awning as he watched Tramp Juice Ron's hunched back and tobacco smoke vapour trail as he ambled down the road. He unhooked the crank and went back into the shop, placing the crank behind the deli counter. He then kicked out the doorstop and pulled the door behind him, turning the red open/closed sign round in one motion. He then pushed the deadbolts at the top and bottom of the doors before using the large Chubb key to lock the door. Like most of the shopkeepers in Heathview, they didn't have an alarm as burglary was generally extremely low and on the rare occasion a break-in occurred the sole village bobby would round up the two or three usual suspects and coerce the one who didn't have a solid alibi to make full reparation, no forensic evidence required! He could hear the till whirring, which meant that Marilyn was in the process of getting a Z reading printout to reconcile the till to the cash and cheque receipts. Due to Eddie's dexterity on the till, this process would often be laborious, involving a forensic check of the complete till roll of the day's transactions to find the numerous keying errors that he had made, that would have inevitably led to an incorrect total of the day's takings. The till frequently screamed out with a long bleep as Eddie pressed an incorrect key. Whenever this happened he would invariably press the key at least another two or three times and say to the patiently waiting customer, 'Name that tune?' then frantically call for Marilyn to reset the till. That was one of Eddie's idiosyncrasies that particularly got under Marilyn's skin as she tried to promote customer care, but not as much as Eddie's greeting whenever he answered the shop phone.

'Battersea Dogs Home, Chief Beagle speaking,' was Eddie's preferred salutation, but he had some alternatives to provide variety to the confused, usually elderly, customers ringing through. 'One Hung Low Chinese Takeaway' or 'Lunatic Asylum, Mad Hatter speaking'.

'Eddie, can you get some hot soapy water from the kitchen to clean down the deli counter please while I'm cashing up?'

Eddie grimaced as he didn't feel either willing or actually physically able to clean the deli counter and meat slicer in his current state of inebriation. The process of cleaning the meat slicer required a methodical approach and the disassembly of the blade guard to ensure that the inner chamber, where the meat and fat remnants from the blade dropped, was properly cleaned. Unfortunately, when they had first taken over, they had been unaware of this essential hygiene requirement and had simply turned the blade on and washed it with a plastic brush and soapy water. It was about a month before Marilyn noticed a putrid aroma wafting up from the meat slicer when she was cleaning it. It took about 20 minutes to work out how to remove the guard, and when they finally removed it, to their absolute horror they witnessed a green mulch of decaying ham. Eddie had tried to put a positive spin on it by pointing out there weren't any maggots… yet! It also later transpired that was their best month for toilet roll and Imodium sales.

'It's OK Eddie, just get the water I'll clean it.'

Eddie moved behind the counter and put his arms around Marilyn, and whispered, 'We'll be OK love, don't worry about Salter's.'

'It's not just that. Did you take any money out of the till for anything or pay any suppliers without getting an invoice Eddie?'

Eddie vaguely remembered 'borrowing' some money for his vodka earlier that morning, although it was somewhat hazy after his daily medicinal ingestion; yes, that was it! He had taken cash from two customers when Marilyn was out the back having a coffee break and had just popped the money straight into his trouser pocket. He was fairly sure that he hadn't rung the transactions so it wouldn't show in the end of day receipts.

'No, but I expect I have rung something through incorrectly love, like I usually do.'

'Even after I have amended all of your errors the till is £20 short. Only you, me and Shirley have used the till today, Eddie.'

'Maybe I did make a mistake, gave someone the wrong change perhaps?'

'Not 20 quid though surely, Eddie?'

Even Eddie could see this was unlikely, but with the news earlier in the day he had hit the bottle harder than usual and couldn't be sure that he had operated at his usual efficiency levels. Eddie sometimes had to admit that he gave functioning alcoholics a bad name. He refused to consider that Shirley would help herself to their hard-earned money, no, she wouldn't do that, it was out of the question.

'Well, wrong change to a few people then? I couldn't say I

didn't love, it's been a stressful day.'

Marilyn thought that it certainly was a possibility. She had seen him short-change and overcharge numerous customers. Why couldn't Eddie be more diligent? It was so frustrating! She had been thinking for a while of installing a surveillance camera so that she could watch proceedings when she was on her break, or retrospectively review the tapes in the evening if she had been out of the shop on a rare excursion making deliveries or picking up stock from the cash and carry. The cost seemed excessive to the benefit, but this latest incident seemed to tip the scales, combined with the potential thefts from the spotty locusts she was now thinking it was a necessity.

'We'll have to keep an eye on it, Eddie, we can't afford to lose that kind of money each day, we are struggling as it is, without a supermarket or superstore opening up on our doorstep.'

'I know love but…' Eddie threw his head back and belched in one continuous phrase, 'tomorrow's another day.' Even his well-honed party trick didn't make Marilyn smile.

CHAPTER 5

The newspaper article had galvanised and united the village community and the 'Save Our Shops' campaign was well and truly underway. Trevor and Leslie were standing in The Corner Stores proudly showing Marilyn the placards and posters they had professionally made.

'Do you want two or three posters?' asked Trevor, and before Marilyn could respond he answered his own question.

'You could put one in the front shop window and take down one of those ghastly tangerine Happy Shopper posters, and one in the kitchen window next door, oh and one in young Danny's bedroom. How is Danny we haven't seen much of him?'

Trevor and Leslie had emerged as the natural leaders of the SOS campaign, mainly due to the fact that Caligo Blue, Leslie's advertising agency based in the City, had ready access to free graphic design and printing facilities. That, combined with Trevor's passionate environmental credentials which made him a natural and vocal enemy of the expanding superstore phenomena, made the couple the obvious campaign leaders. Mr Bowford hadn't responded well to his flamboyant next-door neighbours leading the way; neither of them had done a minute of military service and Mr Bowford was not ashamed to say that he didn't agree with their overt display of their sexuality. He accepted of course that 'funny business' had always gone on, and had even been known in his army days – he shuddered as he remembered that time in the barracks when he was stationed in Germany, best forgotten that, Bowford old man, you were young and naïve and it was a confusing time – nothing more. His standpoint was that it was never overt, openly flaunted, it was kept firmly behind closed doors – and that chap Trevor, well he was just so, so camp. Trevor always made a point of knocking loudly on the lounge window when he saw Mr Bowford walking past for his morning visit to The Corner Stores and then waved frantically at him while adorned in a short ladies' leopard print bath robe and matching silk head scarf. It always cheered his day to see the furtive glance from Mr Bowford as he scuttled across the road, his balding grey head bowed, praying to some higher body that they would get some net curtains installed. On Mr Bowford's 80th earlier in the year, Trevor had performed the morning ritual but this time jumping as he waved, and had made sure that he had gone commando to provide a nice birthday surprise for the bigoted old prig. He was fairly sure he had seen the top of Mr Bowford's balding scalp flush.

'Leave us four posters if you can Trevor, thank you. Danny is doing well, he's out doing weekend deliveries for us at the moment. I don't know what we would do without him.'

'He's such a lovely boy,' cooed Trevor, drawing a disapproving glance from Leslie as he tentatively enquired whether Eddie was still unable to drive in the afternoons.

'No, it's still not a good idea.'

Trevor and Leslie knew only too well Marilyn's struggle as Trevor was a recovering alcoholic. He had been a binge drinker for many years, going on massive benders that would last one, two or three weeks, and as a consequence he had never been able to hold down a job. He had been sober now for nearly five years – a month after they had moved in together. It was following a combined party for Trevor's 40th birthday and their house-warming that morphed into a two-week-long bender that Leslie had delivered him his final ultimatum. They both recognised that Trevor's self-destruct mode was never far from the surface. The 'A' word was never openly mentioned in their discussions but all three were aware of their respective battles and beverage-damaged history.

Just as the discussion lulled into silence there was an almighty crash and shriek that sounded like a wounded animal emitted from the adjoining kitchen. Marilyn tore from behind the counter and threw the kitchen door open. On the other side of the kitchen she saw Eddie on all fours with his head wedged in a small gap between the oven and the sink unit, making what could only be described as a high-pitch yelping. Ronnie and Reggie came tearing in from the yard to investigate the commotion; they took one look at their once again forlorn master and retreated from whence they came.

'Oh my god, Eddie what's the matter?'

Eddie wailed like a wounded animal.

'What the hell does it look like? I'm stuck, me heads stuck, ahhhhh!'

'What an earth were you doing to get your head stuck between the oven and the sink?'

'To be honest, the events are rather hazy. Can you just help pull me out?'

Marilyn reached into the oven and sink crevasse and tried to grasp Eddie's neck. She pulled but not only would his head not budge, he continued to shriek in pain as she tried to move him.

'It's no good, I can't move you. Leslie and Trevor are in the shop I'll get them to help.'

'Don't you dare, I'm not having those two sausage jockeys interfering with me. I'm in a vulnerable position here, I'm on all fours and totally helpless. Believe you me, I'm not an unattractive proposition to those two, Marilyn.'

'For heaven's sake! Don't be so bloody rude and stupid. They wouldn't give you a second glance. Trevor, Leslie?' she bellowed. 'Can you get in here, please?' Then whispered to Eddie '…and for your information mister, they aren't both likely to be the jockey!'

Trevor and Leslie burst into the kitchen. They took one look at Eddie's position and then each other; it was all they could do to contain themselves. They got either side of him and tried to pull him out but to no avail.

'Oh Eddie, it's no good, we're going to have to try and take your trousers off,' squealed Trevor with glee.

'You will do no such fucking thing! You're not going to ogle my family jewels. Marilyn? Marilyn?'

'She's gone back in the shop Eddie, there are customers that need serving. What we really need is some lubricant,' said Leslie, winking at Trevor who was now biting his hand to stop himself exploding.

'Get Marilyn… NOW!' Eddie forlornly wailed.

'We need to lubricate your big head, Eddie, it got in there somehow so it must be able to come out of there.'

Shirley appeared from the shop. She had just started her two-hour shift. She stood and admired the scene that lay before her.

'Divna mind me lads I've just come to put the kettle on, as you were,' she grinned, flicking the kettle on. 'Is this likely to be a long job, lads? I'll put a brew on for youse two, thirsty work ken? Fancy a brew, Eddie?'

'NO I DO NOT FANCY A FUCKING BREW!'

'Is there any cooking oil in the cupboards by you, Shirley?' Leslie enquired.

'Aye, there you go son.' She threw it across to Leslie.

'Right, here we go,' said Trevor, 'let's get you nicely lubed up, Eddie.'

'Fine, but can you two fellas please hurry up… I really need the toilet. Have either of you ever heard of Eddie Van Halen by any chance?'

Shirley watched as Leslie poured some cooking oil on his hand and started applying it to both sides of Eddie's head. She could see what suspiciously looked like the lid of a vodka bottle peering from between Eddie's feet in his enforced praying position. She could visualise that the bottle had probably slipped out of his grip or was inadvertently knocked off the draining board into the gap between the sink and the oven, which probably led to a frenzied and panicked retrieval before its precious contents emptied. Shirley watched as Eddie's oiled head popped from the crevasse and he fell back on the floor like a drunken newborn babe. She smiled, grabbed her mug of tea and opened the interconnecting door and returned back into the shop.

'They've got him out, though he may need a wee lie doon to clear his heid.'

Marilyn was balancing precariously on a footstall endeavouring to put one of the SOS posters on the shop window.

'If I'm being honest I don't know what worries me most Shirley, Eddie or Salter's Supermarkets.'

Shirley's sympathetic smile immediately dissipated as she saw old Stanley Simpson hobbling towards the door. She was due to pop next door to assist him with his domestic chores after her shift in the shop had finished, and that hour spent with him was more than enough for one day without having to serve him in the shop. His morose nature could suck the joy out of a small child's Christmas day. He was wearing his long raincoat and trilby hat, his hair would be slicked back with Brylcreem if he had it, margarine if he didn't. Although he shaved every day, there were always clumps of grey hair on his throat or cheeks where his blunt razor ineffectually just skimmed over the resolute bristles. He didn't enjoy spending money or 'good brass' as he referred to it, and it was his son who used to pay Shirley, primarily to ease his own guilt as he rarely visited his joyless and increasingly forgetful father.

'Hiya Stan, what can we get you love?' said Shirley with a forced smile.

'Why aren't you round sorting my tea out, what are you doing working here? I don't pay you to work here.'

'I'll be round in a wee while, is there anything you want from the shop?'

'I'm quite capable of looking myself woman, I haven't completely lost my marbles you know,' snarled Stanley with his usual aggression.

Stanley forcefully yanked a wire basket free from the pile and proceeded to hobble slowly around the shop, lifting and scrutinising the labels on various packets and tins, and tutting loudly at the price. Shirley raised her eyebrows and whispered to Marilyn, 'The boy's getting proper tapped in the heid.'

Stanley Simpson lived in the bungalow next door to The Corner Stores. With each passing day his confusion grew. He would often find himself sitting in his own lounge in the darkness trying to work out where he was and where his parents were. He recognised that heavy set loud-mouthed Scottish woman when she turned up but didn't know who the hell she was. He sometimes thought she might have once been his wife, but he didn't mention it for fear of making a fool of himself. But to give her credit she did look after him. He often felt a rising panic that something was wrong but he didn't know what. He also knew that he had a family but couldn't remember their names or even visualise them in his mind's eye. Several months ago he had written their names and details of his life in a note pad, which he would get out each morning to study, then one morning he couldn't find the note pad. He didn't mention it to the Scottish woman as he felt embarrassed – and after all, what right had she to know his intimate business! The next day he had forgotten about the note pad and it lay undiscovered on top of the wardrobe in the spare bedroom, its final resting place. The one thing that he managed to grimly hang on to, like an unsecured climber desperately clinging onto the edge of a cliff face, was his pride. Paradoxically, the thing that kept him fighting was responsible for destroying him as he struggled to cope with the harsh day-to-day realities.

Leslie and Trevor emerged from the kitchen.

'We've sorted him out Marilyn. He said he had to go to the shed to sort out the coal. I trust you are both coming to the SOS meeting this evening? Salter's have said they are sending a representative to listen to our views, Trevor's going to minute the meeting so we have a proper record of what is actually said.'

'...and we've got some lovely leaflets printed up,' Trevor proudly added.

'Aye we'll all be there. Looking forward to it, is that tadger breath Beaton coming too? Nay offence lads,' said Shirley.

'Who knows? He's suddenly become the invisible man, but someone from the Parish Council should be there, they have provided the hall for the meeting.'

'Yes, he's lying low, we haven't seen him in the shop since that newspaper article broke,' said Marilyn.

Stanley turned round abruptly at the back of the shop and bellowed, 'I wouldn't piss on that man if he was on fire; he tarmacked my driveway the shyster. Not only did he cover over the fire hydrant, the whole driveway lifted up in one solid sheet a week after he laid it, one solid sheet. The man is a shyster, absolute shyster.' He turned back to the tin of spam he was holding and put it in his inner coat pocket.

*

Eddie sighed as he ran his hands through this cooking-oil hair, recoiling slightly as he touched the abrasions on each side of his forehead. He had retired to the dark sanctuary of the storage shed to lick his physical and psychological wounds. Now that really was embarrassing, he thought to himself and he was no stranger to humiliating situations. He inwardly cringed as the devastating scene replayed in his head. He had been cautiously retrieving his kitchen beverage of choice, discretely housed in the gap between the cooker and the sink, and carefully unscrewing the lid of the bottle of vodka when Ronnie and Reggie jumped up behind him like two silent assassins pushing against the back of his knee joints causing him to drop the bottle and career forward as his legs simultaneously collapsed beneath him. As he fell, he valiantly lunged even harder in a vain attempt to catch the bottle and its precious cargo, his momentum pushed his head into the unofficial storage gap like a cork being squashed back into a wine bottle – he was wedged fast. As he knelt in a praying position, he contemplated the village fire crew arriving and dismantling the kitchen. To add to his woes, he was forced to watch the bottle gently empty. Could it really have been any worse, those two extracting him, with Lurch gleefully watching the entertainment? He had seen them glance at the now empty bottle after they extracted him, but they didn't say anything.

He jumped as his thoughts were rudely interrupted by a loud thumping on the wooden gate that allowed access from the pavement to the rear of the shop and the storage shed.

'Hello Mr Rogers, it's Scotty, Ron's son, I've got the delivery. Are you there, Mr Rogers? Hellooooo?' a youthful voice rose from behind the gate. Eddie launched himself from the shed out of the exposed open end and unlocked the gate.

'For fuck's sake, keep your voice down.'

Scotty stood there blinking with his jaw hanging open.

'Sorry Mr Rogers.'

Scotty was nothing like his father in physical appearance, he was a short wiry youth with a black shock of hair. He wore a garish orange tracksuit, which had become his trademark as he seemed to change his clothes about as often as Father Christmas.

'As I keep saying, it's Eddie, call me Eddie.'

'OK Mr Rogers. I've got the delivery for you. Dad said it was forty pints?'

'Yes, that's right.' There was absolutely no reaction from the slack-jawed Scotty. 'Well, can you unload it and bring it through to the back of the shed?' Eddie irritably barked.

Without a word or sign of acknowledgement, Scotty turned and marched back to the old rusted-out Bedford van and opened the tail gate, and started to slowly lift out the four-pint kegs that sat on the flatbed at the rear of the vehicle, placing them carefully on the pavement.

'Quick as you can Scotty lad,' said Eddie, furtively glancing right toward the front of the shop, hoping that no customers would want any fruit and veg which would require Marilyn or Lurch to come out to the front of the shop. He looked left and saw the ray of sunshine Stanley appear from the shop entrance. He hobbled past, pockets bulging, and glanced at the beverages being unloaded onto the pavement, and without halting his step muttered 'That muck gives me the runs' and shuffled on towards the bungalow he once called home.

Under instruction, Scotty kicked into another gear and had loaded the ten kegs in the rear of the shed in double quick time.

'Tell your Dad I'll pay him when I next see him.'

'OK Mr Rogers. Do you know what the time is please?'

'Yes, it's just gone one o'clock.'

'Oh no! I'm running late for Councillor Beaton.'

'I didn't know your dad sold to Councillor Beaton.'

'He doesn't, I go over every Friday and wrestle him in his lunch hour. He pays me *£10* for it and it's less than an hour Mr Rogers.'

'Really, I didn't know he liked wrestling, tell me more. What do you do exactly?'

'Oh yes, he really likes it Mr Rogers. We always wrestle in the lounge. He pulls the curtains shut and puts down a large rubber mat and a big plastic sheet underneath so the oil doesn't damage his carpet – he said his wife wouldn't appreciate that.'

The 'wrestling' was Gary Beaton's real peccadillo, and by implication his Achilles heel. He happened to stumble across this callow youth by pure chance, and immediately recognised that he was absolutely perfect with the combined attributes of being slow on the uptake and in need of easy money. He had answered the door when Gary Beaton had knocked to tentatively enquire about buying the property as a part of his grandiose Heathview development scheme. It became apparent that his Yeti-like father was out, but Gary Beaton seized the day, and talked the young imbecile in to joining his 'wrestling club'. He told Scotty that he needed to record the sessions to improve his technique, which wasn't totally misleading. So every Friday afternoon when his wife went to visit her mother he would set up the video camera on a tripod and lay out the plastic sheet and the 'wrestling' mat and spend an hour grunting and groaning, then another half hour grunting and moaning after Scotty had left when he watched the action back on the video recorder. The boy is as dim as a five-watt bulb and doesn't have a clue what is going on, he gleefully thought to himself as he stashed the video away in its secret location in the garage, alongside the numerous other 'wrestling' tapes of other young lads that had succumbed to his deviancy and money.

Eddie grinned as he opened one of the kegs and took a heavy slug. He felt this news warranted a silent toast.

'Tell me young man, what sort of outfits do you wrestlers wear these days?'

'Well, I always wear my normal swimming trunks, Mr Rogers. Councillor Beaton has some black rubber wrestling trunks that he said he had specially made. He's training to go professional and doesn't want anyone to know about it, Mr Rogers, so please don't tell anyone.'

'No of course not, that sounds really interesting. What sort of training do you do with him?'

'Just grappling Mr Rogers. He puts baby oil on me to make it more difficult for him though, as he wants to go professional.'

'I bet he puts some effort in Scotty, does he groan and make this puffing noise by any chance?'

Scotty thought for a moment.

'Yes he does, Mr Rogers, he really does. I'd better go, Mr Rogers, or I'll be late.'

'OK son, can you please give my regards to Councillor Beaton though, mention that I was asking after him.'

Eddie smiled to himself. This was the best news he had heard for many a long day. He was actually really looking forward to the next time he saw Councillor Beaton, which as fate dictated would be much sooner than he thought.

CHAPTER 6

The campaign team had adorned the entrance to the village hall with a large banner proclaiming their intentions – 'SOS' in large red letters with and an equally impressive exclamation mark following closely behind. Trevor and Leslie were in the doorway handing out leaflets to all those attending. There was an air of anxious anticipation inside the village hall for the presentation by Salter's Supermarkets. There was already a large turnout with most of the small business owners present, with Mr and Mrs Bowford diligently ushering those attending to what they considered an appropriate seat for them – naturally Brigadier Bowford had reserved the front row for the campaign members, each seat decorated with a cardboard name plaque, beautifully crafted in ornate calligraphy by Mr Bowford's own fair hand.

Marilyn had managed to evade the attentions of the Bowfords and situated herself and Eddie towards the back of the hall. This was largely due to Eddie's 'tired and emotional' condition that Marilyn didn't think was conducive to a front row seat. Unbeknownst to Marilyn, he had got rather carried away with the tramp juice in light of the salacious and rather joyous news about Councillor Beaton, and both his frontal cortex and bowels were seriously affected in contrary ways – one was numb and the other incredibly angry, although he wasn't sure in which order.

They sat next to Brenda Garwood who owned Garwood's Convenience Store, the other corner shop situated at the furthermost end of the village. She had also managed to evade the officious Bowfords and her card remained untouched on her reserved seat, albeit not in splendid isolation. Brenda Garwood had been struggling to manage her shop for the past two years since her husband of 30 years passed away from a heart attack at the wheel of their van parked at the rear of their shop after driving back from the cash and carry early one evening. The article in the parish magazine had said that it was an *'unexpected heart attack'*. Brenda wondered when a heart attack was ever expected – although in Harry's case it was probably more in the 'expected' than 'unexpected' camp – he smoked like an industrial chimney, drank like a fish and ate like a malnourished pig, hence his 25-stone frame and faint heart. They found a half-eaten pasty in the passenger foot well of the van; it transpired the heart attack had been induced through choking. At the inquest, the coroner concluded that Harry had been frantically trying to consume a second pasty before unloading the van as he was an avid *Coronation Street* fan and didn't want to miss his favourite programme. Unfortunately, his mastication was inadequate leading to the pasty lodging in his windpipe with the ensuing panic causing a massive coronary. It always made Brenda feel sad that he hadn't finished the pasty as Harry hated to see food go to waste. She was perpetually exhausted from the emotional strain of the bereavement and the physical demands of 14-hour days, six days a week (five hours on a Sunday).

The Salter's news had weighed heavier on her than Harry did on Valentine's night. Brenda smiled and greeted the Rogers; she was not surprised to see Eddie's puce face and inane grin, she had heard he was getting worse but it felt good that they were all sitting together united against the common enemy. On her other side sat Cloth-Eared Jack, who was playing with his whistling hearing aid, and his corpulent wife Dot who had made an extremely rare excursion from the living room and was busy polishing off a family bag of Maltesers.

In the car park, Councillors Mike Brooks and Sally Holmes were nervously having a cigarette before entering the lion's den; they were still waiting for Gary Beaton and really didn't fancy answering to the thronging hoard without him as he knew the scheme and their decision-making rationale inside and out, an almost encyclopaedic knowledge. They were now secretly hoping that the representative from Salter's didn't turn up as it would give them a legitimate excuse to postpone the meeting. They turned their heads toward the throaty roar of a red Porsche screaming into the car park and coming to a halt with the screech of tyres and the accompanying regulation smell of burning rubber. They were more than surprised to see a wind-swept Gary Beaton, his plump frame wedged in the passenger seat and what looked like, at first glance, the rock guitarist Rick Parfitt in the driver's seat. JBJ turned off the engine and unbuckled her seat belt.

'Now remember Gary, leave all of the talking to me, it's important that we keep the locals onside – I've been through this many, many times – and whatever the provocation do not lose your shit.' JBJ nodded at the back seat. 'Now be a honey and bring those boxes of leaflets for me.'

The raucous chattering in the hall gradually diminished to a murmur as JBJ led the three councillors, like the Pied Piper, to the stage where they took their seats. Salter's had provided comfortable chairs and microphones, and one of JBJ assistants was floor walking with a roaming microphone for the audience questions. They had a professional sound rig with a mixing desk and a qualified sound technician operating it. At the back of the hall behind a screened off area the caterers were laying out wine, beer and nibbles for the end of the session. At the entrance to the hall they were also piling up Salter's mini hampers to hand out to each person in attendance – JBJ was highly experienced at the charm offensive and no expense had been spared. As the audience fell silent, JBJ picked up her microphone and walked to the front of the stage.

'Good evening ladies and gentlemen, I'm Jerry Bailey Johnson, Head of UK Business Development for Salter's Supermarkets. As you can probably tell I'm not from these fine shores, but what I can tell you I come from a small community in the northwest of the States and I grew up from the age of 12 working in my daddy's grocery business, so I understand the importance of family, community and the role of the small business. What I want to reassure you today is that Salter's are totally committed to working for your community and helping to support and work alongside all the existing businesses. We will help to ensure that the infrastructure of the village can support the plans for expansion and help attract new members to your community. We will also create job opportunities and our policy is very clear, we will always look to put local applicants first – and as an employer we offer excellent benefits such as healthcare and a funded pension plan. This is for you, your children and your children's children. We feel honoured and privileged to have this wonderful opportunity to serve and be part of your community. I know you have lots of questions and your parish councillors are here too; they will introduce themselves shortly. We will do our very best to answer all your questions with honesty and integrity. Before the councillors introduce themselves, I would like to say that if you don't want to ask your question now we have put on some free drinks and food at the end of the session and the councillors and myself will be here for an hour or so after, so please come and have a chat with us or just have a drink and chat between yourselves. If you do speak with me you can call me JBJ, it's much easier to remember and less of a mouthful. We have also outlined all of the frequently asked questions and the key dates and timelines in a document that we have put in a mini hamper for each of you to take when you leave later this evening. Right, councillors, would you like to give your personal introduction…'

JBJ's opening speech was greeted with a deathly silence, almost as if there had been a collective holding of breath until its conclusion. The councillors introduced themselves, two very briefly but the third, Councillor Gary Beaton, went into great detail describing his resume and the planning process. Trevor was struggling to keep up as he was taking the unofficial minutes. He had learned shorthand when he was training as a journalist when he first left school, but even shorthand couldn't keep up with a free-flowing Councillor Beaton – he was a man on a manic mission. JBJ glared at Beaton as she realised his second mad dash to the toilet before they went on stage was nothing to do with his stomach, more to do with his nose and the copious amounts of

Colombian marching powder he had clearly just hoovered up. She had known Beaton was a liability and it was a calculated risk bringing him along to the meeting, but his non-attendance would have immediately created a relationship of mistrust with the locals – but right now she was regretting her decision. As he drew breath and reached for his water, JBJ seized the opportunity and picked up her microphone to intervene, mindful of the knowledge he could be heading for a crash before the end of the session unless he powdered his nose again. She wasn't sure which would be worse.

'Thank you Councillor Beaton for that extremely thorough 15-minute walk-through of your entire career and passions in life, it was most enlightening.'

There was a solid laugh in unity from the audience. However, Beaton was totally oblivious to it as he was champing at the bit to get back to the toilet. In his own mind the cocaine was, as always, purely for medicinal purposes as he had put his back out performing – what he had described to Ron's boy as – a half-nelson. In fairness, the Nelson reference was apt as it was probably a manoeuvre performed in desperation by seamen holed up on a boat for months on end, and it also led to Beaton's own production of semen, mostly after the youth had left.

'Can we please now invite you to ask us any questions you may have. Please raise your hand and one of my team will bring the microphone to you – it's helpful if you wait, just so that everyone can hear. Can you also introduce yourself so everyone who can see you knows who it is.'

Four or five hands immediately sprang into the air. JBJ scanned for the one that looked like the least trouble and pointed to the back of the room. As her assistant attempted to move towards them from her position by the front row, Brigadier Bowford, who had his arm still raised, snatched the microphone from her with his spare hand. He immediately sprang to his feet and cleared his throat directly into the microphone, with a sound like a flooded car trying to start, causing a shriek of feedback from the speakers. The sound engineer nonchalantly looked up from the paper he was reading and made a token adjustment to the desk, then got straight back to the intrigue of the *Melody Maker*.

'Byron Bowford.'

From the back of the room, Eddie screamed out with laughter receiving a rebuking 'shush' and glares from those near him, Mr Bowford briefly turned his scowling head to the source of the interruption.

'Fuck me Byron, Byron! I never knew that or would have EVER guessed that… he's a poet and he didn't know it,' he loudly whispered to Marilyn as his convulsing shoulders gave away his continued mirth. Ron's tramp juice elixir was really pumping in his veins.

'…retired military logistics officer, 80 years young, ma'am.'

'Hello Byron, firstly can I just say thank you for your service to your country and to the free world. Without our servicemen that fought in World War Two, where would we be today? Byron, what is your question please?'

Brigadier Bowford noticeably swallowed hard and, bristling with pride, his voice started to waver before he composed himself.

'Question for Beaton. We have set up an action group, of which I and Mrs Bowford, are the prominent members. When you made the decision to approve planning permission, you didn't consult any of the local businesses. We want, no, we absolutely demand, a proper consultation process before this project proceeds any further. We want the Parish Council to speak to the planning authority and put this project on ice until this appropriate and necessary consultation has occurred.'

There was an eager but short round of applause from the room. Gary Beaton was now feeling rather fragile and on a delicate edge, and this stupid old fool was calling into question the decision of an elected body. No fuck that, calling into question Gary Fucking Beaton! How fucking dare he! I'll rip his scrawny head off! JBJ saw the wild look in Beaton's saucer eyes and stepped in front of him; she had already taken the precaution of having his microphone turned off before the Q & A session.

'Thank you Byron for your so eloquently expressed question. I think it is more appropriate that I explain the legal position as the planning and appeal process was completed several months ago. However, what I really want us to do is to consult with all of the businesses in Heathview. We want to know what this business community fears and what they want. I've got that as an action for me. Does that satisfactorily answer your question, Byron?'

The Brigadier nodded as his anger and frustration totally dissipated. He felt a ball in the pit of his stomach, a feeling he hadn't felt for 25 years. Admittedly, she didn't look conventionally attractive, but right now she was the most attractive woman he had ever met. The way she spoke to him, so confident and recognising him and what he had done for this country!

JBJ spotted a woman with a weather-beaten face and dreadful perm toward the back of the room.

'Yes, madam, you with the lovely contemporary hair style, what's your question and who is it to please?'

'Aye, I'm Shirley, I'm nae gonna give yis my life story, like yer man there. I was gonna put the question to tadger breath Beaton but I could hear from here he's oooff his tits on the showbiz-sherbet, ken?

There was a mix of laughter and chatter, those not laughing wanted to know what 'showbiz-sherbet' was, primarily from those who laughed.

'…so you'll do hen. I'm nae a fan of you, and that's fucking putting it mildly, I can see right through you, with yer drinks and hampers. This is all fake, community this, community that do yer think we were fucking born yesterday…'

The microphone was snatched from Shirley before she could actually ask a question.

'Sorry to interrupt you, Shirley. We really believe in the community past, present and future. You are so wrong Shirley, we do care. Can I just say, can we all please, please mind our language, let's keep it clean and respect our families.' JBJ looked out for the next question and saw that Jack was holding his hand aloft. He looked fairly harmless.

'Yes, you sir,' as the assistant with the microphone walked towards the man with the whistling hearing aid.

'Hello, I'm Javas some people call me Jack, anyway I'm the taxi driver in the village and I'm livid, bloody livid. I rely on fares from my customers taking them to town to do their shopping. You are taking my bloody livelihood away.'

'Thank you, Jack, let me just say that we as a company have need for the regular use of a taxi in the village for the monthly visits from head office. I will make sure that you are designated as our official taxi for all Salter's needs.'

'Oh right, errr thank you Mrs errr Jennifer.' Jack felt a sharp dig in his ribs from Dot to remind him of 'his' other question.

'…oh, can I ask what the nibbles are and what's in the hamper?'

This drew a raucous round of laughter. JBJ assumed it was some English joke that passed her by so she laughed too and moved on to the next question without addressing the issue of the nibbles. Jack lowered himself back into the seat to a torrent of abuse from the ravenous Dot directed to his right ear. He surreptitiously turned his hearing aid off.

'Yes please, you sir, the one in the wonderful cowboy outfit. That looks original and so reminds me of home, thank you sooo much! Tell us your name hon?'

Bruce 'Jesse' Wyatt did all of his weekly shop in The Corner Stores, although that wasn't great in volume or value. He worked long hours and for convenience often ate breakfast and lunch at the greasy spoon café which was a mere stone's throw from his garage in the village centre. Eddie loathed him for how he treated his children, and called him 'Whistling Rufus', due to the pronounced whistle on every 'S' that passed his lips. To continue his career and lifestyle after his wife passed away, Jesse had both his children put immediately into foster care. He told the local care authority that he would have them home occasionally, but when business permitted. The squalor in the flat above the garage had provided the evidence the social worker required to progress his request. His two boys were 14 and 15, but in Jesse's mind they could look after themselves – after all, he was no stranger to the care system and it had done him no harm, just an absence of empathy. He changed his name by deed poll to incorporate his passion of country and western, attending gun-slinging events in the wild east of England – he went from Bruce to Jesse Wyatt, many thought an unsuitable moniker for a proprietor of a garage, although it was actually quite apt with his fairly shady handling of insurance claims and age-rejuvenating treatment of vehicles on their MOT.

'Thank you kindly, ma'am.' He tipped up his Stetson hat. 'My names Bruce… I mean Jesse, Jesse Wyatt.'

'Yeeha Jesse! You make me feel right at home! What's your question, Jesse please?'

'I shop at The Corner Stores every week, which is a tiny little shop not very far from where you are building your massive store. I have seen your stores all over the country. You will wipe out these little stores… it's happened everywhere you've been, despite what you say. We want these little shops that know us. We want to put in a shopping list at the start of the week and pick it up later or have it delivered if we are unable to collect, a place where we can get tick and they trust us. We really don't need a superstore in this village, our message is a simple one, please go home, ma'am.'

The meeting erupted with everyone on their feet applauding and whistling. Marilyn felt a pang of guilt as she didn't care for Bruce Wyatt at all, due to the way he treated his children and openly physically and verbally abused them in the shop on the rare occasions they stayed with him. She didn't know his sons' names as he only called them 'the boys' but had witnessed the overweight six-foot brute club them round the head and verbally abuse them if they asked for or said something that he didn't think was appropriate. Marilyn sensed they were brought into the shop as a bizarre display of his dominance. Their reaction was even more chilling, they didn't cry or even bat an eyelid, merely carried on as if nothing happened – truly the next generation.

JBJ waited for the euphoria to subside then spoke.

'This is a special model to us, we have learned by our previous mistakes. If The Corner Stores, or any other business selling the same as us, want to join us we can offer them a franchise deal so that we are working together, or they can stay independent. We believe all the businesses in Heathview can expand in the next ten years. Can I ask please, are Eddie and Marilyn Rogers from The Corner Stores here tonight?'

JBJ's earpiece linked to her assistant had already told her where they were located in the room and that Eddie was already comfortably numb.

Much to Marilyn's horror, Eddie stood up and beckoned the microphone. A strange thought went through her head, whenever you describe a woman as 'glowing' it is complimentary, in Eddie's case his luminous head was anything but.

'Hello, everyone, most of you know me, but anyway I'm Eddie from The Corner Stores, the shop she was shaying about.' He noticeably slurred on the tricky tongue twister and he attempted, unsuccessfully, to erase his mistake by repeating it '…the shop she was shaying about, that's easy for me to shay. Anyway, I just want to ask Brown Envelope Beaton how the Parish Council made that decision and did he have to WRESTLE with his conscience – and I don't want an answer from you Jenny Bailey Brown or whatever your name is, I want it from him, Big Daddy himself, Brown Envelope Beaton, the corrupt bastard.'

The hall erupted with cheers and laughter. Leslie leaned over to Trevor. 'Don't minute that.'

'How dare you! You fucking piss-pot!' Beaton screamed, more concerned at the wrestling references than the allegation of impropriety. Surely he didn't know? He sprang to his feet, threw the microphone on the floor and leapt forward, launching off the stage and running as fast as his Colombian marching powder legs would carry his rotund body to his target. In his own mind, he vaulted from the stage and ran like an Olympic sprinter breathing slowly with absolute control, increasing his speed as he approached his prey for the kill. To all that were watching, he stumbled off the stage then started running slowly at first then increasing speed, screaming 'Come on then you fucking pisshead'. When he got within six feet, he launched himself snarling like a rabid dog, he was invincible, he was superman, he was going to rip that pisshead apart. His journey was brought to an abrupt end by the giant iron fist of Tramp Juice Ron sitting next to Eddie. It was one solid punch that efficiently compressed Beaton's nose flat against his face. A small amount of white powder floated in the air as Brown Envelope Beaton, as he was to be known as from now on, crumbled to the floor.

Eddie then started the wrestling chant of 'Easy, Easy, Easy…' unsteadily swaying as he rhythmically clapped his hands, arms arching above his head. Most of the village attendees were cheering and laughing, some were even joining in the chant, as JBJ's assistant and the councillors rushed to the aid of the prone semi-conscious Brown Envelope. JBJ realised that things had gone very wrong and a sharp exit was required. She pulled the microphone to her lips and above the cacophony of noise she said, 'Right then ladies and gents, I think it's time for drinks and nibbles. Please collect your hamper on the way out too. Thank y'all for coming tonight, I can only apologise for Councillor Beaton's unacceptable behaviour, although I want to make it absolutely clear he is nothing to do with Salter's Supermarkets or this exciting project.'

'Please tell me that you have minuted that that last bit, Trevor?' Leslie burbled excitedly.

JBJ smiled as she grabbed her bag to make for the door. It wouldn't be wise to be around when this lot get stuck into the free booze, she correctly reasoned. At the same time, she was also thinking about what to do with the publicly crowned Brown Envelope Beaton. She needed to contain this night – Salter's could never hear of this or her ass was grass. Fortunately it wasn't recorded, and all the key Salter's employees would be briefed on a version of the events. If push came to shove, she would get her assistant to testify that Brown Envelope Beaton was taking illegal Class A drugs and was out of control. She had thought earlier after his 15-minute cocaine fuelled presentation that giving him a large amount of that stuff was a mistake, she had only wanted him to make a fool of himself and further undermine his credibility within the village; she hadn't envisaged him turning into a mouth-frothing raving lunatic. But she had to admit that despite all of the potential problems it had caused, seeing his supercilious face caved in by that Neanderthal was total vindication.

CHAPTER 7

A little white rusty Subaru van with no livery motored through the Wisdom Estate. At the helm was Danny Rogers making The Corner Stores Christmas deliveries, and as this was on a 'non-working' Saturday he had no need to don the disguise. Over a month had passed since the infamous SOS meeting which was now recorded in the annals of the village history. Although he hadn't attended the meeting as he had a band practice, he had heard from several different colleagues at Heathview Manufacturing of the evening's entertainment, the common opinion being 'Your old man is an absolute legend Dan'. He never actually heard the uncensored version of events as most confidants were too embarrassed to mention his father's condition; his feedback was confined to Eddie calling out Brown Envelope Beaton who had then endeavoured to launch a vicious 'unprovoked' attack only to be brought to abrupt and timely justice by the hulk-like fist of Tramp Juice Ron.

The band practice had been equally memorable. They had been auditioning a new keyboard player and Simon the bass player recommended a girl he had known from school. They had trundled up the off-road winding mud track in the Subaru van to the Old Hut where they were allowed to rehearse for free as a 'community project'. The Old Hut was used by community groups like the Cubs, Scouts, Brownies and Guides, the main attraction being that, unlike the village hall, its charging regime was the whispered suggestion of a donation or help in kind with the upkeep. There were a few hardy souls, mainly parents of the various troops, that helped keep The Hut patched up and reasonably watertight. When the rain drummed loudly on the corrugated roof, all the amps needed to be turned up a notch or two, and the circuit breaker that the extension leads were plugged into became the most valuable piece of equipment – with the propensity for sudden leaks in the roof, it was potentially a life saver.

As Danny turned the last corner to The Hut, the lights of the Subaru illuminated a figure in the car park. There she was leaning on the Bowles Bakery Van with a beaming smile on her face. She pulled up her sleeve up and tapped her watch as they were nearly five minutes late. 'Thought you said you were professional,' joked Jenny.

'I didn't realise you played,' Danny stammered.

'You never asked Danny. In fact, you've never asked me very much at all,' she teased, pulling her parakeet-blue hair back and securing it with a colour-clashing purple scrunchy.

Danny had driven past the site of Salter's new superstore and the progress was quite staggering (largely due to the work being commenced behind closed doors before planning permission was granted). The boarding round the site had only just been removed at the front at the request of Jerry Bailey Johnson to ensure transparency and openness. Those protesting villagers had been aghast at how quickly the project had progressed, it was only just over three months ago that planning permission was granted yet the massive store and car park looked near to completion.

Danny pulled the van into Granny Smith's driveway, its tyres leaving tracks in the virgin snow. She was the last delivery of the day as her order wasn't urgent and she normally had some 'little jobs' that needed doing which invariably had the propensity to make him late for the other deliveries. In all honesty, he rarely had the time to help Granny Smith and didn't always offer the helping hand with a glad heart, often unfairly cursing Shirley for not doing her job properly. He was too young and naïve to realise that it was his company that Granny Smith craved and the 'little jobs' provided an excuse for her to hear about his band, job and his loves in the outside world. Granny Smith would prompt and then sit back and listen as Danny told her the latest about some idiotic apprentice at work who had attempted to clean the blades on one of the wood saws as he had been instructed but without the wherewithal to first turn the blade off and was now missing two fingers. Then for comic effect Danny had added the old joke that he hadn't realised he'd lost the fingers until he was signalling goodnight to the foreman. The good-hearted banter always flowed while he cleaned out the fireplace, moved furniture, caught and ejected a spider or simply made a nice cup of tea with a slice of cake. She loved hearing the timbre of his young voice. He wasn't to know that Granny Smith's teenage son had been killed during the Normandy Landings; his picture sat alongside her late husband's on the sideboard but it was a loss she never spoke of, and of course no one asked about. Who was really interested in those dusty black and white memories of an old lady?

The back gate had a lock and a latch. Danny reached under the ornamental frog next to the gate to retrieve the key and let himself into the small garden. He saw a robin bouncing merrily across the snow to some remnants of food that had fallen off the busy bird table. He noticed some footprints to the bird table that were now partially covered with the light continuous fall of snow. He rummaged in his pocket with one hand while cradling the box of groceries in his other arm, and plucked out the back door key and let himself in to the kitchen.

'Hello, it's me, Danny,' he loudly announced to ensure he didn't scare Elvis or his owner. He heard Elvis snuffling as he came through from the lounge. Danny placed the groceries on the small kitchen table, made a quick fuss of Elvis and stepped into the lounge, where he saw Granny Smith was asleep by the window; she had been watching the activity on the bird table. It was gloomy in the lounge so he turned the centre light on. Granny Smith was dreaming of George, her son, hugging her for the last time. She hadn't had the old recurring dream for decades. She woke with a start.

'Sorry, I didn't mean to make you jump. I've made you a nice cuppa and a couple of chocolate biscuits.'

'Oh, George, I didn't think…'

'It's Danny.'

'Danny?' Granny Smith squinted at the figure coming into focus.

'Ah Danny, thank you love, that's very kind of you. You are a lovely young man a real credit to your mum and dad.' She reached out and clasped his hand between her own.

'I've put your groceries away, for you. I'm afraid we didn't have any tangerines but we had satsumas which we put in for you as a substitute. Mum also included a small piece of stilton as we got some in on the deli counter for Christmas. I hope that's OK? I've left the bill on the table – Mum's added it on to your account.'

'That's lovely dear, thank Marilyn very much, you are all so good to me. I know you're really busy but have you got ten minutes to have a cuppa and a chat? I bet you've been rushed off your feet running around on your day off after silly old fools like me.'

'Of course I've got time,' Danny lied, frantically calculating how long it would take to get back and changed and bathed before heading out and picking Jenny up to see a potential rival band playing in town '…and I wouldn't do it if I didn't enjoy it, would I? It's always lovely to see you.'

'Sit yourself down then Danny, how is that band of yours going?' Granny Smith placed the cup and saucer with the biscuits on the little table next to her and leant forward to the apron dangling from her frame to retrieve her tobacco tin and lighter. She was delighted to find that she had a few already rolled. A plume of acrid smoke soon followed.

'Excellent thanks, we've got a new keyboard player – Jenny, she's excellent,' said Danny, awkwardly coughing from the tobacco smoke and feeling himself start to blush at the same time.

'We've actually got our first gig on New Year's Eve at the Kings Arms Pub – apparently Dad knows the landlord really well. We've got quite a few practice sessions lined up as Jenny needs to get familiar with the set, but I have to say we clicked straight away, the band and Jenny that is. We are being paid though – it is ticket-entry only so we have to try and sell them up front. Jenny is going to try and sell them to customers on her rounds. Bakery round… she works for Bowles the Bakers.'

'That's really wonderful Danny love, I'm so pleased for you. I know all the hard work you have put in over the last year or so. It sounds as though this young lady Jenny is quite the catch. Did you know that I used to play the piano?' Even though her memory was now failing, she was certain she hadn't mentioned it as she hadn't spoken to anyone about it for many decades. It was another painful memory locked away with George.

'I was classically trained, my father made me attend lessons from the age of seven or eight, I think. I loved playing but when I married and had my son when I was 17, we couldn't afford furniture for our rented flat let alone a piano. I never played properly again. Just the occasional rendition when we were at a party where there was a piano. But I can still remember a piece I learned to play by Chopin, 'Nocturne Opus 9 No 2' – funny isn't it, as I can't remember what I had for breakfast this morning,' she said with a hollow laugh. 'You know Danny, you should always follow your dream, always follow your heart not your head, and never be put off by others. Do you have anything of yours I can listen to?'

'I do! We have a demo tape that we had recorded in a local studio, but that was before Jenny joined though. I'll bring it round next time – do you have a cassette player?'

'I'm afraid I don't dear.'

'Not to worry, I'll bring my portable one round. If you like, I'll see if I can dig some *Showpan* out of the library, I see you have an old record player over there in the corner.'

'That would be lovely Danny. All my old classical records warped when my husband put them in the loft of our house back in the 60s so we threw them out – it's the heat you see – never put records in the loft. In this life Danny, you always live and learn by your mistakes.'

Danny realised he was going to be late again.

'I'll put some more coal on the fire for you Granny Smith, it looks as though it on its last legs. I need to make a quick call on your phone if that's OK, I'll leave 10p for the call, it's only local.'

'Of course you can, it's not to someone called Jenny, is it by any chance? Don't keep her waiting lad, you get off now,' Granny Smith chortled.

*

Laurence Padbury didn't enjoy the three-mile cycle in the snow to The Corner Stores. His 1960's racing bike wasn't exactly built for these treacherous conditions and he struggled to keep control, especially round some of the winding lanes before he got to the estates. But he had no viable alternative option for groceries and toiletries. Technically there were a number of shops that were closer to his dilapidated bungalow but his poor interaction with other human beings and own limitations in shopping acumen meant there were really no other options.

He had always used The Corner Stores since his mother died a few months ago – he had been passing on one of his daily cycle rides and forced himself to stop at the shop for a cold drink. He parked his bike up against the fence by the fruit and veg and stood pondering his approach. If he went into the shop, where would the drinks be? Who would be serving? Would there be any children in the shop to make fun of him like they did when he left the bungalow? Despite being nearly 65 years old he had been sheltered from his withering social ineptitude, but his mother's passing had left him cruelly exposed. It was Marilyn emerging from inside the shop and asking him if he needed anything that had been the catalyst for his ongoing dependence on The Corner Stores. When he had said that he wanted a can of pop, she had headed back into the shop emerging with a cold can of Coca-Cola, which she handed to him and he paid her the money. She introduced herself and husband – who Mr Padbury had shrewdly observed over time seemed to spend most of his time in the storage shed at the side of the shop – and asked his name. He had replied 'Laurence Padbury' and she had said that it was 'lovely to meet you Mr Padbury'. He would have loved to say 'call me Laurence' but of course he couldn't. Since that time, his bi-weekly shop had been conducted in the same unusual method. He would park his cycle and wait patiently in his bicycle clips for Marilyn to emerge, sometimes it would be ten or 15 minutes if the shop was busy, but he didn't mind at all. The first time he started to read item by item from his prepared shopping list, and Marilyn politely interrupted and suggested it might be easier if he gave her the list and she would do the shop for him. She would bring it out in a cardboard box and he would remove the items and carefully place them (in a defined order of course) into the pannier bags hanging over the rear wheel of his racing cycle. He knew the exact weight and distribution ratio that each bag could safely hold and its likely effect on the handling capabilities of the cycle as he had designed the bike, both the numerous prototypes and the eventual production models.

Laurence Padbury was an extremely wealthy man from his designs and patented inventions but had never married and had no family. He dedicated his life to design, engineering and ingenuity, and his appearance had developed over time into a caricature of a Mad Professor – white goatee beard, wild grey hair and round-rimmed glasses. The bungalow where he had lived his whole life was in complete disrepair and his overgrown garden was a blot on the landscape as far as the neighbours were concerned. In his view, he was cultivating a habitat for the wonders of nature, and apart from the hours he spent in his workshop at the end of his garden, the other love of his life were the long cycle rides in the neighbouring country, documenting and drawing the local flora and fauna. His overgrown garden was now a refuge for a family of foxes and sometimes he could see from the conservatory the cubs lying and playing on the patio. In his world, this was a thing of immense beauty and worthy of celebration, and he would sit motionless for as long as they stayed. His neighbours didn't quite share his love of mother-nature's creations when they were ripping open their bin bags and defecating on their gardens.

He propped his cycle up against the fence and looked into the shop. He could see some figures moving around, and there was a taxi parked in the lay-by so he imagined he could have a bit of a wait. While he was waiting, he often took his small pair of binoculars from his jacket pocket to survey any wildlife of interest, mainly birds. There was a beautiful old oak tree that was situated at the back of Trevor and Leslie's bungalow opposite the shop. Mr Padbury had located a squirrel nest on his last visit and was trying to pinpoint the location, although he had assessed that in this weather the chance of any activity was fairly remote. As he was scanning the tree, he caught a dazzling reflection from the cul de sac road running to the side of the bungalow which housed a number of garages. He rolled his finger on the wheel of his binoculars to bring them into focus.

Eddie was standing behind the till and could see Mr Padbury standing in the snow by the fence with his binoculars peering at something across the road, his warm breath freezing in the chill air. Marilyn was busy serving Cloth-Eared Jack who had come in for Dot's 'elevenses'. She was valiantly attempting to squeeze three Danish pastries alongside two jam doughnuts into a large paper bag. Finally she admitted defeat and tore off another bag which hung next to the cakes, bread, pies and pasties on the middle aisle. She held it in one hand and opened it by blowing on it and promptly deposited the second part of Dot's elevenses with the help of a pair of baker's tongs.

'Oh, I see your Professor Yaffle is out there with his spy glasses again, I'll leave the mad bastard to you,' said a rosy-cheeked Eddie. Although he hadn't got the spotty locusts to contend with on a Saturday, he had still decided that he had to have something warm to keep the cold out, so had put some coffee in his large early morning brandy.

Marilyn glared at Eddie. She didn't like him making disparaging comments in front of other customers.

'He can't hear, he's mutton Jeff, aren't you Jack?'

As if it was choreographed, Jack fiddled with his hearing aid which emitted its usual shrill whistle.

'What's that?'

'I said anything else we can get you, Jack?' Eddie shouted, already reaching behind him for the Superkings.

'Oh, yes, 40 of my fags, can you put it on my bill? I'll settle up at the end of the week.'

'Technically this is the end of the week!' blurted Eddie.

'Oh OK, what's the damage Eddie?' as Jack reached into his pocket and produced a huge wad of ten-pound notes.

'Blimey Jack, have you come up on the premium bonds or the pools?' Eddie exclaimed, wondering why he was running a tab when he had that amount of cash in his pocket. The truth was that Jack had really struck gold. Jerry Bailey Johnson had been true to her word and the taxi contract was proving to be incredibly lucrative; not just the fees for the shuttle runs to and from the station but for the very healthy tips that Jerry Bailey Johnson gave him for information on the SOS campaign, most of which he made up. Although in all honesty he had come to realise he didn't really like the hard work the extra money entailed.

Marilyn placed Dot's 'elevenses' alongside Jack's cancer sticks and left Eddie to play *Name That Tune* on the till as he attempted to enter the cost of the precious late-morning bounty plus the balance owed on Cloth-Eared Jack's account. Customers who had a credit facility had a small red notebook which they kept in an old ice cream tub under the till. Each book had a running total, which they put a signature on with every new entry following purchases in the shop. The only exception to this were selected (not all as some were strictly cash on delivery) housebound customers where it was all based on a trust system. Most came to settle their accounts when they got paid, usually on a Friday, or received their pension or dole money. As they paid they were asked to watch as the previous entries were crossed through for a clean slate. This facility wasn't strictly legal but had been inherited by the Rogers who realised it was a way of securing a reliable customer base. They always had about 20 customers that ran their lives on credit or 'tick' as it was referred to. It did have its drawbacks however. Often customers would 'go missing' for a few weeks when they didn't have the funds to settle the account, and the more brash would demand a larger line of credit until they managed to source the funds, and some would never be seen again!

One such character was an illiterate delivery driver known as

Plug due to his facial resemblance to the Beano comic character. Plug had an unpleasant job delivering animal entrails for a local pet food company and the miasmic aroma that followed him into the shop made him a less than desirable customer. However, the money he spent each week on his family of four made his presence tolerable, although he had explained that the hours he worked were variable depending on the level of business that the company were doing – so his level of credit gradually grew. Sometimes at the weekend his short fat wife with her lank greasy hair would come to the shop accompanied by Plug and their grotty, snotty and unruly child entourage. When Plug stopped coming in on Friday to pay off his account, he owed over £150, and with horror it occurred to Marilyn, as an inherited customer, they didn't know where Plug lived or his real name. Emblazoned on the front of his red book in block capitals was 'PLUG' – nothing else. Marilyn knew they lived somewhere on the council estate but didn't have an exact address. Then about a month later his greasy-haired wife came into the shop, with Satan's spawn in tow, asking for credit! When Marilyn explained that she would need to pay off the existing balance, Chip Pan Hair nonchalantly explained that Plug had upped and left her, and that his debt was nothing to do with her as he wasn't her husband or even the father of her children! The Rogers had decided to write that debt off and put it down to experience. They kept Plug's book under the till on the infinitesimal chance he would one day miraculously return to serve his debt, but more realistically as a salutary reminder not to over-extend a line of credit. Needless to say, they didn't extend the offer of a little red book to Chip Pan Hair, who merely shrugged her shoulders at the children as if to say 'I tried', walked out of the shop and they never saw her again.

'Good morning Mr Padbury, how are you? What can we get for you today?' Marilyn stood shivering on the frontage of the shops next to the veg. Mr Padbury was intently focused on something across the road; Marilyn briefly wondered if he was up to something less than salubrious.

Without moving the binoculars from his eyes, Mr Padbury

mouthed in a strange loud theatrical whisper, 'Did you know you've got someone spying on you? He's parked up at the end of the cul de sac in a nappy-brown Ford Escort – he's been watching the shop with a pair of binoculars for the last five minutes, we are looking directly at each other now.' As he spoke he held his free hand aloft in a theatrical wave to his fellow spy. With that the nappy-brown Escort sprang to life and tore out of the cul de sac, veering right away from the shop at unnatural speed.

'He seemed to be making notes and watching you, most odd. I'll also have a bunch of spring onions,' said Laurence Padbury, handing over what was his second Christmas shopping list of the week. He always jabbered the request for spring onions whether they were actually in season or not; it was a nervous affectation, his late mother had always considered them to be a key differential between working and middle-class salad.

'Why on earth would someone be watching our shop? We don't have any spring onions, they aren't in season.'

A number of thoughts were running through Marilyn's head. Was it the council – either Trading Standards or Environmental Health? But why would they have a covert stakeout for them selling the odd ciggie to the spotty locusts or not cleaning the meat slicer for a month? Surely they would just present themselves? It must be something to do with Salter's, what else could it be?

'It is certainly most curious, Mrs Rogers, the surveillance that is, not the spring onions. Once I've got my shopping home, I'll have a ride around the village and see if I can locate the vehicle. I can cover all the residential roads in the Heathview vicinity in approximately three hours and 25 minutes.'

'If you do, can you let us know what you find out as soon as you can, our number is in the phone directory. It might be worth starting at the new supermarket site, then Beaton's yard. Thank you, Mr Padbury… do you mind if I call you Laurence?'

CHAPTER 8

The boardroom at Salter's Supermarkets had a resplendent walnut-panelled interior, with a 30-foot centrepiece table crafted with a simple elegance from the same beautifully polished wood – these aspects of the room furnishings dated back to the 18th century. However, the 18th-century historic fine art that had once graced these fine walls had been confined to the basement in wooden tea chests with no environmental protection, at the crass instruction of Colin Salter. They made way for various incarnations of the garish livery of the supermarket chain and blown-up photographs of the egotistical chairman, and substantial shareholder, Colin Salter grinning inanely in front of their various flagship stores. His corpulent frame and ruddy moon face had been skilfully adjusted to ensure his ego was suitably massaged when approving their production. He had also dispensed with the ornately carved chairs, which, though restored several times, were undoubtedly of a similar era. They were also consigned to the damp basement where they now lay slowly perishing next to the tea chests. He had replaced these with armless black leather swivel chairs, that were incredibly difficult to find a comfortable position in – a design plus as far as Colin Salter was concerned as he wanted to make life for anyone visiting that boardroom as uncomfortable as possible. He also ensured that he sat on, what looked to all intents and purposes, a throne. It was a solid high back George II library chair, a highly desirable genuine antique. He had paid handsomely for the privilege and added to his outlay when he had it re-upholstered in black leather so as not to unbalance the ambience of the room, and had extensions put on the legs so that he could be elevated a couple of inches higher than those around him, so he could literally look down on them. The problem he found was that although he was sitting higher than those surrounding him it was now quite a struggle to squeeze under the table with the gradual increase in his thigh size, through the intensive workout of his hand throwing food and drink down his throat 12 hours a day.

He was now feeling rather irritable as the fronts of his thighs had been chafing against the underside of the table for over 20 minutes. He had already scrawled on the notepad in front of him for the end of the table to be adjusted to accommodate his ever-increasing bulk. He didn't for one minute consider reducing the chair height, or heaven forfend a diet! Surrounding him were the five other sycophantic board members and the next item on the agenda was a report on delays to new flagship branches .The first to be considered was the Heathview Superstore.

'Before we get JBJ in for the next item, don't minute this…' he snapped at his PA (for the life of him, he couldn't remember her name – it was Suzie Kent and she had worked with him for just over six months which was a new record of longevity in the post).

'…we wanted this store open for Christmas and now we are told that it won't open until the new year, two weeks after the peak time. Now gentleman, I don't have to tell you that is about as much use to us as tits on a nun. Every day we overrun we incur additional costs and loss of revenue. When we get Rick Parfitt in here I want us to give her a right working over, metaphorically speaking.' He turned to address his unknown PA, who was looking rather perplexed, primarily as she was totally unaware that a member of Status Quo was involved in the building project.

'Right, go and get her in…'

Jerry Bailey Johnson was ushered into the boardroom by Suzie Kent who looked both ways down the corridor to see if there were any denim-clad rockers sitting in wait. Unsurprisingly there weren't, so she followed JBJ back into the boardroom.

'Welcome Jerry, please take a seat…' oozed Colin Salter, pointing her to the chair at the far end of the table where she would sit in splendid isolation with the spotlight firmly on her. JBJ nodded and took her place at the table. She placed her handmade leather briefcase on the table, opened it and placed her papers in front of her.

'...it's so lovely to see you. How has your adventure been in the wilds of Essex? You've survived clearly!' His eyes had a gleeful glint as he prepared the ground for the demolition.

'It has certainly not been without its challenges but nothing we can't handle. I assume you want to discuss the late project milestones ultimately leading to the late opening of our Heathview Superstore. We clearly need to understand these to ensure they are not repeated on future projects that we already have in the pipeline.'

Colin Salter's sore thighs had made him irritable, but JBJ's opening gambit heading him off at the pass and completely destroying his swinging wrecking ball had notched his annoyance up to ten. Bradley Ellis, Salter's finance and resources director, noted the change in his chairman's demeanour and decided he could earn some brownie points by landing a heavy blow – metaphorically speaking.

'Hi Jerry, Brad Ellis, I'm Salter's global director for finance and resources...' he preened. He always liked to add 'Global' into his designation, despite Salter's presence only extending to the home shores. He had also added the 'Resources' into his designation as he had heard other finance directors use it at various conferences he attended. He did this without a full understanding of the meaning of 'resources' or the implications. When he floated it to Colin Salter for approval, he was astounded to hear him immediately agree with an uncharacteristic zeal. It transpired that 'resources' actually meant the company staff and responsibility for any purchasing or procurement. It was with great pleasure that Colin Salter made the director for resources redundant and her own staff transferred to the leadership of Brad Ellis, or Brad 'Bullshit' Ellis as he was more commonly known among staff that had dealings with him. There was no additional remuneration for Brad but a whole new magazine of bullets to dodge – another spectacular own goal scored by his inflated ego.

'Hi, so great to see you again Brad, I remember you so well from my appointment. You were on the interview panel.'

The vague memory came flashing back to him as soon as she said it.

'Err quite, good to see you again too.' Although initially rattled, Bullshit Ellis was soon back in the groove. He leant forward towards JBJ and pointed his pen at her to emphasis each point.

'Obviously we have some concerns on the loss of revenue and particularly how you intend to recoup that in the first six months – we can come on to that. But firstly we need chapter and verse on the reasons behind these unforeseen delays, and why wasn't a contingency plan enacted far earlier, to at least have some part of the store open for the Christmas rush. You really should have approached the board much earlier and not present us with a fait accompli. We pride ourselves on being an agile organisation that responds with speed and rigour to any challenges that are laid before us.'

He reclined back in his seat like a barrister who had just completed a successful cross examination, and smugly surveyed the faces of his fellow board members for reaction, mainly focusing on the chairman who he observed had taken on a seemingly more relaxed demeanour and seemed to be thoroughly enjoying the show.

'Sure, I can talk you through my report if that would help? It covers all the points you need to address and I have also included an action plan which can be built into the future strategy and be used to inform the corporate risk register and of course any ongoing project in flight stage. I am advised it's been included in your board pack on appendix 5, which I think starts at page 238 in the pack after the interim mid-year draft accounts. I am really interested in getting you guys to give me your thoughts before finalising it, as there were some pretty fundamental flaws in our corporate governance and operational processes, which this size of project with an accelerated timetable has exposed. Hey guys, it's my ideas but it's whatever you want, you're the bosses.' JBJ threw in a Status Quo classic that went unnoticed, she had been listening at the door and wasn't in the mood to take any prisoners.

The room fell silent except for the sound of agenda packs being frantically thumbed. JBJ had phoned Suzie Kent when she was putting the report together for some advice on the house style for reports. Suzie Kent had only just received a dressing down from Colin Salter's wife for failing to pass on a message which had led to her husband being out until all hours instead of coming home for a hastily arranged meeting with the school. Suzie had of course passed the message on, but took the abuse meted out as part of her job. 'Good girl,' said Colin Salter, struggling again to remember her name as he hovered behind her as she fielded the call from his irate spouse. So in that frame of mind, Suzie had confided to JBJ that the board members really never bothered with the detail of the agenda packs and certainly didn't bother reading any paper of substance. She further explained that generally the meeting wouldn't last longer than an hour due to Colin Salter's chafing thighs, which JBJ didn't really want to explore further.

'Would it be helpful if I just went over the key points of failure in the executive summary on page 241 of your pack?' As there was no response, JBJ continued.

'I will also ask Suzie if she would be so kind as to pass you guys this project Gantt chart, which maps all of the planned milestones against all of the deliverables so when I go through the key issues it becomes far easier for you guys to visualise.'

The board members were a mixture of two old family members now in their 70s who had worked in the fledgling business which bore no resemblance to the complexity and size of the business today. The other board members comprised a retired banker and a retired solicitor, who were paid a healthy remuneration for their attendance. Their main credentials for appointment were primarily their professional qualifications but also their obsequious nature which paradoxically would transform into unbridled aggression towards anyone that dare challenge the authority of the board. Colin Salter and his henchman Brad 'Bullshit' Ellis were the decision makers, the rest were dispensable patsies to be thrown under the bus when the situation demanded.

'The major point of failure in the project occurred on the 20th September when there was an unplanned corporate suspension put on supplier engagement and payments which lasted for a total of 35 days before it was lifted. This led to the inability to both engage specialist contractors that were required for the completion stages of a project of this nature and also, more importantly, to make payments to our contractors, which was in breach of our contractual obligations. This in turn led to their own cash flow pressures, and of course an inability to pay their own suppliers who in turn refused to extend credit or provide further materials until the already exceeded credit limits were settled. In one case, one of our smaller contractors went into administration; we weren't able to engage a replacement due to the aforementioned suspension. As you gentlemen are well aware, this meant that other planned works also had to be suspended that were reliant on the delivery of earlier milestones – again causing us some future legal difficulties as these delays fell well outside the defined agreed which are documented in the terms and conditions of our contract with them. In short, gentleman, a shitstorm of epic proportions. Not only did it lead to the late delivery of this project, but I assume it will have affected our grocery and household product suppliers across the whole business, pretty much every store. As well as the breach of contract, it may well have impacted sales which we won't realise until we get the quarterly figures in about a month's time – although I must add the caveat that I may be wrong as it isn't within my remit, and there may have been some mitigation put in place for our grocery suppliers. But from this project alone we have incurred several contractual breaches that we will either have to reach a negotiated settlement or look to enter into litigation which will be costly, time consuming and of course damaging to our brand as our dirty linen is aired in public resulting in our share price going down down, deeper and down. Any questions guys?'

JBJ drew breath after getting in the latest Status Quo song reference; however, she did have some regret that she had wasted it when they were in a state of shock as clearly it hadn't registered. She noted that Colin Salter's head had taken on an unhealthy puce appearance; sitting on his throne it would have been highly appropriate to call him King Crimson at that time. His hands thundered down on the desk and turned to address Brad 'Bullshit' Ellis, who in contrast to Colin Salter's crimson hue had himself turned a whiter shade of pale.

'Why the fuck and who the fuck ordered a suspension on supplier engagement and more importantly payments and why didn't I know about this?'

Brad 'Bullshit' Ellis was frantically trying to remember what had happened. It did certainly ring a bell but he didn't like to get his hands dirty with the detail. His brain had gone into survival mode, so as well as trying to recollect the problem it was also valiantly searching for a sacrificial lamb or two. Then he remembered. It felt as though he was swallowing something hard and jagged as he prepared to speak, an unfamiliar feeling to someone whose main skill was blagging it.

'We were installing a new state-of-the-art supplier management and payment system housed on our own mainframe which would give us unrivalled capabilities to our competitors. I know we experienced what we initially thought were some 'teething' troubles when we flicked the switch to 'live' status, so we had to get the company in to do some tweaking to the operating system I believe. We had assurances it could be remedied in seven days, when they exceeded that timescale and an extended deadline it became apparent it wasn't going to be remedied – so we reinstated our old, largely manual processes, but we had to put a halt on all activity to do this.'

'You fucking idiot, why the fuck wasn't I informed of this?' flecks of white spittle appeared on the corners of Colin Salter's mouth.

'The initial proposal was included in August's agenda and approved by the board,' Brad 'Bullshit' Ellis proffered, based more on hope than knowledge. He had switched to full bullshit mode to buy some time to allow him to get back to the office and construct a timeline of events that saved his own skin and allowed him to throw some poor unsuspecting soul to the lions.

'We'll see,' hissed Colin Salter who certainly wasn't taking Ellis's word for it. He knew him of old. Staring stonily at Brad 'Bullshit' Ellis, he continued.

'I still want to know why I wasn't informed of this whole fucking fiasco. Have all our suppliers been impacted and have sales fallen?'

'Well, as you know from the last agenda item, our mid-year interim position is a strong one, overall sales are up over 7% and that growth is on an upward curve...'

'I don't give a flying fuck about the mid-year position, I want to know what the fucking position is after then, you dozy twat. Answer the question and cut the bullshit,' was the vicious retort from the chairman, glancing over to his anonymous PA who was frantically using her Pitman's Shorthand to ensure she had an accurate record for the minutes.

'Don't minute this, you fucking stupid cow!' screamed Colin Salter, jabbing his stubby finger towards her as if she were responsible for this predicament. Suzie Kent smiled back and placed her pencil and notebook on the desk. 'Him and his sidekick couldn't organise a fire in a match factory,' she thought as she sat constructing a plan of revenge on these supercilious buffoons.

In truth, she didn't need to as JBJ had a recording device built into the bottom of her briefcase which still sat on the table in front of her.

'We have a really strong relationship with our key suppliers so I'm confident any impact to our stores would be minimal...' blustered 'Bullshit' Ellis, a thin film of sweat had now formed on his forehead, which was like blood in the water to a corporate shark like Colin Salter.

'You don't fucking know, do you? You haven't got a Scooby fucking Doo, this is just more of your bullshit. Get someone up here now that does fucking know.'

Brad 'Bullshit' Ellis rose unsteadily from his seat to use the phone situated at the end of the room. He then realised with horror he didn't actually know how to make an internal call or even the extension of his head of finance, when JBJ stepped in to his rescue.

'I did take the liberty of making some enquiries when I was re-calculating my projections for the Heathview Store. Unfortunately, there are some limitations as my sample size was restricted to six of the largest stores, the sales figures when compared to last year are down 2.2%, however, factoring expected market growth which had materialised in our mid-year position that equates to a 7.3% reduction in expected sales. The figures are only available up to the end of November. I spoke to the store managers who inform me that several key lines ran out, which means that customers may have decided to switch their allegiance away from our brand, so it is possible the trend may continue. I would suggest that we need to collate the numbers across the whole group as a matter of urgency. I'm sure we will already have them.' She didn't even bother glancing at Brad 'Bullshit' Ellis as she knew he wouldn't be able to confirm or otherwise. '…and if the results of my sample correlate to the rest of the group, then there needs to be a strategic campaign to win back any customers we have lost.'

Colin Salter understood the implications of such a significant drop in sales; not only would it impact profits, it would also significantly damage the share price – and more importantly the valuation of his own share-holding – if it became known to the market and impede their future ability to raise capital to fund the grandiose growth plans that he had in the pipeline. The late opening of the Heathview Store now paled into insignificance. He wondered what other ticking time bombs lay in wait. The governance structure he had established meant he was protected from any wrong doing but he also now realised he didn't really know what was happening in the business and the advantages of having a malleable director of finance and resources now seemed to be outweighed by his blithering incompetence. He would need to keep him under his wing for now as he was a potential trussed and oven-ready sacrificial lamb that would be ritually slaughtered once Colin Salter had got the auditors in to do a confidential root and branch review for him.

Later that afternoon as he sat nursing his third very large brandy, Colin Salter made a mental note to ensure that he got his hands on those minutes before they were seen by anyone else. He couldn't trust that stupid bitch not to document something that was said 'off the record', he would literally have to rewrite history – not for the first time, he chuckled to himself. Reflecting on JBJ's performance, he painfully concluded that she had given them, to quote his own planned intentions for her at the meeting, a right working over. He was equally impressed and intimidated by JBJ, her knowledge of the business was superior to his and she had only been with them for five minutes. The jury was out on her though, as Colin Salter's well-honed conniving instincts told him that something wasn't quite right.

CHAPTER 9

It was a unique day for Eddie and Marilyn Rogers. It only happened once a year, they had a day off. It was Christmas Day and a smattering of snow still lay on the ground, although most of the Hawtrey Estate's roads were now a grey slush as the thaw had started on Christmas Eve, The Corner Stores busiest day of the year. The Rogers family had collectively risen in the pitch dark at 4 am on Christmas Eve to make up dozens of orders for fresh fruit and veg which Eddie kept in the storage shed alongside the turkeys that were supplied on Christmas Eve by a local farmer, who was also their regular egg supplier. All the orders were paid up front and nothing was allowed in the red books – that was known and understood by all customers.

Danny had first cleared the snow from the shop frontage and the footpath outside, which he had then liberally salted to ensure they didn't freeze and cause catastrophe to befall either customer or Eddie. He then helped Eddie set up the fruit and veg and made a decent start on the orders by the combined light of the shop interior and streetlights shining on the shop frontage, before he had to leave for work at Heathview Manufacturing. He was only working a half day as the factory and office shut down for the Christmas holidays. Nothing had been said but he, and Marilyn, had already assumed he would be making deliveries most of the afternoon and into the early evening. Marilyn had taken all the orders in the weeks leading up to Christmas. They were written in an order book with carbon paper providing the duplicate copy. The written copy was torn off and placed in a file ready to be made up on Christmas Eve; it would then be placed in the customer's box containing their Christmas order. It had to be a well-oiled machine as there were dozens of orders as well as the inevitable rush in the shop. On the plus side, Shirley had agreed to work extra hours to help them. However, this positive was perhaps neutralised by Eddie embracing the festive season with full bonhomie. It provided him with lots of legitimate opportunities to indulge in his favourite – and only – hobby as many regular customers came bearing gifts, usually something sweet for Marilyn and something wet for Eddie, and if it was something for both of them it was normally a box of chocolate liqueurs.

The now infamous Christmas Eve had started off so well. By the time Danny left for work, a good proportion of the orders were completed and safely housed in the storage shed; those for collection front left, those for delivery far right. To get in the real spirit of Christmas, Eddie had ditched the vodka for the day, and replaced it with a nice bottle of Glenfiddich whiskey that Cloth-Eared Jack had kindly dropped off for him on the previous evening. It seemed far more in keeping with the festive season – and was almost medicinal in this weather, Eddie reasoned to himself. He was blissfully unaware that this was part of a massive hamper that Jerry Bailey Johnson had sent Jack for all his assistance as her personal 'grass' on the comings and goings of the SOS campaign. The greatest joy of all was that it was a legitimate gift that Eddie had graciously received in front of Marilyn and placed it under the counter alongside the thoughtful tray of dates Jack had presented as a gift for her. He came bearing gifts with the withering explanation, 'I don't like whiskey and she don't like dates, they go right through her.' Eddie had mused, my god something the Spacehopper doesn't eat, well adequately digest, but managed to keep that to himself.

Eddie had found some dust-laden disposable plastic tumblers under the back of the confectionery display and after getting stuck in early Christmas Eve morning he proceeded to offer a Christmas tipple to the regular customers, much to the annoyance of the scowling Marilyn, to which he would respond 'Lighten up love, it's Christmas'. It was a really nice Christmas treat not to have to neck his remedy in the bitter cold of the storage shed.

Throughout the morning, as the level on the bottle gradually reduced, fresh provisions were continually arriving. Shirley enjoyed a quick pre-breakfast livener as she nipped in to pick up Granny Smith's order before going to attend to her and Elvis. At 11 o'clock, Brigadier Bowford and his good lady wife came through the door singing 'We Wish You A Merry Christmas' holding a tray with four glasses of sherry and three mince pies. His face dropped when he saw Shirley at the back of the shop refilling the shelves.

'Oh, sorry Shirley, I only bought four glasses,' said Mr Bowford, thinking that the superior quality of the aged cask sherry would be wasted on her tobacco-ravaged taste buds.

Shirley shoved the crisp box into the corner and strode purposefully down the shop and snatched a glass off the tray and threw the contents down her throat without it seemingly touching the sides.

'Aye, nice aged cask drop that, I'll pass on the mince pie Mr Bowford if that's all the same to youse, I divna eat that shite.' Shirley gave him a wink then punched her chest to help the sherry on its way, let out a loud belch and squeezed past the affronted Bowfords heading for the shed to smoke a much needed Superking to further ravage those stubbornly discerning taste buds.

After lunch, the shop had a continual stream of customers with no real break. It was also impossible to have three staff serving in the tiny shop. So Shirley manned the deli counter, Marilyn the till, and much to his annoyance to be separated from the remnants of the Glenfiddich, Eddie was posted outside to weigh and serve the fruit and veg. It was a case of posting the weakest link in a place he could do minimal damage to the shop and himself – the deli with its meat slicer and cheese wire were clearly a bridge too far. However, manning the fruit and veg was by no means plain sailing for Eddie in his now Christmas scotch-induced haze. The heavy-duty scales were white enamel and manual, and consequently required some arithmetic skill to convert the weight to the cost as pretty much all of the fruit and veg was charged up by the price per lb. It was then necessary to write the cost on the paper bag to be rung up at the till. Normally Marilyn would assist this process as they never had a queue of people. Eddie was currently trying his damnedest to read the scales as Trevor was patiently waiting for 'a couple of lbs of tomatoes'.

'Errrm, that's just over two pounds in weight I think?' Eddie lifted his glasses to his forehead to scrutinise the scales. He squinted but it was still just as blurry with or without his glasses. The tomatoes were 57p per pound, Eddie was trying to do the calculation in his whiskey-soaked brain.

'So that's two times 57. Two sevens are…'

'It's £1.14, Edward.' Trevor's patience was wearing thin as that was the first of eight items he needed from the fruit and veg. He snatched the pen from Eddie and emptied the tomatoes into a paper bag and wrote '*£1.14*' on the side.

'I'll serve myself with the rest of my order Eddie, it will probably be easier.'

Within the hour, Trevor was 'assisting' Eddie with the fruit and veg to deal with both the continued footfall through the door and the outstanding paid orders. The system was actually working extremely well. Trevor was standing instructing Eddie who was running round doing the fetching and carrying, while he managed the orders and did all the mental arithmetic.

'We make quite the couple, Teddy boy,' Trevor teased. Eddie was in need of a drink as he had been working solidly for the past half an hour – Trevor was a worse slave driver than Marilyn, he thought. The perfect opportunity soon presented itself as the unmistakeable sight of the old beaten-up Bedford van pulled into the lay-by and Tramp Juice Ron and Scotty alighted from either door, jumping without hesitation into the slush that still remained, their already filthy clothing getting a much-needed wash. Standing side by side it was difficult to comprehend that they were father and son – Scotty, a slack-jawed youth with short wiry frame and dark hair, and Ron the man mountain with a weather-beaten face, unkempt grey hair and matching whiskers, his gnarled club hammer right hand the most famous in the village after it flattened Brown Envelope Beaton's Columbian marching powdered nose at a highly emotionally charged village meeting. Their attire couldn't be more contrasting, Scotty stood shivering in a weather-inappropriate loose fitting garish orange Holland tracksuit and Ron in a tatty herring bone overcoat with a moth-eaten fur collar, the buttons were a distant memory so it was held tight by a piece of old yellow nylon rope. The only commonality of their ensemble was their filthy old paint-splattered dealer boots they both wore. They did share one noticeable common trait – they were both men of few words, comfortable with silence.

'Sorry Trev, can you hold the fort? I've got to get Ron's order.' Without waiting for a response, Eddie intercepted Tramp Juice Ron as he strode to the shop and beckoned him, assuming the role of the ultimate liberty taker by leaving poor unpaid Trevor to manage the growing throng of customers.

'Your orders out back Ronald my good man – follow me.'

Tramp Juice Ron scraped a match against his whiskers and sparked up his ever-present rollie perched on his bottom lip and followed Eddie into the storage shed. Ron's Christmas order wasn't fruit and veg or a turkey – the boy would be going to his mother's as Ron didn't really celebrate Christmas, although he always went to the midnight service on Christmas Eve. The 'Christmas order' was actually ten pouches of tobacco, two dozen green Rizla papers and half a dozen boxes of matches, and three tins of spam. Without instruction, Scotty automatically trailed behind holding a wire milkman's carrier that he had retrieved from the back of the rust bucket, the carrier was weighed down with half a dozen old milk bottles.

'Have you got it?' Eddie enquired, finding it difficult to contain his excitement. Tramp Juice Ron had been extending his product range after constructing a homemade still, and was now selling his first batch of 'Christmas moonshine', albeit at the last minute to his trusted customers.

'Ya boy.' Ron nodded to Scotty who placed the carrier down in front of the wide-eyed Eddie. In the crate there were six old milk bottles filled with Tramp Juice Ron's Christmas moonshine recipe. Ron looked at Eddie and nodded at the carrier. Eddie pulled out the massive cork stopper and took a long draw from the bottle, then immediately found himself gasping for air. The Heath Robinson overhead lights in the shed sang in the murky winter half-light. Eddie could feel the liquid burn as it made the descent down his oesophagus, he could now imagine what swallowing acid or bleach was like. He felt an immediate paralysing effect and as he tried to form words there was a total disconnect between his mouth and brain, his legs had also started to malfunction and he took an involuntary step forward.

'How strong is it, Ron?' Eddie finally croaked, tears edging out of the corner of his eyes.

'It's straanger than you've ever 'ad boy – yer don't need much o'thart. Deal we agreed?' As he spoke, a long line of ash off the rollie glued to his bottom lip dropped onto his threadbare coat. He made no move to brush it off; after all, it was no fashion parade. He then plucked the rollie from his lips to spit on his hulk-like hand, which he offered outstretched. Eddie shook it without a word, just tears rolling down each cheek.

It was about half an hour later that, as Danny returned from work, he could hear the manic barking of Ronnie and Reggie from the concrete yard next to the storage shed. He found his father spread-eagled across the shed floor, the orders for delivery had broken his fall and their contents were now strewn across the floor with the invoices blown to all parts of the shed and concrete yard. Eddie managed to lift his head from his prostrate position; it wobbled like a nodding dog toy on the parcel shelf of a car driving over multiple speed bumps. 'I've taken a tumble shun, I schlipped on a sodding satshuma… that's eashey for me to say,' he slurred, then laughed until he cried, Ron's Christmas moonshine recipe being the final nail in his coffin after a day's heavy ingestion. It finally took him down at three o'clock, as he would fondly recall as a glowing reference when endeavouring selling the illicit fire water to prospective customers. Danny sighed and helped his befuddled father to his feet, and scraped the squashed tomatoes and Brussel sprouts off his back, before helping him to his bedroom for a lie down. He told his mother and Shirley that Eddie wasn't feeling too good – Shirley had shot him a knowing glance, but Trevor hadn't taken the news at all well, as he was already finding handling the vegetables, in particular the mud-encrusted fresh potatoes, was playing havoc with his skin. Marilyn had broken open a new pair of bright orange Happy Shopper washing-up gloves for him to wear, which went a small way to placating his ire, even if the 'small' fit was looser than a politician's promise on his 'medium' male fingers.

Danny then set about collecting up the invoices and re-packing and replenishing the devastated orders before heading out to start the deliveries. The customers that had ordered Ron's Christmas moonshine were going to be bitterly disappointed as it remained hidden at the back of the shed, tucked in the gap behind one of the freezers, while its guardian lay in the land of nod snoring like a wildebeest with defective adenoids – testament to the potency of the new line from Tramp Juice Ron's home brewery – and there would always be New Year's Eve. It was going to be a much longer day than Danny had ever anticipated.

The Rogers decided they would have a much-deserved lie-in on their day off. Feeling shattered after the Christmas Eve frenzy, they planned on staying in bed until at least seven o'clock on Christmas morning. Eddie had risen again like Lazarus around five o'clock on Christmas Eve to help with the evening rush. He had a thumping head which was soon sorted out with a quick snort of the hair of the pooch that had mauled him, and they had worked through until nine o'clock that night. Their ambitions to have a lie-in were thwarted by frantic knocking on their front door at five o'clock on Christmas morning. They had already been woken by a banging on what sounded like the shop door. All of this commotion they could faintly hear from their bedroom at the back of the accommodation. Danny's bedroom was an old converted storeroom on the ground floor next to the front door, so he had already made his disquiet known

'Shut the fuck up, I'm coming,' he bellowed through this bedroom bay windowpane which sat next to the front door, as the relentless knocking continued. He put on an old Iron Maiden

T-shirt and staggered with bed head hair to the front door, carefully negotiating the new stock obstacle course that was stored in the hallway to replenish the Christmas-ravaged empty shelves. He opened the door to see old Stanley in his long raincoat and trilby hat in a state of high agitation. He had numerous pieces of blood-soaked tissue paper dried to his face where it looked as though he had been attacked by a crazed psychopath wielding a Gillette razor – it was in fact the result of a self-inflicted dry shave as he had forgotten to use shaving cream.

'Why aren't you open?' barked Stanley, pointing to his watch. 'It's not even five o'clock yet, that's too early to close, and where the hell is everyone? The streets are deserted.'

'It's five o'clock in the morning!' Danny rubbed his right eye to wipe away the sleep that had accumulated and to see if he was actually still dreaming.

'How dare you, you insolent young whipper-snapper! No it isn't. I've not long had my lunch, that Scottish girl was round. What on earth did she make me…?' The old war veteran trailed off, suddenly looking old, confused and frightened. The confidence drained out of him and he felt like the nervous youth on his first date standing at her front door not knowing what he was going to say, a small seemingly inconsequential matter that suddenly presented as a looming catastrophe.

He had fallen asleep fully dressed in the armchair and woken up around 2 am. He didn't know where he was and called out for his mother. He started to search round the bungalow for his mother and something, anything that looked familiar. In the tiny kitchen he had found a newspaper which he thought might give him some clues as to what was going on. He had managed to turn on the light and sat at the table reading the paper; he kept reading the date and the headline story, it didn't make sense it couldn't be 1989. He spent an hour re-reading the same page; then the motor in the fridge sprang to life which made him jump with a start. He opened the fridge and looked at the cans of tinned food on the shelves – what sort of fool puts tinned food in a fridge, he thought. He then remembered an afternoon not so long ago when he had run all the way home from school as he knew mother was baking him one of her wonderful apple pies for tea, with thick creamy custard. Then it occurred to him, perhaps she has gone to the shops. He rubbed his stubble and thought he would need to shave before going down to the shop to find mother, it simply wouldn't do for a soldier to be unshaved on duty. It suddenly dawned on him for some peculiar reason that his mother was Scottish, nevertheless no reason to lower his own standards he would still have to get himself spruced up before going out – now this damn place must have a bathroom somewhere.

'It's Christmas Day and it is pitch black outside because it's five o'clock in the morning, trust me, you've just woke me up.'

Marilyn came down the open staircase tying her dressing gown, and stood beside Danny at the door.

'Now then, what's the matter Stanley?'

'Fellow-me-lad there reckons it's five o'clock in the morning, not the evening. I've not long had my lunch, Mum's homemade apple pie I'll have you know.' Old Stanley pointed, jabbing his bony finger accusingly towards Danny.

'It is five o'clock in the morning Stanley, it's Christmas morning. You've just woken us all up.'

'I need to get some bits and bobs but for the life of me I can't remember what they are… are you going to open this bloody shop or not? Was my mother here earlier?' Danny took a step forward and grabbed the old man's arm as he started to topple backwards.

'Better come in for a cup of tea or coffee Stanley and I'll give your son a call. If you grab one arm Danny I'll get the other and we can steer him into the kitchen,' she deliberately bellowed to the once again snoring Eddie as they passed the stairs to get up and put the kettle on.

So, on the morning of their annual lie-in, Eddie and Marilyn sat round the battered old oak table in their dilapidated kitchen at half past five nursing a hot beverage alongside their befuddled cantankerous neighbour as they waited for his irate son Malcolm to come and fetch him.

'What is this place? When I used to dig my own latrine, it

looked a darn sight better than this out-house.'

Danny stretched and yawned then leant against the corner of the kitchen door frame, caught between two rooms.

'Did you serve in World War Two then Stanley?'

'I served Queen and country but I can only give you my rank and number, while those two are sitting there eavesdropping. Absolute scum of the earth they are! How quickly they turn young fellow-me-lad, one minute they can't do enough for you and the next you are branded a felon, nothing more than a common criminal.'

He hadn't taken kindly to Marilyn taking his coat and, due to the unanticipated weight, immediately conducting an investigation to ascertain the contents of the bulging pockets. The search revealed two tins of Happy Shopper pilchards, a box of Happy Shopper candles and a Fray Bentos steak and kidney pie. Marilyn disapprovingly shook her head.

'Oh Stanley! Really?'

She silently placed the items on the table and then opened her address book to find Malcolm's number. When his son finally arrived just after ten o'clock and he heard the full story his mood changed to one of eternal gratitude as he ushered his father back to his own property. It could no longer be called home.

'What are we going to do with you, Dad?' he said as he helped the frightened and confused old man shuffle through the slush on his own tarmac-less driveway. It was a rhetorical question, but one that scared him as he really didn't have any answers himself. He planned on getting some clothes together and taking his dad to stay with them over Christmas and then think about the next steps. His main thoughts now were how he was going to break it to his Filipino wife Jasmine. The last time his father had come over for Sunday lunch about three months ago he had been unceremoniously ushered out with his wife screaming 'You're never going to set foot in my house again!' after his father had meted out a totally unprovoked torrent of vicious racial abuse, believing her to be of Japanese descent and therefore wholly responsible for the horrendous war crimes of World War Two.

'Oh well, so much for our annual lie-in! We might as well start pricing up and restocking the shelves ready for tomorrow, and I don't even need to cook Christmas dinner today,' laughed Marilyn.

'I'll drink to that. Merry Christmas love,' said Eddie, raising his cup of coffee that had been given a secret Irish identity.

CHAPTER 10

It had only taken Laurence Padbury about 30 minutes after dropping off his groceries to locate the nappy-brown Escort, Mrs Rogers had been absolutely correct in her assumption! He had found it parked up in Beaton's yard. He was now squatting again in the field opposite the yard, where it looked like Beaton and his merry men liked to dispose of waste product as there was hardened discarded cement strewn in the ditch that ran round the perimeter of the field, and old packaging of various building products entangled in the hedge that he now hid behind. Mr Padbury was peering through his binoculars that were held stationary in a tripod that he had purpose built (essentially three metal stakes that he could push into the earth with a large magnet welded on top) to allow him to document his wildlife finds. He was now compiling a dossier with similar rigour, hoping to document the comings and goings of the barbaric animals residing in the builder's yard. This was his second session of surveillance as the first time proved fruitless – but he was finding this the best Christmas Eve that he could remember in recent years and he felt a pang of excitement in the pit of his stomach. He had already made up his mind to refer this ghastly bunch to the Environment Agency for fly tipping and destroying the natural habitat, and planned to undertake a thorough survey of the whole surrounding area, having no doubt there would be further evidence of their wanton destruction of the countryside.

It was bitterly cold, and although he was wrapped up in his thermals he didn't think at his age that realistically he could remain in situ for longer than an hour. He had foolishly exceeded this on his first day of surveillance and spent yesterday with his feet in a hot bowl of water in front of a blazing coal fire, slurping on some soup and shivering uncontrollably. The binoculars he was using were high powered and he could easily see into the grey Portakabin and could see Beaton on the telephone, highly animated with a cherry-red blood pressured head – he seems a permanently angry man, thought Mr Padbury. After another hour of inactivity, he was all set to return to his open coal fire to warm his chilled bones when he saw the Escort pull into the yard.

The man who Mr Padbury had waved to at the shop strode the short distance from the car to the Portakabin. Mr Padbury scrawled in his dossier, 'heavy set/ balding/50s?/tatty brown 70s suit/ kipper tie half-mast/briefcase/private detective???' He noticed that Kipper Tie didn't knock on the door, just swept straight in. Mr Padbury focused on Beaton for his reaction. He immediately put the phone down and started pointing at Kipper Tie. His anger hadn't desisted, thought Mr Padbury. Kipper Tie placed his briefcase on Beaton's desk and handed over a large envelope. Beaton tore into the envelope and pulled out what appeared to be a number of blown-up photographs. Mr Padbury then witnessed something he hadn't seen before, a broad malicious grin appeared on Beaton's battered face – his nose still sporting a large plaster after his operation to have it re-broken and reset following his altercation at the village meeting. He subconsciously touched his nose as he threw the envelope on his desk, and reached into his desk drawer and threw a large wad of notes into the still open briefcase, then leaned across and vigorously shook the exiting Kipper Tie's hand.

Ten minutes later, Brown Envelope Beaton found himself talking to an eccentric old boy in his office about a possible extension to his bungalow. He inwardly chuckled as he wondered to himself if it was for a laboratory as he looked like the archetypal mad professor. It then dawned on him who this was, the kooky old boffin who had made an absolute fortune several years ago. He was a recluse and word was that his place was an absolute shit hole so this was a potential endless gold mine to be tapped! Things were certainly starting to look up, he thought as he afforded himself another smile and threw three heaped spoons of sugar into the steaming hot tea he had brewed to warm the shivering odd bod up. 'Chocolate biscuit with that Mr…?'

'Mr Davidson – yes, thank you,' Mr Padbury lied, quite clumsily, frantically recalling the name of his old English teacher.

'I've just got to nip next door to the workshop and grab a packet from the lads' stash, bear with me, won't be two shakes of a lamb's tail.' He grabbed the photographs and locked them in his desk drawer. What Beaton really went to retrieve from the workshop was his main builder to help load the sales pressure on the old nutcase. Their well-honed plan involved both of them giving the client a lift back to their home (if they didn't have a car, following behind if they did) to give a formal quote for the works, then of course an immediate escorted visit to the bank to help grease the wheels of a large cash withdrawal for a substantial up front 'deposit', normally 100% of the works value. Of course, the initial quote would increase massively with structural damage or dry rot that would inevitably be 'discovered', even some defective electricals that required a complete rewire of the property. All of the remedial works would of course be superficial as there were no defects to start with, or at best some very minor works that could be fixed at minimal cost. Beaton was already planning to try and work out how just much he could milk him for – the crackpot looked like the sort that lived on his own, unkempt and scatty, a perfect candidate. So it was just a matter of instigating a search when they got back to his bungalow to find his bank statements and/or building society books – generally he would keep the client chatting in the kitchen while his colleague went to 'measure up the job'. This would help Beaton determine the value of the likely 'works' Mr Davidson would be having to his rats' nest of a property. Even though Beaton potentially had bigger and legitimate opportunities with the new developments in Heathview, he viewed this opportunity as easy and quick money that could work wonders for his cash flow – after all he had wages to pay and showbiz sherbet to buy! He would pride himself on being able to bleed someone dry in a couple of months or less, and as a bonus if he did it with a superficial sycophantic charm he had been known to find himself written into their last will and testament, much to the annoyance of some remote family, who usually kicked off. He didn't want to get too far ahead of himself, but if he was right about this old kook being the inventor, he had hit the jackpot – and the old fool had presented himself gift-wrapped on a silver platter. Yes, his luck was definitely changing.

Laurence Padbury had worked on an inbuilt bike lock as part of his prototype, but it had been quickly dropped by the manufacturers as it was far too cumbersome to suit the streamlined model. But this meant that he had a detailed knowledge of the inner workings of quite complex locks and it took him less than three seconds to open the flimsy desk lock with a skeleton key housed on his own key ring. He had lost his own front door key years ago and now always opened it with the skeleton key. He had calculated that it would take Beaton probably four or five minutes to get to and from the workshop which was based on the other side of the small yard, and that was if he didn't get talking to any of his henchmen. He pulled the photographs out of the envelope and afforded himself ten seconds to study each one. It transpired there were 24 photographs in total but six were essentially repeats of a former, leaving 18 unique prints to burn into his photographic memory. His now shaking hand hurriedly shovelled the photos back into the envelope and locked the drawer. The door to the Portakabin sprung open as Mr Padbury drained the last dregs of his tea and thumped the mug on to Beaton's desk, ensuring it left a permanent mark.

'I'll take a rain check on those biscuits. I've just realised I've got to set sail.'

'We'll give you a lift back and we can size up the job and sort you out a good deal,' said Beaton rather too eagerly. Mr Padbury saw one of Beaton's knuckle scrapers lurking outside through the half-opened door.

'Oh, that's OK, I've got my push bike you see.'

'Absolutely no problem, Mr Davidson, we'll pop it in the back of one of the vans and you can sit in the front with us, just tell me where we are going to Mr Davidson?' Beaton gesticulated towards the van parked out front.

'I've got a doctor's appointment, I'll pop back tomorrow and we can sort out the finer points of the job and estimate,' stammered Mr Padbury.

'No need Mr Davidson, I'm pretty sure I know where you live. Isn't it that bungalow with that lovely weeping willow in the front garden just on the outskirts of the village? Remind me, Mr Davidson, what's the road called again?' Beaton grinned, knowing the answer to his own question. He was used to his customers getting cold feet and consequently was a seasoned veteran in reeling flailing fish in once they were hooked.

'Willow Drive,' Mr Padbury weakly replied, realising that Beaton had known where he lived all along.

Ah, yes Willow Drive! We'll pop round first thing after the Christmas break, let's say ten o'clock on Monday, Mr Davidson, save you the effort of cycling up here, and we can get you a more accurate estimate if we are on the job, so to speak.' Beaton gave a mirthless cackle and added, 'Have a nice Christmas Mr Davidson' emphasising Mr Padbury's "new" surname.

'Errr, yes you too,' stammered Mr Padbury as he retrieved his bike from the Neanderthal that was holding it for him. As Laurence Padbury exited the Beaton & Son's yard he flicked the gear lever and the racing bike slipped effortlessly into third gear. His legs felt strangely feeble and as soon as he was out of sight he stopped to catch his breath and found his hands shaking again, but this time not from the cold.

CHAPTER 11

The whole frontage of the bungalow was festooned with fairy lights; Leslie was precariously balanced on a set of aluminium stepladders trying to locate the rogue bulb that had temporarily curtailed the invisible morning pyrotechnics. The melting icicles had made the cuffs on his Rudolph Christmas jumper sodden as he tested the bulbs, the only one flashing was Rudolph's nose. He had been twisting sockets and replacing bulbs for a good 20 minutes before the day lightshow recommenced. Christmas morning always made him think of his former wife and his now grown-up son, and the excitement of present opening in those distant years past. The only contact he had in the last five years was when a maintenance payment failed to clear when he was changing banks, and that contact was only via her solicitor. He had sent his son numerous letters but hadn't heard anything in return. He wondered if they were thinking of him this morning, but thought it was fairly unlikely, and all things considered he couldn't really blame them.

'It's always the last one you check isn't it,' crowed a voice rudely interrupting his reminisce. Leslie turned carefully to his right and saw Brigadier Bowford, as Eddie called him, peering chad-like over the top of his back fence which backed onto the side of their property.

'Oh yes, sod's law isn't it? Merry Christmas, Mr Bowford.'

'Merry Christmas to you both Leslie, and please do call me Byron, we are neighbours for heaven's sake,' exclaimed Mr Bowford with unusual conviviality.

'What are you two up to today?' Byron casually continued,

then suddenly struck by the potential sexual connotations '…I mean celebration wise,' he awkwardly blurted in redress.

'Oh we've got a few friends coming over for drinks and Christmas dinner, that's why I'm out here trying to repair these poxy lights. We've got even more inside, it's like Santa's grotto in there. Are you and Mrs Bowford going to your son's?' Leslie enquired, his thoughts trailing off to his rapidly approaching deadline before their guests started to arrive.

'No, that's the funny thing, just heard from them. The whole lot have been laid low with a nasty tummy bug – you know, blowing out of both ends. Obviously we haven't got anything in as we were expecting to spend the day with them. Mrs Bowford is absolutely distraught.'

'I bet she is! I'm sure they will be OK, Mr Bowford.'

'Oh quite, quite, she's absolutely distraught,' repeated Mr Bowford, recognising that it wasn't the family's alleged malaise that was at the root of Mrs Bowford's disquiet, it was Christmas food and drink, or rather lack of it. If they had known they would have got a Fortnum and Masons hamper in like they had in the past. It was damned inconvenient. He was sure she blamed him for the blight of the 'tummy bug' – deep down they both knew it was probably linked to last year's festive altercation when he had come to physical blows with his daughter-in-law's older hippy brother, over the reintroduction of national service and the birch. They were separate discussions but the culmination of both events and the ridiculous steadfast opinion of the left-wing looney that neither had a place in modern society had led to a port-wine befuddled Mr Bowford grappling on the floor with a startled middle-aged Conservative bank manager, who had just been accused of being a 'fucking disrespectful looney left pot-smoking hippy' before being violently rugby tackled to the ground by the psychotic geriatric. Since the incident, their contact with his son's family had been infrequent and somewhat fraught.

There was an awkward silence, eventually broken by Leslie who capitulated before Mr Bowford.

'Well you could come to us if you like – I'm sure we can squeeze you in.'

'Excellent, I'll let Mrs Bowford know right away. Who else is coming?'

'Oh just the Rogers, Shirley and Granny Smith.'

'Your neighbours then!' came the curt response from Mr Bowford, taking umbrage that he hadn't been originally afforded an invite.

'Well technically they are not all neighbours, Mr Bowford.' Leslie looked across the road and could see figures bustling around in the shop. He wondered how the Rogers and Shirley would take to sharing their Christmas day with the Bowfords. He knew it was their only day off in the whole year, and they had decided to invite them for Christmas dinner as they knew the trials and tribulations that Marilyn experienced on a daily basis with Eddie's peccadillo. Leslie had first-hand experience with Trevor's own alcoholism. Leslie had gone out of his way to support Marilyn although she was either in denial or didn't realise the extent of the problem – they never mentioned the 'A' word in connection with Eddie but had been very open with Marilyn about Trevor's previous problems. He wasn't surprised to see the Rogers working on Christmas morning, even if the shop wasn't open, the two of them running it with Eddie's issues would be a constant strain, and without Danny impossible. It made him reflect on his own problems, Caligo Blue, the advertising agency he ran hadn't won any contracts for the past four months and cash flow was now critical. Last week he had been forced to re-mortgage their bungalow; Trevor was blissfully unaware of their perilous financial situation. He wondered what on earth was happening now across the road as that eccentric old mad professor with the racing bike was banging furiously on the shop door.

The pricing gun was feverishly clicking as Eddie shot the white adhesive price labels onto each Happy Shopper baked bean can housed in the opened cardboard tray. Marilyn now ensured that she always set the price on the gun as they couldn't afford a repeat of the 2p cans of Coca-Cola that Eddie had erroneously labelled up and proceeded to sell to the spotty locusts – they were queuing up en masse in a silent mob outside the shop door and halfway down the street before she realised what had happened. But Eddie wasn't a stranger to hard graft – he had left school at 15 years old and had naturally followed in his postman father's footsteps who arranged for him to work in the sorting office to serve his time before rising through the ranks to the heady position of postman. It wasn't until he did his national service that he had ever taken an alcoholic drink, instead preferring to frequent the West London cafés in the early 1950s that served milkshakes and frothy white coffee. It was at a little Italian café that, as a callow 17-year-old youth, he first met Marilyn. His best friend Brian had just met a girl who worked as a secretary at the engineering company he had just joined and had asked Eddie along on a double date as a favour. Eddie hadn't known but it was the 16-year-old Marilyn's first date, his own nervousness and inexperience had led to him acting the goat. After five minutes, he was hanging a spoon from the end of his nose, then his party piece which involved opening and closing a jam scone as it sang Nat King Cole's 'Mona Lisa'. Marilyn didn't stop laughing on the first date or their second date when they went to see Ken Coyler's Jazz Band and Eddie's theatrical jazz dancing had tears rolling down both cheeks, it was only much later she realised he hadn't been jesting with his dancing.

Six months later, Eddie was posted to West Germany to do serve his 18-months National Service, but by then they were already engaged to be married on his return. It was a mixture of the newfound freedom of West Germany, his longing for his fiancé and the encouragement of the other home sick conscripts that led him to start enjoying more than the odd stein of beer. Although he should have been saving for married life, he found more and more of his pay helping him blot out his loneliness and the futility of National Service. The army did teach Eddie how to drive and got him his HGV licence which changed his career path when he was discharged from military service. It allowed him to continue in his carefree ways as a lorry driver as he often worked away for days at a time. On his return, Marilyn had noticed a change. He was as comical and fun as ever but preferred a night out at a pub rather than the café, and although they still went to see skiffle and jazz bands, he preferred to go where there was a licenced bar. He also spent the most of the savings he had accumulated on an Ariel motorcycle and she would be seen frantically clinging to Eddie as they tore through the deserted streets of London, dropping her home well after her parent-enforced curfew. Her virtually teetotal father had taken a dislike to the post-army Eddie and counselled his daughter about dating a man who he believed was wedded to the bottle. 'He will amount to nothing, mark my words'. When Eddie had asked his permission for his daughter's hand in marriage, he served up the ultimate protest by not giving his blessing and effectively extinguishing any wedding plan – sending Eddie away to seek the solace of a nearby pub. But Eddie was persistent in his love for Marilyn and sold the motorcycle to raise the money for a deposit on a flat, forcing Marilyn's father to agree to the wedding rather than endure the social stigma of his daughter living out of wedlock. These days, Marilyn often thought of her father's portend of their future life.

Eddie heard a banging on the shop door and turned to see Laurence Padbury in a state of high agitation.

'For fuck's sake… Marilyn!' screeched Eddie, thumping the price gun down on the freezer.

'No need to shout.' Marilyn rose from behind the confectionery counter about ten feet away; she had been restocking the cigarettes in the wall shelf behind the counter.

'It's Professor Yaffle, can you deal with him? Hells bells, can't they just give us one day off a year!'

Marilyn lifted the deadbolts and used the Chubb key to unlock the door.

'Merry Christmas Laurence, what can we do for you? Is everything alright?'

'Can I step in for a minute? I have something to tell you, Mrs Rogers, I wouldn't normally trouble you but I haven't been able to sleep, it's been playing on my mind,' Laurence Padbury excitedly jabbered.

It became quickly apparent to Marilyn that he had no

recognition that it was Christmas Day. She also noticed that he looked more unkempt than usual and had developed some form of nervous tic that was causing his top right lip to spasmodically lift and fall that reminded her of the famous Elvis Presley 'uh-huh-huh' sneer. For the first time ever, Mr Padbury stepped into the shop, and Marilyn closed the door behind him, as he passed her she noticed that personal hygiene was somewhat compromised. He frantically pulled a notebook from his anorak pocket and proceeded to read his hastily written notes, although his photographic memory meant that the notebook was little more than a theatrical prop.

'Observed Brown Escort pull into the yard of Beaton & Sons Ltd on the 23rd of December and again on the 24th of December – you were absolutely correct in your assumption Mrs Rogers.'

Marilyn had forgotten about the vehicle that Mr Padbury had spotted, seemingly spying on them, and his vow to track it down.

'I'm certain that the individual in the aforementioned car is a private detective in the employ of Beaton.'

'Do you think he was watching us then?'

'I know so Mrs Rogers. He was doing more than watch you, he had been taking photographs over a period of days and nights – he must have used some sophisticated specialist equipment for the night-time photographs.'

Eddie was trying to unblock a jam on his pricing gun, digging at the snarled-up labels with an old biro as he listened in.

'I managed to get a look at the photographs that he handed over to Beaton. I gained access to the office under the pretence of commissioning some building works to my property, using a pseudonym of course. I also suspect that he is guilty of numerous environmental breaches in the proximity of his own property on greenbelt land, I need to collate further empirical evidence before I can refer the matter to the appropriate authorities, which believe you me I intend to do as soon as I have finished here…'

'Sorry to interrupt, Mr Padbury, the photos? What were the photos of?'

'Oh, it was a bit strange. There were two photographs taken

at night of you and your husband at the deli counter, seemingly weighing what looked like two long-haired miniature dachshunds on the electronic scales. He managed to get a photo of each dog being weighed while the other stood on the deli work surface.'

Marilyn smiled awkwardly realising that Mr Padbury normally ordered cheese and ham from the deli counter, both of which required use of the scales and deli cutting area.

'Errrm, we needed to have an accurate record of their weights to ensure they were growing as they should.'

Eddie then chimed in from across the shop.

'I always have the job of cleaning the whole shooting match thoroughly after the pooch weigh-in,' he truthfully explained. The pooch weigh-in was always after Ronnie and Reggie's tea – and after they had closed the shop for the day. Eddie was always given the job but in practice rarely bothered, he either lacked the capability to complete the job after a day's ingestion – ironically through the rather thorough application of his own hangover equalizing 'hair of the dog' – or he just plain forgot. 'It's like the meat slicer all over again,' Eddie mused rubbing his chin.

Mr Padbury seemed totally uninterested at the environmental health breaches, if there was any question of ill treatment of the two dogs he would have been appalled and called to arms, but he viewed this as a quite sensible approach to ensure the pooches' well-being.

'That's not all I'm afraid,' he continued. 'There were several photographs of customers making purchases from you on different Sundays. They had written the time and dates on the photographs. But this wasn't confined to you, the same Sunday trading photographs had been taken of the other corner shop, at the other end of the village.'

Mr Padbury paused thinking how best to phrase his next finding.

'There is also photographic evidence of Mr Rogers in the storage shed at the back of your shop buying what looks like fairly large quantities of what appears to be alcohol beverages from a rather unkempt looking individual. Frankly he looked like a gentleman of the road. It looks as though some form of static hidden camera had been installed – this is a professional and costly job. There are also some photographs of this individual in a ramshackle outbuilding seemingly brewing the beverage, whatever it may be.'

Marilyn shot a look over at Eddie who had unblocked the jam and was now whistling while sticking price labels over those stamped minutes earlier.

'Mrs Rogers, I would say that it looks as though Councillor Gary Beaton is collating a body of evidence against you. Why would he do that?'

'I wonder why, Laurence,' she said loudly, never removing her gaze from Eddie whose whistling had noticeably increased in volume.

CHAPTER 12

A wonderful aroma of mulled wine greeted Granny Smith as Shirley and Danny lifted her frail body over the doorstep and into Trevor and Leslie's hallway, where the house-proud hosts stood in waiting. Trevor steadied her walking frame and Leslie approached with a silver tray of steaming bone china mugs of mulled wine. The distant strain of carols rang from the lounge where Trevor had a tape of Christmas songs playing gently in the background and Eddie and Marilyn were already mingling with the Bowfords.

'Season's greetings to you both,' Mr Bowford had exclaimed, raising his mug of mulled wine, as Leslie ushered the Rogers into the lounge. Leslie promptly thrust a very oversized mug of mulled wine into Eddie's hand as he witnessed a look of incredulity on his face at the sight of Bowfords.

'Mr and Mrs Bowford are joining us as unfortunately their son's family are unwell so their plans have fallen through, last minute.'

'Bad business, blowing out of both ends,' the Brigadier grimly elaborated as Eddie drained his mug of mulled wine in one fell swoop.

Danny could hear his father laughing manically as he and Shirley helped Granny Smith along the hallway, which was no easy feat with the multitude of garish Christmas decorations adorning the walls and hanging from the ceiling. After successfully squeezing past a newly purchased antique mahogany side table, housing a full blown china nativity scene, they helped Granny Smith into the lounge and an armchair of suitable height (they had to put down a cushion to raise her up).

Shirley flicked her tightly permed head towards a highly

animated Eddie on the other end of the lounge. 'Yer man's already away wi' the fairies son.'

'I'll go and get Elvis from the car.' Danny took the opportunity to remove himself from the already awkward situation that he sadly had seen many times before. He was planning on getting away early to pop over to Jenny's, they were going to run through some of the tracks before the New Year's Eve gig. It was just the two of them. 'It's simple Danny, my Mum wants to know who I'm playing with…' giggled Jenny with the deliberately provocative statement. '…and your mum has seen me every day for two years already, lugging in bread, cakes and pasties!'

'There you go hen!' Much to Leslie's chagrin, Shirley lit two cigarettes and popped one into Granny Smith's mouth. Simultaneous plumes of tobacco smoke were exhaled from their tar-filled lungs, mixing with the sweet mulled wine aroma to produce a rather rancid odorous cocktail. Shirley wiped her mouth with the back of her hand as she crashed her empty mug back onto the tray the astonished Leslie was holding, and then she picked up his mug of mulled wine and attacked it with similar alacrity. He excused himself to the kitchen to bring some more mulled wine and an air freshener; more importantly he wanted to forewarn Trevor who was on cooking duties of the ensuing chaos, realising that as a recovering alcoholic and ex-smoker, today could prove to be the straw that broke his recovering partner's dromedary back.

Eddie had now started to really enjoy himself, feeling a warm glow of satisfaction from the inevitable ensuing carnage he had helped create. On first sight of the Bowfords, he had immediately made his excuses for the toilet; making a swift detour to the kitchen he surreptitiously pulled a milk bottle of Tramp Juice Ron's Christmas rocket fuel moonshine from his inside coat pocket and emptied virtually the whole contents into the large stainless steel mulled wine warmer. He then drained the last remnants and hid the bottle in the nearest cupboard, where he took the opportunity to help himself to a large mug with 'Dog' and a cartoon image of a beaming mongrel, it sat next to a similar 'Cat' mug – they were in fact Trevor and Leslie's treasured cocoa mugs that they had exchanged on their first anniversary. He then pressed the lever tap of the mulled wine warmer and decanted a brimming mug full of the elixir and inhaled the deep aroma with the solemnity of an expert sommelier.

'Ahhh, Bisto!' he purred in reverence of its restorative powers.

The kitchen was a mass of pots and pans boiling and bubbling away. Trevor was red-faced and sweating profusely with steamed-up glasses as he shut the oven door on a goose that was cooking far too slowly for his liking. As an ex-smoker he hadn't appreciated the news that Puffing Billy and Fag Ash Lil were busy staining their newly painted Dulux-white Anaglypta wallpaper tobacco-lung yellow, and Leslie's warning about the potential for alcohol-fuelled carnage made him wonder what on earth these people were doing in their lovely bungalow on Christmas Day. It was Leslie who had inadvertently invited them, feeling sorry for Marilyn he had invited her and Eddie for a drink on Christmas morning. He hadn't realised Shirley was crouched stacking tins into the carousel at that back of the shop. After ten minutes he had left the shop shell-shocked and wondering how he was going to let Trevor know that he would be cooking Christmas dinner for the Rogers, their rough and ready Scottish shop assistant and the old lady she was a home-help for. He needn't have worried, Trevor knew how difficult Christmas Day was for his partner and the memories of his old life, so he had agreed with a glad heart – but perhaps with not quite the same level of joy when he was told of the Bowford's impending arrival on Christmas morning. He could hear that the music in the lounge had been cranked up and it didn't sound like Aled Jones singing 'Walking In the Air' and there were sounds of raised voices interspersed with raucous screams of laughter – he pressed the lever tap of the mulled wine warmer and poured himself a steaming mug full.

'This punch is a canny wee bevvy Lesh,' slurred Shirley as a line of ash fell from the cigarette perched in the corner of her mouth, landing on the cream shag pile carpet. She continued, 'Yis is a lovely, lovely mon, disnae matter to us one jot, not one jot that yeez a jobby jabber – we're a' Jock Tamson's bairns.'

Elvis lay asleep under the chair at Granny Smith's feet. She had wisely decided against the punch and was still sipping the small Harvey's Bristol Cream sherry that she had been given nearly two hours ago, but she was secretly longing for a nice strong cuppa. Her daughter had made her customary call from Newcastle first thing this morning while she was having a brew. She had been delighted and relieved to learn that her mum wasn't going to be alone on Christmas Day; Granny Smith knew that the guilt of the festive period weighed heavy on her daughter's heart, but it really shouldn't, she always had Elvis and her memories.

Trevor came giggling and staggering into the lounge, his face flushed.

'Ladies, gentlemen and Elvis, dinner will be served in about an hour or two, give or take an hour or two.'

Elvis's ears pricked up at the sound of his name and his mum's sigh of resignation as she reached into her apron tied to the walking frame and pulled out a half-eaten family-sized bar of fruit and nut chocolate, snapped off two chunks which she popped into her mouth and washed down with the remaining sherry. Thankfully her expectations had been fairly low and the apron was fairly well stocked. She also had a satsuma, a box of 'Eat Me' dates, and a half a cheese and pickle sandwich wrapped up in tin foil from yesterday's tea.

'I'll get you some aperitifs, no, I mean Hor's Douves, or an aperitif if you want. I'm an absolute whiz with a cocktail shaker!'

'I'll get them, you concentrate on the dinner,' snapped Leslie now in a belligerent punch-induced mood. It had been months since Trevor had touched a drop of alcohol to his knowledge and he was now clearly under the influence, this didn't bode well.

'I'll have a very large Scottish wine if your wonderful mulled wine is all gone… what? It's Christmas!' said Eddie, dispelling the chastising glance from Marilyn who had proffered her disapproval through instinct rather than genuine sentiment, as she was also feeling the warming effects of the poteen punch.

'Scottish wine?' An unfamiliar sounding beverage to Leslie's city palate.

'Scotch, malt whiskey if you've got it… aka Scottish wine,' explained Eddie.

'Make that two Lesh, the good stuff mind son, none aye that White Horse pish,' slurred Shirley.

'That would be very civilised indeed, Mrs Bowford and I will have a wee dram with you both,' the Brigadier gave a conspiratorial wink.

'Sounds like the dirty old sod Bowford's after his Nat King Cole,' Shirley shouted across to Danny who was sitting cross-legged on the floor thumbing through the extensive record and cassette collection, a pile growing next to him was today's play list. He was pleasantly surprised to see some of the latest releases that weren't particularly mainstream. They had the Waterboys some Prince, Tears for Fears and U2's seminal 'War', on the negative they had Dire Straits 'Brothers In Arms', Sade, ABC. He made a note to come round at a future date and see if he could borrow some of this stuff to tape. Danny would never have put either of them down for having any of this contemporary music – he wasn't to know that Leslie got them through Caligo Blue as promotional material from the record companies and they never even bothered to take most of them out of their record sleeve. Deliberately ignoring Shirley, he pulled out a record that caught his eye, as he read the track listing it dawned on him that his understanding of the pronunciation of the artist had been way off. As he waited for the dulcet tones of Aled Jones to fade out on the tape that Trevor had so forcefully reinstated, he pulled the record from its sleeve and blew the dust off its surface and placed it on the turntable, lifting the stylus arm to the track he had identified. He turned the volume up so that it could be heard across the raucous alcohol-fuelled chatter and screeching laughter which didn't abate. As Danny looked across the smoke-filled room, he saw Granny Smith's immediate recognition as she shared a smile in that esoteric moment before closing her eyes to fully absorb the piece. He thought for that split second he had seen from the merest glint in her eye the excitement of that young pianist she once was; he watched as her gnarled fingers moved slowly, re-enacting the distant memory of the piano piece – Chopin's Nocturne 9 Opus No 2.

A parlour game had seemed like an excellent way of curbing the rather over-enthusiastic consumption of Leslie's drinks stock, which he had purchased with the intention of servicing the entire festive period not just Christmas afternoon. They had all placed a piece of paper with film, TV programme or book into a bowl – it had been decided to exclude plays, much to Leslie's growing irritation, as it had been unanimously discarded after Shirley's rather barbed comment.

'Nay chance of that, you're barking up the wrong tree there son! The only theatre maist of ays have ever visited is the type that whips oot our tonsils.'

Eddie was now valiantly trying to focus on the piece of paper he had drawn, before he embarked on the monumental task of trying to act out his charade for the audience in waiting. He started with the action of a camera and held up three fingers.

'Film, three words!' Granny Smith proudly exclaimed as she thrust another date into her mouth.

Eddie paused for a second, and then held up one finger.

'First word,' they chimed in unison.

Eddie pointed at Mr Bowford.

'Scrooge!' shouted Shirley, immediately receiving a withering look from Mr Bowford.

'I know the whole thing…' screamed Leslie.

'Dirty Rotten Scoundrels?'

The Brigadier bristled at the indignity of the situation. Then it dawned on him that it was actually his suggested film that the drunken idiot was attempting to act out. An ever more excited Eddie continued to jab a finger in his direction.

'Creepshow,' sniggered Mrs Bowford. Seeing an opportunity too good to miss, Danny joined in.

'Day of the Dead.'

'For heaven's sake, it's supposed to be the first word ONLY,' pleaded Mr Bowford.

'Nightmare on Elm Street!' screeched Shirley at the top of her voice.

'Heaven forefend woman, that's four words for goodness sake, enough of this utter bunkum... if you must know it's 'Fanny By Gaslight', a 1944 classic, my own offering, am I correct Edward?' A deflated Brigadier Bowford gave an expectant glance over to Eddie who was now lying prone on the cream carpet with his legs kicking in the air trying to catch his breath as he roared. The whole room had spontaneously erupted in a cacophony of laughter. Shirley had been in the process of swallowing a rather large mouthful of a sherry, rum and Blue Bols cocktail that she had made from the nearest bottles to hand, when Mr Bowford delivered those immortal words – the muddy blue contents of her mouth came to rest alongside the fag ash on Leslie's (formerly) cream carpet.

By the time they eventually sat down to their Christmas dinner they had absorbed the Queen's speech and demolished the entire contents of Leslie's drink cabinet. The wine with the meal was all that remained. A swaying cracker-hat-crowned Eddie was using the phone in the hall to urgently call in more supplies from Tramp Juice Ron.

An hour later, a malodorous Tramp Juice Ron was sat at the table ravenously devouring the leftovers as Leslie proposed a toast, holding aloft a glass of Tramp Juice Ron's Christmas moonshine.

'Merry Christmas and thank you all for sharing this day with us and of course special thank you to my Trevor for a wonderful meal.'

His words were said with heartfelt sincerity, with no hint of sarcasm, despite the charcoal roast potatoes (Elvis had taken care of Granny Smith's as she fed him under the table – she had recognised that her dentures were in jeopardy) and solidified gravy. Trevor coyly smiled holding a glass of the poteen brew in one hand and one of Tramp Juice Ron's rollies in the other. A rapturous round of applause ensued with Eddie raucously wolf-whistling in approval.

'...here's to Marilyn and Eddie and to stepping up the SOS campaign – they may have built that monstrosity but it needs customers to make it work. We won't give them that... United we stand!'

'United we stand!' They all raised a glass to the accompanying sound of Elvis hacking up the indigestible roast potatoes.

CHAPTER 13

'I said we needed someone that's fucking box office...' Colin Salter screeched down the speaker phone at his global director for finance and resources - Brad 'Bullshit' Ellis.

'...The Chuckle Brothers and Dave out of Chas and Dave aren't fucking box office, you dozy twat.'

He was discussing the forthcoming opening of the Heathview Superstore and he had tasked Brad 'Bullshit' Ellis with the task of hiring a so-called celebrity to cut the ribbon. However, as it was mentioned over a rather heavy lunch at his Gentlemen's Club Brad 'Bullshit' Ellis, in a rather champagne and brandy-befuddled state, had made a note onto a paper napkin which he had used later that evening at Diamond and Pearls pole dancing club to wipe vomit from his suit lapel. It wasn't his own vomit, rather that of one of the escorts he had been unnecessarily plying with champagne. It was only when Suzie Kent called asking him to speak with Colin Salter, just to confirm the identity of the surprise celebrity who was performing the opening the Heathview flagship superstore, that he remembered. He broke out in a cold sweat as he realised he hadn't delegated the job, which was his normal modus operandi, or made any enquiries whatsoever and the opening was in less than a week; time to switch on full bullshit mode. He picked up *The Sun* newspaper and frantically flicked through to the celebrity gossip page as Suzie Kent put him through to Colin Salter. There was an article on the Chuckle Brothers so he tentatively tested the water and withdrew his toe as the shark snapped at it. He remembered that one of his team (he couldn't actually recall his name but could picture his flabby inane grinning face) was related to either Chas or Dave, so he took a punt at Dave to an equally vicious response.

'I'll just have to do it myself, I'm more well-known than those clowns,' preened Colin Salter not noticing Suzie Kent's shoulders moving up and down as she put her notepad in front of her mouth to hide her guffawing.

'Oh, of course sir – who better than one of the most well-known faces in Britain today,' fawned Bullshit Ellis while sticking his middle finger up at the phone handset.

'Please tell me you haven't forgotten our little discussion about the outturn figures for the last quarter that we need to present to the next board meeting, hang on a minute I've got you on speaker phone…'

Too lazy to pick up the phone, he looked at his PA trying to remember her damn name, in irritation at his own inadequacy he snapped at her.

'…go and make me a coffee, I need a private word here,' and gave a dismissive flick of the hand in the general direction of the grand oak door. As she left, Suzie Kent closed the door behind her and hurried over to her desk to listen in to the call.

'OK, talk to me.'

'Yes, I've had my trusted generals working on the third quarter outturn and year-end projections. We have deferred a number of operating costs as extraordinary items so that we don't have to reflect them in the quarterly trading figures. We have also, shall we say, extended the duration of the quarter to enhance our sales figures…'

Brad 'Bullshit' Ellis spoke with confidence as he read verbatim from the confidential memo that his deputy had prepared for him, unwittingly not realising that it was a back-covering exercise, as the manipulation of profit reporting was potentially illegal, but Bullshit Ellis had little understanding of the technicalities of proper accounting practices and financial management – he left that to the bean-counter boffins that worked for him. They would also field any of the questions that the auditors may have when the accounts were signed off at the year end. He was rudely interrupted as he was getting into full flow.

'OK, cut to the fucking chase – are the declared profits increased on the previous quarter, despite the reduced sales due to your monumental cock-up?'

'Yes, as we discussed, there is no drop in profit, and the year-end outturn looks equally as healthy, I can send a report over to you?'

'No need for that!' roared Colin Salter. He didn't want any paper trail linked to him. He had already arranged to offload a significant proportion of his own personal shareholding to market in the next month when the price was likely to reach an all-time high with their new store openings and false market projections, news of which he had got his stooge Ellis to obliviously provide to several financial journalists on a recent boozy night at his Gentlemen's Club. He was going to maintain the family majority shareholding but fully intended to purchase back his shares after the price inevitably crashed when they published their year-end audited accounts. He would make a tidy personal profit after buying back the shares he sold at a lower value and at least maintain his shareholding, although he had grander ambitions of using the profits to purchase additional shares from other shareholders that like lemmings would panic at the share price drop and misreporting of profits and be grateful to off load what they would perceive as falling stock.

He was confident that the auditors would go through their accounts with a fine toothcomb and identify the 'accounting irregularities' – leading to public disclosure to shareholders and a subsequent plummet in the share price as the market analysts reacted to the incorrect profit forecasts. He would then be able to throw Brad 'Bullshit' Ellis under the bus as a result, and as all of this mess was Bullshit Ellis's fault in the first place, Colin Salter's vindictive nature meant that his desired outcome was to see Ellis not just unemployed but languishing behind bars for false accounting. There would probably be some job losses on the front line to bolster future profit projections – the market had to be thrown a bone, but that's life. He certainly saw potential in Jerry Bailey Johnson and had already earmarked her as Brad 'Bullshit'

Ellis's replacement. Ironic though he pondered, once again, he, Colin Salter, had yet again managed to turn an unmitigated disaster into a potential personal goldmine, so he'd better not be too hard on the bullshitting buffoon; after all he had a tough few months ahead, no job and a porridge-based diet.

'Thank you Brad for all you are doing. We all make mistakes but you have stepped up to the plate and dealt with yours, I'm impressed and I can honestly say I won't forget this. I hope to see you later on this afternoon at the club – I won't take no for an answer!'

Suzie Kent carefully replaced the receiver and put her personal notepad into her handbag.

CHAPTER 14

It was the Sunday before the grand opening of the Heathview Superstore that Trading Standards made enforcement visits to both The Corner Stores and Garwood's Convenience Store, following covert surveillance they had undertaken on the previous two Sundays.

The laws on Sunday trading were utterly ridiculous and convoluted, constructed in a bygone age when most of the population attended church. They were primarily designed to enable workers to have that day of rest. The small shops were permitted to open for only three or four hours but there were restrictions on what could be sold. For example, the sale of fresh fruit and vegetables was permitted but not those that were tinned or bottled; similarly it was permissible to sell cigarettes but not bread (without an exemption order). They could sell tripe but not cheese or butter. The Rogers and Brenda Garwood, like most shopkeepers, were oblivious to the finer details of the regulations, and Trading Standards tended to have a relaxed enforcement approach unless the opening hours were obviously out of acceptable parameters.

The Council's head of trading standards had received a detailed dossier with accompanying photographic evidence from a parish councillor, Gary Beaton, seemingly showing multiple breaches by The Corner Stores. He was demanding enforcement action for this flagrant breach of regulation on Sunday trading and also alleged sale of illicitly produced alcohol. Minimal Sunday trading by small businesses was something they would normally turn a blind eye to, but the fact that a councillor had referred it to them and had requested a full briefing on the action they were undertaking meant that some form of action was required. They would need to visit both of the village stores to ensure equity in the process, and this fool's errand required the skill set of a pedant to carry it out.

The assignment had been passed to the officious Brian Bishop, who was known by his own Trading Standards colleagues as Mini Hitler. He was a short fat balding man (albeit sporting a comb over) with an encyclopaedic knowledge of legislation and procedure; he lived and breathed enforcement. His wife Eileen Bishop was also a trading standards officer, known by colleagues as EB (which they esoterically knew stood for Eva Braun). She was thin and taller with a fierce pinched face and shared her husband's zeal for enforcement. They were often assigned to work together despite this not being an appropriate arrangement due to the obvious conflict of interest; it was a coupling out of operational necessity as none of their colleagues could endure more than five minutes in their tedious, overzealous and officious company.

'These are very serious offences, Mr and Mrs Rogers, we are prepared to issue an official enforcement notice which serves as a warning but any repeat of these offences will lead to prosecution and significant fines…'

Marilyn stood perplexed, mainly at the attire of the trading standards officers who were both wearing orange hard hats (which admittedly blended well with the Happy Shopper livery), yellow fluorescent jackets and tightly gripping clipboards. They both had walkie-talkies attached to their belts which seem to be totally superfluous.

'…do you accept that you were working extended hours and selling products that were in direct contravention of the Shops Act 1950?'

'Well I have to say we don't actually know what the requirements are. We work shorter hours on a Sunday to have a half day off – the shop has always had these opening hours as far as I'm aware. We will accept what you say as you have obviously been spying on us over the past couple of Sundays.' Marilyn looked to Eddie for support.

'Come on, we all know this is all engineered by Brown Envelope Beaton and his interests in the new Salter's superstore. He is basically playing you for a couple of mugs. What does it really matter if we sell a bit of cheese or some nappies and are open for half an hour longer? We are helping the community out, for fuck's sake…'

'Please moderate your language, Mr Rogers! I cannot disclose the nature or source of referral, Mr Rogers, we ensure strict confidentiality. We have a free copy of the Shops Act 1950 in the car, to assist you both in the future – my colleague, Mrs Bishop, will furnish you with that on our departure. Now I need access to your storage area at the back of the property.'

'Proper jobsworth, aren't you? You're loving this, aren't you? Have you got a warrant?'

'I can assure you, Mr Rogers, I don't require a warrant if I deem there is potential for non-compliance with licensing laws.'

'Well, we don't have a licence as we don't sell alcohol so you are barking up the wrong tree – so the answer is go forth and multiple.'

EB snapped at the insolent oaf's blatant disregard for their authority and revealed their evidence much to Brian Bishop's visible annoyance; she triumphantly presented the photograph of Eddie taking a delivery from Tramp Juice Ron and Scotty.

'Mr Rogers, I can tell you we have unequivocal photographic evidence of you loading what looks like a large quantity of alcohol into the aforementioned storage area.'

'Well for your information it isn't alcohol its apple juice for my personal consumption. If you must know I have a chronic bowel disorder and to enable me to successfully evacuate my bowels on a regular basis I need fresh apple juice and lots of it, otherwise I'm spending half the morning on the shitter screaming like a chimp on fire…'

Eddie was now really enjoying himself. He had long since moved the tramp juice and moonshine from the storage shed to the adjoining garage that housed the Subaru van. The only alcohol in the shed were the half bottles of vodka safely stowed away in between the coal bags.

'…besides I can't open it up now, can I? You've just told us we mustn't work any longer or we will be prosecuted – make up your mind Adolf, shit or get off the pot!'

'Please don't be obtuse, Mr Rogers, I will be forced to serve another enforcement notice for non-compliance, and I have already warned you about your use of foul and abusive language,' Brian Bishop pompously blustered.

Although they had shut the shop door and turned the sign to 'closed', they hadn't locked it and an out of breath Cloth-Eared Jack burst through the door.

'Forty of my fags, and 'er pasties,' he panted.

With more than a modicum of sarcasm Eddie responded.

'Sorry sir, we are closed, and in any event these good people here from Trading Standards won't allow us to serve you 'er pasties on a Sunday, we would be breaking the law apparently. We could however sell you half a pound of tripe if we stocked it – no problem at all.'

Jack pushed his NHS glasses up to the bridge of his nose then fiddled with his whistling hearing aid, more through habit than necessity.

'Just my fags and 'er pasties – pop it on my slate. I can see you're busy, I'll give you a knock and pick it up later Mrs Rogers, I've got a bloody fare in the cab so I can't stop.'

Brian Bishop's ears pricked up and his thin smile returned.

'Mr and Mrs Rogers, you surely know you are not permitted to lend monies which is precisely what running a credit facility of this nature is, it is in direct contravention of the credit regulatory framework…' Marilyn curtly interjected, cutting the bombastic Brian Bishop off in full flow.

'Just take him round the back Eddie, let's get this whole charade over and done with. They clearly all want us out of business and won't stop until we are.'

Marilyn was unsuccessfully fighting back the tears, though determined they wouldn't see. She was at the end of her tether, physically and mentally exhausted, and the till had been short again last week. It pained her to admit it but Eddie's drinking was getting worse, earlier in the week when he had been putting the fruit and veg away in the storage shed she had heard him loudly singing 'You're Adorable', but belching out the letters, starting with a long deep belch to produce the 'A… you're adorable', then a rasping belch for the 'B… you're so beautiful', then it sounded as though he was almost sick trying to produce the 'C… you're a cutie full of charms'. What hurt the most was the memory of him singing that to her when they were first courting, and more often than not without the belching. The camera she had installed to monitor the till had long since revealed the truth that she had always known, that it wasn't Shirley taking money from the till, it was her own husband. The imminent opening of the new superstore meant things were only likely to get worse, far worse.

CHAPTER 15

The opening of Salter's Heathview superstore was on track to be delivered in accordance with the revised timetable submitted to the board by Jerry Bailey Johnson. There had been some superficial vandalism to the new superstore that had seemingly occurred on the early evening of Christmas Day when Beaton & Son were supposed to be providing site security but Gary Beaton, in his wisdom, had decided that he didn't want to pay treble time and gave the 'security guard' (his own yardman) the evening off – without pay of course. The new-fangled CCTV cameras weren't yet operational but the six-foot letters 'SOS' daubed across the shop front doors in white gloss paint gave a clue to the potential suspects, and if JBJ had heard Leslie's rousing post-Christmas dinner toast she would have been able to narrow the list of suspects even further. In fairness, Tramp Juice Ron, with his permanent rollie hanging from his bottom lip, was the only one that was still able to balance on the packing crates that they found lying around. Under an inebriated Trevor's somewhat slurred tutelage he eventually managed to paint the campaign insignia. They didn't need to break into the site as the gate was left unlocked, as were the building supplies housed in a compound next to the superstore. The unlikely trio of Trevor, Leslie and Tramp Juice Ron carried out the act of rebellion under the full Christmas moon. Later in the early hours of Boxing Day morning, Tramp Juice Ron returned in his empty van with Scotty to take full advantage of the unsecured materials and equipment; it turned out he did get a rather nice Christmas present after all.

On the morning of the grand opening, there was no sight of

any building materials or the unsightly SOS daub as JBJ's red Porsche flew into the virtually empty car park. She always liked to make an early start and this was her big day, the culmination of several months' work. The great and the good of the village were attending, which unfortunately included Brown Envelope Beaton whom she hadn't seen or spoken to directly since he had his nose flattened at the engagement event at the village hall. Though on reflection that seemed to be the least of her worries since she received a call from Colin Salter's PA asking for details of the opening to be sent over to his office as the great man was performing the opening himself.

The last proper shop opening in the village was some ten years earlier and had been performed by one of the chimps that advertised PG Tips. JBJ had heard a rumour (emanating from her inside man – Jack) that the chimp, attired in a bowler hat and three-piece suit, had managed to cut the ribbon only to be spooked by the clapping and screaming crowd and went on the rampage round this shop, pulling down shelves and light fittings, before the trainer finally managed to fire a tranquilizer dart into its neck (just about the only part of exposed flesh with its three-piece suit ensemble). This whole sorry performance was conducted to the live soundtrack of adults screaming hysterically and petrified children sobbing uncontrollably. She held out great hopes that Colin Salter would certainly be able to out-perform the chimp in the opening ceremony; he did after all have the advantage of the power of speech. That said, her main concern would be what he said to the press – not only would the local hacks be in attendance but also some of the nationals and trade journals. The press engagement would need to be very carefully stage-managed and she intended to stick like glue to Mr Colin Salter. The store manager would deal with all of the operational and security teething problems they would inevitably have – this wasn't JBJ's first rodeo and she knew full well that the day wouldn't run without the odd hitch or two. Her own mantra was a time for quick thought and a calm head.

In the village hall, the motley SOS crew were assembled, holding placards that were made by Leslie's advertising agency but handed out by Mrs Bowford under the supervision of Brigadier Bowford who was proudly brandishing a battered olive-green megaphone that he had managed to borrow off an old army colleague. He surveyed his troops that stood before him with feelings of despair and impending doom – Tramp Juice Ron and his half-wit son, Trevor (Leslie was working), a rather unsteady Eddie (Marilyn was manning the shop and young Danny was working), that dreadfully coarse Scottish woman that worked for the Rogers, Bruce 'Jesse' Wyatt the garage owner that periodically dressed up as cowboy for some unknown reason, the dotty old mad professor, and the only saving grace – three colleagues from his very own amateur dramatics society that had agreed to come along with the opportunity to get into the character of a protestor. The Dirty Dozen, thought Byron Bowford, just as, on cue, a rather unpleasant aroma from Tramp Juice Ron wafted his way.

At the end of the consultation meeting only weeks earlier in the village hall, there had been an angry mob protective of their own business community, but during that time the employment of dozens of residents at the new store and a charm offensive targeting other initial protesters – such as £10 coupons off their first shop posted through every door – had somewhat abated the locals' ire. It was always the same predictable story – there would be a hard core of protestors that would eventually peter out before the store had even opened. Even Mr Bowford had wanted to throw the towel in some time ago, as in reality the opening of the superstore would make life much easier for him and Mrs Bowford; it was only a five-minute walk and a minute or two in the car. Currently they did most of their large shop in a supermarket several miles outside the village – he only bought their milk and the occasional stamp from the Rogers, though he liked to pop in for a jolly good natter to keep their spirits up. It was Mrs Bowford who offered a sharp rebuke when he had tentatively suggested that they may wish to take a back seat. A women of few words, she simply snapped, 'We spent Christmas Day with these people and if we can't support our neighbours in their time of need then we aren't really neighbours at all.' Byron Bowford had been taken aback. 'Quite so dear, I'm just saying perhaps we shouldn't hog all the limelight.' Mrs Bowford didn't need to say another word.

'Good morning, ladies and gentleman and welcome to this historic day. My name is Byron Bowford,' he boomed through the whistling megaphone.

'Turn it in Mr Bowford… please,' said Trevor with his hands over his ears.

'…we can hear you without that thing, there's only a handful of us so just come a bit closer and talk to us.'

'Oh, fair enough,' he said, somewhat crestfallen as he lowered the battered megaphone to his side, immediately thinking how he would be able to use it for his clarion call later on in the battlefield.

'We are all here today to protect the integrity of this fine village and the way of life that we know and love. The impact of this abomination on our existing business community could be devastating, and it's disappointing so few have turned up here today – it's appreciated that they have to open their shops, but when David fought Goliath, did he worry about his assigned household chores or paper round or whatever the equivalent was in those days? No he did not! He stood and fought! We will fight them in the car park! We will fight them in the shopping aisles! We will fight them in the boardroom!' He pulled his shoulders back and waited for the applause as he surreptitiously pushed his speech that he had written on the back of a postcard of the village pond into his back pocket. Trevor broke the stony silence and started to outline his plan of action to the motley crew.

The Brigadier haughtily stood aside as Trevor carefully explained the strategy that he had devised with Leslie over the past week. Leslie's passion and anger had come as a surprise to him, mainly as he was still oblivious to the failings of Caligo Blue, the stress of which had instilled real vitriolic venom in Leslie that needed to be channelled into a safe outlet. The placards were directly aimed at Colin Salter. This was the output from a brainstorming session that Leslie had organised at Caligo Blue during their now all too common down time. One of his creative team's girlfriends knew Salter's PA and she had provided a lot of feedback on him

– essentially he was a rather unpleasant narcissistic sociopath. They had also learned that he was conducting the grand opening, which given his personality profile made perfect sense. As Trevor now looked at the highly provocative placards, he tried to remind himself it was done with the best of intentions.

A Rolls Royce Silver Spirit wended its way through the unfamiliar roads of Heathview. The driver was struggling to see through the cigar smoke purposely blown from the back of the vehicle. He had lowered the middle window at the request of his boss who proceeded to level abuse at him for not knowing where the new store was.

'What are you? Fucking stupid? I'm due to open this in 40 minutes and counting. This is a very important day for my public! I'll have your bollocks for bookends if we don't find it in the next five minutes.'

Mikey 'The Iron Fist' Collins was a professional boxer, and always said after his fourth pint, to all that could hear '...still got a punch that could make mash out of a raw potato'. After his eighth pint he was normally letting his fists create a Mr Potato-head from the face of the last unfortunate person to inadvertently upset him. This job was extremely important as his girlfriend was expecting and he needed to provide. He was still boxing, but now at 36 classified as a punch-weary journeyman – he had lost two thirds of his 61 fights – but his granite-like chin meant that he had never been stopped, although the years of absorbing punches had left some brutal scars that were only visible on a brain scan. But this situation was something else. He gripped the steering wheel as though it was his passenger's throat. His little stepsister, who had put a word in for him with Salter and effectively landed him the job, had always been the calming force and he thought of her now. As soon as he dropped this obnoxious bag of shit off he would call her from the superstore, it was sure to have a payphone he could use. This was part of his so-called anger management treatment, and his stepsister would understand how this arrogant weasel could get under the skin of even the most mild-mannered person. After all, she was Salter's PA.

There was a large crowd gathered outside the store angrily jostling for position in front of the podium, which served as the only barrier to the ribbon-encased entrance. Word had spread that there were some absolute bargains placed near the entrance, albeit strictly on a first come, first served basis. The rumours had originally started with half-priced meat close to its expiry date but had grown to colour TVs with remote control being sold at a 90% discount, and even the outside possibility of a brand new Mini Car being sold for a nominal fiver – all of which now had the mob whipped up into a fever pitch. The reality of course was quite different; JBJ had instructed her management team to drop hints to the new workers employed from the village of amazing discounts on fantastic products, with the express instruction that it was a strict company secret to give the new shoppers a surprise on the grand opening and should therefore not be shared more widely, even with their families. The strategy had worked perfectly as there wasn't a person in Heathview that wasn't aware of the amazing bargains to be had, and people had even taken time off work and camped outside the shop overnight. There were some generous discounts, mainly on luxury food items that were approaching their use by date, and there were half a dozen black-and-white portable TVs being sold with a 50% discount. Worryingly though, there was still no sign of Colin Salter as JBJ ushered the awaiting local and industry press photographers and journalists to a suitable position near the podium. A film crew from the regional news programme were supposed to be in attendance but had been diverted to an unexpected breaking news about a local man who's pet parrot, aptly named Yarwood, who had learned to mimic several well-known celebrities and as a consequence had been booked to appear on 'New Faces', a national televised talent show. However, they weren't to know that although the impressions were unerringly accurate, they were interspersed with random profanities, which transpired to be Yarwood's other speciality, rendering the piece virtually redundant without some cover-up bleeps being inserted. This meant the production was taking far longer than expected.

The opening was due in 15 minutes and the crowd was starting to grow. JBJ had prepared the speech for Colin Salter to deliver and was now actually hoping that he would be a no-show so that she could deliver it in his absence. As she looked at her watch, she heard a ruckus coming from the entrance, she could see a ragamuffin band of placard-waving vagabonds trying to get access through the car park to the store. Beaton's two security guards were attempting to hold them back. JBJ had pre-empted this and had given specific instruction to prevent them from coming on site – well, at least until Colin Salter had arrived. She could just about make out that pompous old windbag Bowford leading the pack with what looked like a megaphone, spouting something unintelligible from the distance of the entrance gate. She certainly hoped they had personalised the protest placards as she had suggested to Suzie Kent. The journalists turned their heads towards the commotion at the entrance and started to walk over.

'We have every right to be here to deliver a peaceful protest. Miss Bailey-Johnson would not tolerate such a barbaric treatment of potential customers, get your hands off me this instant, you crude oaf,' blustered Byron Bowford.

'Take it easy Grandad, we have been told not to let any troublemakers on site, and you lot my friend look like troublemakers.'

The shaven-headed goon nodded at the megaphone Mr Bowford was holding. He then leaned down so his nose rubbed against Mr Bowford's, whose only thought was that the Crude Oaf must have eaten a raw onion and excrement sandwich for lunch as he recoiled from the putrid stench emanating from the Crude Oaf's fetid mouth.

'Don't push your luck, Grandad, understand? You're not coming in here with that! Now you can have your protest here at the gate on the public footpath… OK? OK!'

Trevor had manoeuvred his way next to Mr Bowford in an attempt to defuse the situation as he had noticed that Tramp Juice Ron was starting to get quite fidgety.

'Look, if we leave the megaphone with you and collect it at the end can we go in please?'

The Crude Oaf was taken off guard, as he was expecting – and hoping – the situation would escalate. He had also noticed lurking at the back of the group the mad old professor who had come into the yard before Christmas but hadn't been at home whenever they had subsequently called to 'give him a quote' – he made a mental note to tell the gaffer, with any luck they could frogmarch him home after the opening and start the 'quotation process'. The gaffer always bunged him enough for a decent drink if he found their building society books or bank statements when he went off alone to 'measure up' the job.

'Alright then… give it here.' He snatched it out of Mr Bowford's hand, his eyes firmly set on the mad professor who represented a good weekend down the boozer, his feral rat-like instincts calculating that getting the target on site gave him and Gary Beaton a better chance of bundling the old kook into his van and giving him a 'lift' home. Lovely jubbly, he rubbed his hands together in anticipation, already looking forward to that first celebratory lager slipping down without touching the sides.

The Rolls Royce Spirit approached the turning to the store at breakneck speed, its silent elegant approach betrayed the anger within.

'Oh fuck me, bravo, you've found it at last… remind me next time I'm building an idiot to borrow your brain.'

Mikey 'Iron Fist' Collins was now at boiling point, the only thing that kept him going was the thought of his girlfriend and their little one – and, of course all of the horrendous things he wanted to inflict on this worthless piece of excrement, as he had been taught to visualise rather than 'do' at his anger management sessions. However, as he pulled into the approach road, a strange feeling of warmth and benevolence washed over him as he saw the placards of the protestors, and he did something he hadn't done in a while – he started laughing.

'What the fuck is so funny? Have I said something that amuses you?' shrieked Colin Salter, leaning forward and fanning the space in front of his face to escape the fug of his own cigar smoke. At first he struggled to read the signs then he felt his blood pressure erupt.

'I'll, I'll… you fucking ungrateful bastards,' was all his apoplectic red face could spit out to the accompanying soundtrack of raucous laughter from the front of the car.

The photographer was twisting his camera to get the best picture of the various placards. The reporter held a dictaphone in front of Trevor.

'As spokesman for the group, tell us why you have directed this personally at Mr Salter?'

'This is all about this business destroying our village life and the small businesses that care about the community and aren't fixated on profits and work their fingers to the bone helping those less fortunate. I'll tell you what this is, the first step to extinction for a number of the businesses in the village and we are here to demand to know how this happened. How was planning permission ever granted in the first place?'

'The placards are something else. I assume you had legal advice as potentially they are quite slanderous if not supported by facts, and one thing we all know is Colin Salter has deep pockets and a short fuse.'

They were interrupted by Colin Salter as he lowered the window from his Rolls Royce passing the placard-carrying party.

'I'll get your names, all of you, I have the best litigation firm in the City. You're finished, the lot of you, and your whole families, I'll make it my personal mission to ruin you.'

'You already have, fella,' said Eddie, gently swaying. 'You already have.'

JBJ inwardly chuckled as she beckoned to the purple-headed enraged man who emerged from a Rolls Royce like a popstar making their way to the stage through a fog of dry ice, as a cloud of cigar smoke trailed behind him. She hadn't noticed the regional news crew driving into the car park. They had edited and submitted their piece on Yarwood the Impressionist Parrot with Tourette's and were now looking for a two-minute mid-programme filler. There were now a couple of hundred people gathered as she stepped up to the podium and microphone.

'Ladies and gentleman, thanks y'all for coming today, as my old daddy used to say, a new start is a new part of a life and that's what we are offering to y'all today.'

The gravelled lone voice of Ricky Brown from Heathview's dog-rough estate shouted from the back of the crowd, 'Get on with it for facks sake love, it's brass monkeys out here, I've got bollocks like a deep-sea diver.'

'I hear you, good sir, so without further ado, can I introduce Mr Salter's Supermarkets himself… Colin Salter.'

The speakers sprang into life with Fleetwood Mac's 'Little Lies'. Colin Salter bounded to the stage and placed his hand over the microphone and leant over to JBJ as she stepped off the podium.

'Tell me lies, tell me sweet little lies…' Christine McVie's voice rained over the gathered throng.

'I'll speak with you after this! Let me be very clear I want some answers…' Salter hissed, then straightened his tie and fixed firm his fake Cheshire Cat smile as he stepped up to the microphone, as the music faded out.

'Ladies and gentleman, I know most of you will be familiar with me but for the uninitiated the name is Salter, Colin Salter, licensed to dispense quality goods at affordable prices.'

Salter paused for laughter as suggested in the script provided to him, but there was only a general murmuring and one vocal response.

'My bollocks aren't getting any warmer or any bigger mate, so do us all a favour and get the fack on with it!' Much to Salter's annoyance, it raised a cheer and a chain of sporadic laughter at other ensuing jokes from the crowd that were fortunately out of earshot but led to even more raucous laughter. Ironically it was as his script has suggested.

'…I'm the owner of this magnificent store we are opening today for all you good people and your wonderful village. Let me tell you a bit about the story of Salter's and in effect my own story. Some people will say I was born with a silver spoon in my mouth… not so, I had to work for everything I have today…'

His speech was abruptly interrupted by the placard-carrying Dirty Dozen, or more precisely by the rotten eggs that were being launched at the podium, primarily by Tramp Juice Ron and Bruce 'Jesse' Wyatt who were hurling them with vicious precision and power, and to lesser effect Eddie and Shirley. It had been Eddie's responsibility to age the eggs by keeping them next to the warm motor of one of the freezers at the back of the storage shed. However, he was now questioning whether he had got the fresh and rotten eggs mixed up as some of them exploded on Salter's head with a bright yellow and seemingly odourless yolk – his main concern now was the potential for the customers cracking into a rancid breakfast boiled egg. It would be the meat slicer enquiry all over again. He let out an audible sigh of relief as people closest to the podium started to wretch and gag as the foul acrid stench met their nostrils. Tramp Juice Ron had spotted Brown Envelope Beaton standing to the side of the podium and directed his aim at the side of his head. He was throwing with rapid fire now, with Scotty handing the ammunition to him out of a metal bucket, with the urgency and dexterity of a side gunner.

'Wooar!'

Tramp Juice Ron's rollie nearly fell from his lip with the excitement of scoring a direct hit on Brown Envelope Beaton. Instead of the egg exploding on impact, Councillor Beaton was knocked off his feet, falling backwards, his now freshly broken nose spurting blood from the impact of one of the Maris Piper potatoes that were erroneously lying in the bottom of Scotty's ammunition bucket. As the falling Brown Envelope Beaton's head turned on impact, a crescent of nose blood showered over the cowering egg-soaked reeking Salter.

As pandemonium erupted, the crowd saw the opportunity to make a beeline for the awaiting store bargains. The front of the crowd ripped through the ceremonial opening ribbons and as others saw what was happening a frantic scramble ensued. At the sight of his boss being felled, a blind rage switch flicked in the Crude Oaf's tiny brain. The first punch he landed was flush on the chin of the astounded female reporter holding a microphone who had been looking into camera and over her shoulder back at the crowd. Seeing his opportunity, Mr Padbury leapt forward and crouched on one knee, his protest placard scythed the air like a Vikings axe, straight into the groin of the Crude Oaf, who let out a shrill yelp and crumbled to the car park floor, where he writhed, tears flowing from his piggy eyes. He looked up at the sky, through the tears, as he sensed something overhead; the black shape he saw was actually a rapidly approaching microphone boom, deliberately dropped by the film crew's sound engineer. He wanted to move his hands to protect his face but he couldn't as the pain down below was too intense and he couldn't release his protective grip on his throbbing testicles. The weighty boom pole landed flush on his upper jaw. As he was already grimacing, his exposed tobacco-stained teeth flew through the air on impact. Like autumnal acorns making their final journey, they came to rest by his side on the car park floor.

The crowd were now surging, trying to get into the store. The podium was knocked over by the jostling crowd, removing the cowering Colin Salter's cover. He hadn't noticed that Mikey Collins was making his way through the crowd as his potential saviour. Mikey pushed his way through, finding himself in some free space and breaking into a sprint. As he approached the cowering Salter at speed, a grinning Mikey Collins didn't break stride as his foot landed a sickening blow to the base of Colin Salter's spine, propelling him forwards like a demented jack-in-the-box lurching into action. He landed face down on the car park, sliding forward as the skin was removed from his nose and forehead and replaced with blood-soaked gravel.

'Mr Salter, are you OK?' Mikey Collins enquired, ensuring that he stood on Salter's fingers as he asked the question.

'Ahhhhh.'

'Oh, so sorry sir, let's get you on your feet and out of here.'

He grabbed hold of the rancid Salter under the arms and roughly lifted the whining wreck to his feet. Salter was winded from the heavy blow to his spine and so was unable to mete out the verbal abuse that the situation warranted. Instead he meekly lay in the arms of his saviour as he was physically dragged like a bloodied rag doll from what had now become an uncontrolled mob.

As the carnage ensued Jerry Bailey Johnson had stepped inside the store and instructed Old Dave, the in-store security guard, to lock the doors. Before he could employ the shutdown switch, the crowd started pouring in like a pack of hyenas sensing their wounded prey. The newly employed staff just stood watching in a mixture of fascination and delight, realising what was unfolding. JBJ removed herself to the back office so that she could attempt to restore some calm through the in-store tannoy. The crowd soon became aware of the paltry offers.

'Where's the fucking Mini?... Where's the colour tellies?'

A couple of teenage lads from the notorious estate seized the golden opportunity and grabbed a black-and-white TV each. Old Dave could see what was going on.

'Hey, you two... you're Ricky Brown's lads, put those back or I'll tell your father.' He felt a burly tattooed arm across his chest, as he turned to see a rough shaven Ricky Brown at his side.

'You ain't gonna tell nobody about nufink my saaan, right! Bung one of those over here boy.'

One of the Brown boys launched the portable television like a rugby ball into his father's ape-like arms.

'Better still, go and get a couple of trolleys we can get some booze in too – you don't mind Dave, do you?' said Ricky Brown as he gave Old Dave a menacing pat on the head.

That was the point when the crowd turned from disappointed bargain hunters into a baying mob of looters. The choice and range was dizzying as the majority started stripping the shelves, reckoning they had a good ten minutes to fill their boots; even some of the staff were taking the opportunity to slip some cheese, steak or chocolate inside their overalls.

There was nothing that JBJ could do apart from issue veiled threats of prosecution over the tannoy to those found to be shoplifting, and advise of the imminent arrival of the police. The state-of-the-art in-store cameras weren't yet operational so prosecution would be a long shot, and not particularly desirable as this would be a public relations episode best forgotten rather than resurrected at some future date in court. She did inwardly chuckle though as she remembered how she had misguidedly thought before this whole sorry fiasco that Colin Salter would be able to conduct an opening that would improve on the last one – the PG Tip's chimp had certainly won the day with that particular contest!

CHAPTER 16

The opening of the Heathview store had hit the national news headlines, leaving Colin Salter questioning his lifelong mantra that 'there's no such thing as bad publicity'. The image of the Neanderthal security guard punching the female reporter had been repeatedly played on the news broadcasts on all the channels, and published in the inner columns of all of the red top newspapers – but thankfully it only made the headlines on the local rags. Worse though for Salter was the ridicule that he imagined he must be receiving for the images taken of him when he was cowering behind the podium. Never mind 'hell hath no fury like a woman scorned', 'an arrogant sociopath mocked' would put that saying to shame; he vowed to bring fire and brimstone down on those responsible.

He suspected there was a conspiracy with some inside collusion. The placards were professionally made and while some bore simple messages such as 'Save Our Shops', at least two had his face superimposed on Tarzan's chimpanzee with the phrase 'Profit Cheatah?', which seemed a very strange turn of phrase in light of the recent massaging of the last quarter's profit figures. His rage was incandescent when the lawyers told him that it simply wasn't worth taking any legal action for slander as the placards could be interpreted in several ways – and didn't actually call him a cheat, merely a clever pun on the name of Tarzan's faithful companion 'Cheetah' and could also be construed as a reference to the last disastrous shop opening in Heathview by that three-piece-suit-bedecked chimpanzee. To take any action would merely focus a spotlight on the situation at a time when the store opening needed to be forgotten and out of the limelight. In Colin Salter's mind, the way that the baying mob had mobilised and rushed the store must have been organised. He not only had a badly bruised ego but a black and blue body and heavily scabbed face due to those cowardly plebs putting the boot in, and if it hadn't been for that cretin of a driver getting him out it could have been far worse. Every morning when he tried to get out of bed the pain in his back and ribs made his thoughts of revenge on the person or persons responsible, all consuming.

The report he had received from Rick Parfitt in a frock hadn't impressed him; no CCTV operational inside or outside of the building, the police didn't arrive for 35 minutes as they had been called out to one of the farms on the outskirts of the village on what turned out to be a malicious call alleging a livestock theft, namely pigs, the caller left their name as 'Paul Skinback'. So Colin Salter had decided to call in a professional corporate investigator to find the bad apples for him to boil down to pulp. In the meantime, he was going to have to start to unload some of his shares to the market, in small bundles that wouldn't attract too much attention, far sooner than he had intended.

*

The opening of Salter's superstore had a more immediate and profound effect on takings than the Rogers had expected. Their daily sales were down and they were also incurring significantly greater wastage on fresh items such as Bowles the Bakers bread, pies, pasties and pastries that really needed to be sold on the day of delivery. The spotty locusts still attended en masse due to the proximity to the school and the extra time that would be lost traipsing to and from the superstore, not to mention the ready availability of cigarettes (the superstore applied the age check with rigour). However, the constant flow of customers throughout the day dried up to a trickle, to a point where from mid-morning onwards the shop was empty for long periods. They had always taken more money on the few hours of trading on a Sunday than they did on any of the weekdays, and now they were under threat of prosecution if they continued that long-established practice. Danny had just spent an hour of his day release in the kitchen with Marilyn poring over the books of the first month's trading since the opening of the superstore, while Eddie gently swayed over the till of an empty shop.

'There's nothing for it, Mum, you have to reduce costs. At the moment you aren't even breaking even, it's costing you money for the privilege of working 15 hours a day to serve the good folk of Heathview.'

'Are you suggesting that we get rid of Shirley?'

'That is your main variable cost, Mum, and as you have said, most of the time now she is standing around with nothing to do, as you and Dad are stocking the shelves in the quiet periods and with the drop-off of customers the only time you need two people are when the kids descend on you. You haven't really got any choice.'

'How can we compete, Danny, we can't purchase our goods any cheaper? I went down to Salter's as we ran out of Tate and Lyle sugar and they were selling it on a promotional offer cheaper than we can buy it at cost from the cash and carry – so I bought all the stock they had on display, mainly to stop our customers from buying it there.' What had really hurt Marilyn most wasn't the indignity of buying the sugar from Salter's, it was seeing their regular customers shuffling past head down and shamefaced like naughty children as they passed her in the aisles. It felt like infidelity and a betrayal of the worst kind, also knowing that they would now find it too awkward to come back to the shop. Marilyn vowed never to repeat the experience. She had found that particular evening, as they were closing, an unexpected churning anxiety in her stomach as the meat pies and pastries she had put aside for Tramp Juice Ron remained untouched. Eddie was winding in the awning when the shop door thundered open and in bowled Tramp Juice Ron heading straight for his chest freezer perch, while in the throes of the well-honed process of making a rollie; Marilyn joyfully stared at the fag paper drooping and flapping from his lip, while his club-hammer hands fumbled in his tobacco pouch. She had never been so pleased to see a customer, even the accompanying aroma was a familiar friend that evening.

'Even our locally sourced produce is far more expensive, the eggs, bread, pies, pasties, pastries; the cabbages, potatoes, carrots; the strawberries, apples pears and plums. If we don't sell those products, then there is a knock-on effect on the other local businesses. Will they be able to compete if this is being replicated in the other shops that sell their produce? How does it all end, Danny?' Marilyn let out a sigh of resignation.

'But I know you are right about Shirley. I'll have to speak to your father. She's been a loyal employee and a good friend to me – to us. But I'll tell her when she gets in later this morning.'

'There's something else, Mum…' Danny hesitated. '…the margins don't add up. In other words, for the amount of stock you are selling the till receipts are insufficient, even allowing for the new levels of wastage that you are recording. As you are only too aware, there are a number of keying errors so the Z reading figures can't be relied upon, but the margins tell me you are losing hundreds each month. Have you been looking at the surveillance camera footage of the till? I'm not accusing her but perhaps the situation might improve when Shirley departs?'

'I have. It's nothing to do with Shirley.'

'What is it, stock being stolen? Shoplifters?'

'Can we just leave it for now, love please.' Marilyn physically couldn't say the words, nor admit to her husband's theft to support his peccadillo, which was the only way she could refer to it – not by its real name, alcoholism, and not by its medical name, dipsomania.

CHAPTER 17

An exasperated Jenny hammered on the shop door of Garwood's Convenience Store, the other village corner shop situated at the furthermost end of the village. The 'Closed' sign still hung on the door and the lights hadn't been turned on. She peered through the shop window. She could see that the cover was still over the till and everything was as it should have been on closing.

Brenda Garwood had already been struggling to manage the shop for the past two years since her husband passed away from a heart attack, and the opening of Salter's superstore had seen her already meagre takings dramatically drop by half in the first week with further daily erosion. The fall in takings had also been impacted by the decision to stop trading on a Sunday following the threat of prosecution from Trading Standards. She had roughly calculated that she was now losing money by opening the door to her dwindling customer base and would be financially better off just lying in bed and watching Richard and Judy on *This Morning*.

Yesterday Brenda Garwood had taken the dramatic step of engaging a commercial estate agent to value the property. After reviewing the current perilous financial standing, the Blue Stratos-soaked suit paved the way for his valuation with phrases like 'challenging market' and 'changing retail dynamic in rural areas', his piranha-like instincts had smelt blood from the initial phone call and as soon as he saw the books and the beaten owner he was heading in to strip the flesh from the live carcass. Brenda was stunned at the valuation which was nearly £30,000 less than she still owed on the residual mortgage. All the years of grafting with Harry to build the business and now if she walked away she would have a £30,000 debt with nothing to show for it; an insult to his memory.

'That said' continued the Blue Stratos Piranha with cold indifference, 'with the new retail challenges, it is unlikely that you will achieve that valuation, I can't sell this business as a going concern now, not with that superstore on your doorstep. No, it's more likely that a property developer will need to convert this into residential units and the planning process for that could be tricky and costly so you may have to settle for between ten and 15 grand less than the valuation, but let me run it up the flag pole and see if the cat wants to lick it.'

For the first time since Harry had met his maker after choking on that ill-fated pasty, Brenda was glad he wasn't around to witness this farce. If the pasty hadn't killed him, this certainly would have done. She remembered their first day in the shop, no grand opening just the excitement of turning the sign on the door to open, and waiting for their first customer to appear. Everything they did was on their own terms and for each other. They had planned to retire and buy a caravan to tour round Britain and perhaps abroad, although Harry was a stickler for his food and wasn't a fan of 'that foreign muck', but they could have stocked up on baked beans and tea bags and braved the wider continent of Europe. Now their dream lay in ruins; they had worked seven days a week for the past 15 years only to be stripped of their home and the widowed Brenda was left with a life-changing great debt to boot, in the name of so-called progress that lines the coffers of a corporate giant.

*

Two women sat at the back of a little Italian coffee shop, situated a stone's throw from Salter's HQ in London. To the casual observer they were two old friends catching up over a morning coffee. The younger and prettier of the two handed over a large A3 envelope to the older imposing, somewhat masculine-looking woman. They sat in silence as the older woman examined the contents of the envelope.

'He's planning to start off loading his share portfolio then,' said Jerry Bailey Johnson, placing the papers on the table, confidently slurping the foam off her cappuccino.

'Yes, he was speaking to his broker this morning. I put him through and stayed on the line to listen to the call, he's going to start offloading his personal stock next week. My stepbrother says that he has driven him and Bullshit Ellis to that club three times in the last week and he heard them talking about financial journalists that they were going to feed the fourth quarter projections to.' A wicked smile flicked over Suzie Kent's face.

'Oh yes, the projections that Brad Ellis sent over to Salter via you, falsely showing our highest ever return. Well I'm going to have to get busy very quickly. This is good work, Miss Kent, very good work.'

*

The Bowles the Bakers delivery girl decided to try round the back of Garwood's Convenience Store. This was the first time in five years of her round that Jenny had ever experienced any of the business customers not being available to receive a delivery. Annoyingly this was also the last visit of her morning delivery round in Heathview and now she was running nearly twenty minutes late. She placed the tray of loaves back in the rear of van. She normally left the engine running while she made the deliveries but she turned the running motor off to go and investigate. The side gate wasn't locked, just stiff to open where the base of the wooden gate had swollen in the damp and cold. It took a well-aimed kick with her brown ten-holed Dr Marten boots to force it open. She could hear the sound of a television coming from a half-opened upstairs window at the side of the house.

'Hello, Mrs Garwood, it's Jenny from the bakers. Hello, Mrs Garwood?' she shouted up at the window. She listened but could only hear the mumble and occasional applause from the television. She tried the side door and to her amazement it was unlocked.

'Hello, Mrs Garwood, are you OK? It's Jenny from Bowles the Bakers.' As she entered the hall to the stairs, there were boxes of crisps opened and the contents strewn across the floor. She stepped over them and tentatively made her way up the stairs towards the noise of the television.

'Hello, Mrs Garwood, is everything OK? It's Jenny, Jenny from the Bakers.' She opened the door to the lounge. Her head didn't turn to look at the TV screen, she just focused on Brenda Garwood who was lying on the floor, her dressing gown wide open moving slowly with each passing breath, an upturned mug lay by the side of her, eyes frightened and wide open returning Jenny's shocked stare. There was a pungent aroma and dark stain on the carpet around Brenda where she had been unable to control her bladder. Jenny rushed to her.

'Oh my god, Mrs Garwood, don't worry I'll get help.'

Brenda tried to move her now lopsided mouth to thank young Jenny and to ask her to stay with her as she felt her pulse slowing and her life blood ebbing away, but she couldn't, neither could she move her hand as she felt Jenny's cold hands cradle her own. She was paralysed by the massive stroke she had last night after the unbearable stress of the day's events. She would soon be with her beloved Harry, a death tear escaped from the corner of each eye as she closed them for the last time.

CHAPTER 18

'Have ye heard aboot the auld girl Garwood? She's deid, your Danny's wee Jenny from yon Bakers found her lying on the flair earlier this morning.' Eddie was swaying behind the till with his arms folded as Mr Bowford stood in front of him, seemingly in transmit mode himself as Shirley had burst into the shop not pausing for breath as she imparted the news to her captive audience. The startling news even stopped the Brigadier in full flight.

'Aye, they reckon she had a stroke or a heart attack through the stress of the business going tits oop since yon supermarket opened. She had the agents out there yesterday to sell up, she had'nae got a pot to pish in poor cow, been lying there all night too in her ain pish.'

Marilyn could hear Shirley's excited arrival from the kitchen and suggested to Danny that he made himself scarce while she broke the news of their financial calamity and Shirley's redundancy pay – which consisted of her earnings for that shift, and 40 Superkings. She pushed open the adjoining door to the shop and stuck her head through.

'Morning Shirley, can I have a word please?'

'Aye, nay bother hen, I was just saying have your heard the news aboot the auld girl Garwood? I just found out from Cloth-Eared Jack on ma way here.' And Shirley proceeded to recount the story as if she herself had been an eyewitness to the horrific events, only this time adding in some additional gory details such as the aroma of the urine-soaked carpet and the state of Mrs Garwood's soiled night clothes. When she finally drew breath, Mr Bowford interjected, pumping out his chest as he prepared to insensitively deliver his observations of the situation.

'I think this shows that our SOS campaign is more valid now than it ever was, and Mrs Garwood's passing is a direct result of that superstore opening. You've got hardly any customers anymore either and I'm sure there are others in the village feeling the pinch too. It will soon be like a ghost town, or ghost village. We need to go to the press immediately with this dreadful news. Mrs Garwood's passing must not, yea will not, be in be vain – fear not kind heart, leave it to me Mrs Rogers!'

*

There was a palpable air of anxiety around the boardroom table. It was the first board meeting since the catastrophic opening of their new flagship store, which had received national press coverage, none of which had been positive for the brand. The actual table itself was also more uncomfortable for those sitting around it in the armless black leather swivel chairs, as it had been raised three inches to accommodate the ever-expanding thighs of their chairman. Colin Salter was perched at the head of the table in his garish throne, its antique status besmirched by the vulgar black leather upholstery.

'Right, agenda item one, projected outturn for the financial year. Brad do you want to take us through your projections, please?' Colin Salter surveyed the five other sycophantic board members, comprising of outdated family members and well-paid professionals; and, of course, Brad 'Bullshit' Ellis his Global Director for Finance and Resources who stared down at the script that had been written for him by his own head of finance.

'Thank you, Chairman, I am pleased to say our fourth quarter project shows a healthy increase in profit in line with our mid-year projection. If we take out extraordinary costs we have an anticipated year-end profit growth of nearly 8% on last year. This is a very positive story for the market and our share price growth in year has been nothing short of phenomenal, mirroring our commercial performance.'

The board members nodded, the family members with shareholdings afforded a smile.

'We have five other store openings targeted for the next financial year based on the Heathview model, not the actual opening event that is…' Bullshit Ellis felt the eyes of Colin Salter burning into him.

'…rather the rural village model. Based on Jerry Bailey Johnson's marketing report we have five more gold hotspots that are in the process of acquisition and we will have more detailed implementation plans to bring to the next meeting. Any questions gentlemen?'

'My dear boy, what exactly are "extraordinary costs"?' Colin Salter scowled across at his Uncle George, it was the first time that senile old fool had asked a question in two years. Bullshit Ellis smiled and flicked over the first page of his script to the useful background facts and figures his team had supplied. He ran his finger down the page.

'Well George, these are items of expenditure that can be classified as both unusual and infrequent.'

'I see dear boy, oh do humour me what exactly are they then in terms of items and value? And what would our profit position be if we included them. I mean, they are still money going out of the business, correct?' Colin Salter saw Suzie Kent frantically scribing for the minutes and Bullshit Ellis flicking over the sheets in his presentation for an answer.

'I'm afraid I don't have that minutia of detail George, and I wouldn't want to mislead the board in any shape or form without the actual accurate representation. I will commit to getting the information as soon as we have finished here and circulate it outside of this meeting. I trust that is acceptable?'

'My dear boy, if you haven't got the information there simply isn't much else to be done. However, without that vital information and for the benefit of our shareholders Mr Chairman it must be minuted that the outturn projections have not been approved by the board until further relevant information is forthcoming, and must not therefore, under any circumstances be shared outside of this meeting. Can I also suggest we have an extraordinary meeting within the next fortnight to go through the "minutiae" as it has been so quaintly defined? Oh my, there's that word again "extraordinary", how funny.'

'Absolutely George, we really should have had that information Brad, we need absolute transparency for our shareholders – can you ensure that last part is minuted, errr…'

Colin Salter waved dismissively at his PA. Why couldn't he remember her damn name? In any event, he would ensure that he adjusted the minutes to represent his version of history before they were published. His main focus now would be offloading his shareholding before the next meeting as it looked like the house of cards would soon collapse without the scrutiny of the auditors as he had originally planned, which would have been at the earliest another three or four months down the line – what was that geriatric buffoon playing at? He had expected the report to sail through. It wouldn't be easy offloading his shareholding as a substantial sale could trigger alarm in the market and as a consequence a fall in price, which is why he had already started selling small bundles via a third-party agent recommended by their own broker to ensure anonymity to the market. He would also have to plan for Bullshit Ellis's departure and more importantly ensure there was nothing that could be traced back to him, although he was fairly confident that his tracks were well and truly covered, he had ensured that no paper trail linked back to him. So as far as the auditors were concerned, Brad Bullshit Ellis was their Patient Zero.

However, what did concern him greatly was that in his desire not to be implicated he had become so far detached that he had no real idea of the current financial standing of his empire. They had borrowed heavily for capital investment in the new stores and although in the long term the rural village model was like shooting fish in a barrel, he hadn't envisaged the loss of sales this year through the catastrophic blunder that bullshitting imbecile Ellis had made, which had potentially put everything in jeopardy. He resolved to get early sight of the true outturn position before the next meeting and raise the alarm himself with the other board members in private one-to-one meetings over a glass of something special at the club, so he could get them to suggest the removal of Ellis from his position before the extraordinary board meeting. His only real disappointment was that as they were now going to be merely suspected fraudulent projections, the criminal charges against Ellis for false accounting might prove more problematic, but certainly not impossible with his high-profile lodge-based connections in the Metropolitan Police. There was such a lot to do in a very short period of time but Colin Salter felt extremely comfortable, and it wasn't solely down to the adjusted table height.

*

'Leave it hen, I'll put the kettle on, sit yer sen doon.' Shirley intercepted Marilyn's route to the kettle. She noticed till receipts and bills strewn across the kitchen table and the mallard-green ledger accounting book marked 'income' and 'expenditure'. She nodded at the table.

'Young Danny been going through the books? Bet that disnae make pretty reading…' Shirley was no fool and had noticed that the till was half as full as it had been, and that the once steady stream of customers had evaporated into a trickle. She hadn't been looking forward to this chat with Marilyn but the news of Brenda Garwood's demise had seemed to put everything into cold perspective.

'There's nae easy way to say this, so I'll jist say it. I've been offered a full-time job working the deli counter at Salter's. I'm struggling hen, with old Stanley staying at his sons since Christmas, and I can see you and yer man are struggling here too. I know you really canne afford to pay me with what you must be taking now, I can see what's going on, and to be fair you probably should have given me the auld Spanish archer weeks back. But ah still feel like I've betrayed you by sleeping with the enemy, and only Christ knows what how I'm ganna tell Granny Smith.'

Marilyn didn't know whether it was Brenda Garwood's passing

or losing her friend to the very ruination of their life, or the relief of not having to give Shirley the 'elbow', as she put it, but she felt every ounce of energy drained from her as she fell to the ground pulling the tablecloth and its contents with her.

She was woken up by the rasping tongues of Ronnie and Reggie, who tore in from the yard to investigate the latest commotion, giving her face a thorough reviving wash. She was lying on the kitchen floor with her head laying on Eddie's lap, as he sat cross-legged on the floor.

'Get off, you little swine.' Eddie pushed Ronnie and Reggie aside. 'They keep doing that, don't worry love, you just fainted and had a nasty fall. Shirley's called the doctor, he's on his way.'

'Who's minding the shop?'

'Don't worry, I haven't committed heresy, we haven't closed! Shirley is holding the fort, she told me what happened.'

'What happened?'

'She's leaving, going to work for the enemy. She beat you to the punch then.'

Marilyn sat up and grabbed hold of one of the kitchen chairs to help her back to her feet.

'I don't need a doctor, Eddie. Can you phone and cancel it please?'

'You might not, but sitting here cross-legged I do, my back has locked, I can't move!'

*

The waiter who had served a JBJ a cappuccino was on the phone looking over toward her. She was seated at the back of the little Italian coffee shop near Salter's HQ. He had surveyed the tables to look for a customer that met the caller's description of 'middle-aged woman, blonde hair pulled tightly back, prominent nose'. There were only four other customers and by a process of elimination he had worked out this was Miss Bailey Johnson, the other four being of a different ethnic persuasion or clearly of the male gender. He walked over to her. As he got closer he began to question his gender assessment as he saw her somewhat rugged features.

'Miss Bailey Johnson?' he offered.

JBJ looked up. She had been engrossed in completing some paperwork and hadn't noticed his cautious approach.

'Yes, can I help?'

'Telephone for you.' He extended the foot-long silver aerial and handed over the white portable handset.

'Hi, it's Jerry Bailey Johnson.'

'Hello Jerry, it's me. I'm sorry but I'm not going to be able to meet you in the *café*. I'm in a phone box outside Salter's HQ. I think he's got someone following me, he has engaged an investigator to look into the leaks. The bloke called this morning after the board meeting, I put him through and stayed on the line to listen in and he asked Salter to call him back as the line was unsecure and that someone is probably listening in. I got my stepbrother to use one of his contacts to trace the number and it is the switchboard of a corporate investigations company. The good news though, the meeting went as planned, old Georgie boy took the bait and started asking questions about the projections, they are having another extraordinary meeting in the next two weeks and I have been asked to coordinate the diaries to find a date that works, so I wanted to check in with you first.'

'Thank you for taking the time to let me know Mr Ellis, that's greatly appreciated.'

'Mr Ellis? Oh, is there somebody watching you too?'

'Yes, I think that is the case. I'll give you a call back with a suitable date, but knowing the timeline helps. You take care now.' JBJ ended the call and placed the handset on the table, gathered her paperwork and placed it in her briefcase, leaving a tip on the table she waved the phone at the waiter.

'Thanks hon, I'll leave it here.' As she gathered her things to leave, she noticed out of the corner of her eye a man sitting to her right folding his paper and tucking it under his arm. 'This is going to be fun,' she thought.

CHAPTER 19

The little white rusty Subaru van powered through the Wisdom Estate. Danny had just made an emergency delivery of four pasties, two Danish pastries and a family bag of Revels to Dot as Cloth-Eared Jack had been called out first thing to an unplanned pick up in London on his Salter's contract and didn't know what time he would be back. The ever-expanding Dot was to all intents and purposes housebound; the last time she had ventured out was the meeting at the village hall when Salter's had laid on a free buffet, but the disappointment of the quality and quantity of the said buffet and free mini hamper – oh, and the ensuing brawl – had put her off venturing out since. She had gratefully received the bounty from Danny, tactfully pointing out that usually if they needed a few bits, Jack would normally pick them up from the new superstore on his way home as they were open until 10 pm. She left the parting instruction 'put it on our book love, he'll settle up with you' to the expectant Danny, holding out the bill as she slammed the front door shut.

The home deliveries had also dwindled somewhat due to the superstore's longer opening hours and cheaper prices, so Danny only had two deliveries that Saturday morning and the second one was for Granny Smith. He had planned a lovely birthday surprise for her to go with it. He had finally remembered to bring along his cassette player to play her the demo tape of his band that they had recorded in, what he liked to tell all that would listen, a 'proper' studio; although in reality it was in an eight-track studio housed in a converted bungalow lounge in Heathview. The studio owner was an ex-hippy and made what he liked to quip as a 'joint living'

– producing and recording local bands and cultivating a healthy crop of marijuana in the converted loft space, a business model that seemed to be mutually beneficial to his customers, and one that Salter's superstore, for once, could not destroy. Danny also had a tape of Chopin that Trevor had kindly recorded for him. For once he wasn't pushed for time and Marilyn had baked a cake for Granny Smith's 80th birthday which was on the Sunday, with the strict instructions that Danny stayed for a cup of tea and a slice of cake. When Danny felt the weight of the cake as he heaved it into the groceries box he couldn't help wondering if Mr Kipling might have been the man for this particular job; but as Marilyn had pointed out, as she was viciously hitting the bottom of the cake tin with a rolling pin to dislodge its stubborn contents, this actually required both thought and effort, whereas merely giving Granny Smith a cake out of the shop required neither.

*

The Bishops didn't mind working Saturdays, especially when they were offered the rare opportunity to conduct covert surveillance. The head of trading standards had been feeling the heat from Councillor Gary Beaton who had formally complained to the leader of the council about the lack of results following his detailed dossier. He considered that warnings for the two corner shops were inadequate but that he could live with that, providing regular enforcement continued, but the lack of action against one Ronald Froggatt was wholly unacceptable as he was 'running wild and out of control', illicitly producing and distributing alcohol on an 'industrial scale'. His officers had paid Mr Froggatt a couple of visits but there had been no sign of any industrial-scale alcohol production, only a couple of demijohns of home brew for personal consumption. Any further intrusion would be seen as harassment, so to placate the leader of the council he agreed to conduct a covert surveillance operation.

The head of trading standards first thought was to minimise the cost, the second was who could he send on such a fool's errand? One thing that he read in Councillor Beaton's dossier helped crystalise his thoughts on selection – Mr Froggatt had somewhat of a reputation for delivering physical retribution when slighted. So the Bishops now sat in their Austin Allegro parked opposite Tramp Juice Ron's ramshackle bungalow, with its front garden blighted with tyres, car parts, old washing machines and cookers. Brian 'Mini Hitler' Bishop and his wife Eileen Bishop or 'EB', as she was known by the other trading standards officers, had spent their Friday night meticulously planning the operation while their colleagues were relaxing with their usual end of week wind-down drinks, consuming the confiscated alcohol that they had seized during the week. Needless to say, the drinks invite never found its way to the Bishops who remained in blissful ignorance of the weekly event's existence. The seven-year-old orange Austin Allegro was one of the last off the production line and had been Brian Bishop's pride and joy until he stumbled across an article in *Car Mad Monthly* that had, unbeknownst to Brian Bishop, been the catalyst for the cessation of production. It had simply described his beloved Allegro as an 'ugly, obsolete saloon car'. The garish orange didn't make it an ideal vehicle for covert surveillance, and didn't go unnoticed to the ruffled bed-haired Scotty staring out of the window wearing nothing but his underpants and unceremoniously shovelling Happy Shopper Chocolate Krispies in his furiously masticating mouth.

'Dad, there's two people in a horrible orange car over the road; they are looking over here at us.'

As Scotty spoke, the cereal sprayed over the filthy threadbare carpet but didn't stop the mechanical shovelling of replacement Krispies.

'Been there for ages, Dad.'

Tramp Juice Ron was sitting next to the open fire and didn't bother looking up from his morning paper.

'It'll be those council lot again, gar'n let Dog out boy. She'n see to 'em.'

Scotty tipped up the bowl and drained off the residual chocolate milk which was the favourite part of his breakfast. He walked through the haze of tobacco smoke and into the grotty kitchen where, without a blink of an eye, threw the plastic Tupperware bowl and the spoon on top of an overflowing tower of encrusted plates and pots that lay untouched in the sink. Still in just his underpants, he opened the back door and stepped onto the wet grass. He reached down and untied Dog, a six-year-old Rottweiler who remained prone, looking up at Scotty with complete disinterest. Her ears pricked up when she heard the whistle and accompanying roar from the lounge.

'Gar'n Dog!'

Dog sprang to her feet and started to run with such eagerness that she initially lost traction on the slippery grass, resulting in mud spraying over the semi-naked torso of Scotty. Then her claws finally caught on the grass, propelling her forward at breakneck speed to the front of the property, where she came to a sudden halt and threw herself to the ground to lay in wait hidden behind a roll of chicken wire. She licked her lips as she lay quietly watching the front gate.

Preparation had always been the key for Brian Bishop and now four hours into their surveillance he hadn't seen anything apart from some gormless-looking youth standing at the window in nothing but a pair of filthy grey stained underpants that Brian Bishop guessed had once been classified as 'white' on the packaging. He would soon have to move to Plan B, Operation Quick Silver, but for now he had more pressing issues as his bladder was crying out from his early morning cuppa, the urgency exacerbated by his enlarged prostate. Never fear, this was expected and planned for.

'Pass over the flask dear.'

'Oh really Brian! Do you really need to go again, so soon? That's the third time – you've already filled the first flask.'

Brian Bishop unzipped his trousers and brought his member out and breathed a sigh of relief as the insipid flow dribbled into the awaiting thermos flask. It had been his idea to use thermos flasks, as he had proudly explained to EB when she had asked why he had purchased six thermos flasks from Argos.

'A repository for urine my dear, that when left unattended to the casual passer-by looks like an ordinary thermos flask, unlike your common or garden transparent squash bottle laden with urine which could easily give the game away and blow our cover.'

Initially he was stumped when she retorted, 'Fine, but what am I going to use?' but after careful thought he said, 'You can use them, my dear, you just need a funnel.' So their covert urination kit travelled with them in the car in pride of place alongside their first aid kit.

'Brian, quick, there's someone coming, they are coming over to the car… bloody hell, hurry up, what's wrong with that useless thing, can't it go any faster? Get it away, quick, hurry up!'

The knock on the passenger side window was accompanied by a piercing scream, as in his haste Brian Bishop had trapped his now bleeding foreskin in the zip of his urine- and blood-soaked trousers. EB looked at her husband's zip and its unwelcome protuberance that looked a little like Kojak with a nosebleed, and then momentarily froze as she looked over her left shoulder at the extremely dangerous man who she knew as Ronald Froggatt, standing with his hands in his pockets and a rollie hanging from his bottom lip.

'For Christ's sake, Brian drive, drive, drive, get us out of here, our cover is blown!'

Brian Bishop started the car and winced as he depressed the clutch. The urine flask was now laying in the footwell, gently emptying its contents down the clutch and brake pedal and Brian Bishop's shoes. Another thump on the window and Brian Bishop floored the Ugly Obsolete Saloon Car like never before. Unbeknownst to the Bishops, Ronald Froggatt was actually trying to avert a potential insurance claim as his own vehicle had blown a head gasket and emptied its engine oil on the road the day before, just in front of where they were parked. He felt morally obligated to advise them that they may need to drive carefully, especially as he had also just punctured their rear left tyre with a screwdriver on his hidden approach to the Orange Peril.

As Mini Hitler accelerated, he felt the back of the car slip away as it hit the oil deposit. He pulled the gear lever into second and tried to accelerate out of the skid as he had seen in the movies. He merely increased the speed of collision as he found his beloved car smashing through Ronald Froggatt's gate. As the Bishops careered towards the front door, both covered their eyes. As he was later to be reminded by the head of trading standards when he visited him in hospital, he was 'damn lucky he had all that old tat in the garden or we could have been looking at some serious compensation.' They were brought to an abrupt stop by an old Zanussi cooker that Tramp Juice Ron had bought two years ago for parts. As Brian Bishop had undone his seatbelt to use his covert urine thermos flask, his journey didn't end at the spare parts cooker. He flew through the windscreen and landed about three feet from Tramp Juice Ron's hidden brewery and storage cellar. As he lay semi-conscious, Brian Bishop was vaguely aware of what sounded like a small pony galloping across a field. He opened one bloodied eye to see a blurred outline of a brown animal lurching towards him; his next memory was being dragged out of his semi-conscious haze by the most excruciating pain he had ever experienced as Dog set to work on his already battered nether regions.

'Darn't see that often,' chuckled Tramp Juice Ron as he sparked a scratcher on his face to re-light his Rollie. He wasn't a cruel man so he let Dog play with her new toy for a full minute before calling her off; he always believed in reward for a job well done.

*

Danny reached under the ornamental frog next to the gate to retrieve the key and let himself into Granny Smith's small garden. He opened the gate and picked up the old wooden fruit box containing the groceries and his tapes and cassette player and placed the box on the back step so he could search his trouser pockets for the back door key. He surveyed the garden, it looked quite overgrown, and it didn't look as though the grass had been cut yet this year. The robin sat on top of the empty bird table and cocked his head to one side as if observing Danny, seemingly weighing up the likelihood of any scraps coming his way. With the rummaging and patting of all his pockets, Danny found the key in his back pocket. It had a deliberately cryptic label attached by a piece of browning string – 'GS BD'. He unlocked the back door and lifted the box of groceries and entered into the kitchen, nearly stepping on Elvis who was laying by the back door. Danny ruffled Elvis's shaggy head and tangled ears, noticing that Elvis had a little accident on the carpet, but more strangely he didn't slowly wag his little docked tail, which was his usual greeting.

'Hello boy, who's a lovely boy then?' he whispered in his ear, then bellowed his usual greeting toward the lounge so as not to alarm Granny Smith. 'Hello, it's only me, Danny.' Elvis whimpered and pushed himself against Danny's legs. Danny put the box on the kitchen table. 'What's wrong with Elvis? He's really not himself today,' he shouted to Granny Smith in the lounge.

'I've got a surprise don't come out.' Danny lit the solitary candle on the centre of the cake, and yet again was taken by surprise at the weight as he lifted the cake, and wondered how it would lie on poor Granny Smith's stomach.

'Happy birthday to you, happy birthday to you, happy birthday…' He paused briefly, realising he didn't actually know Granny Smith's first name. '…Dear Granny Smith, happy birthday to you.'

He could see Granny Smith was asleep by the window. She must have been watching the robin on the bird table. He put the cake down on the telephone table next to the lounge door and turned the centre light on. He reached over and held her cold hand, it was only for confirmation as he had realised that she had already passed away the moment he had entered the lounge. In the grocery box on the kitchen table sat an unopened birthday card signed by all of the regular customers of The Corner Stores, and of course Ronnie and Reggie. As the trembling Elvis pressed himself against the kneeling Danny, there were only two sounds – the clock ticking on the old oak sideboard and Danny gently sobbing.

CHAPTER 20

The spotty locusts had already started queuing for their morning nicotine and sugar rush. Eddie stood gently swaying on security duty just inside the shop doorway, his 'metro-central' vein-damaged face flushed from an early morning ingestion of Tramp Juice Ron's current batch of moonshine now the home brew was back in full production. He had listened with glee, while receiving the delivery last night, at Ron's somewhat succinct anecdote of the timely demise of the two officious trading standards officers.

'Nar-thing to it boy, he'd been watching our place, then lost the control of the car after having a piss in a flask and drivin' arf – straight through my gate and straight into an old oven, through the windscreen onto my lawn. Then Dog wen o' work on e's wedding tackle. Fair damaged my stock; I was using that there cooker for parts. Still, they're already talking compensation, proper sorry their boss was.'

On the back of the Bishops seemingly long-term enforced absence, Scotty was loading the milk crate of moonshine and jugs of the potent tramp juice into the storage shed, rather than the garage which had been the temporary residence while the investigation was ongoing.

'Splendid news, Ronald, I'll drink to that.'

Eddie lifted one of the milk bottles in a toast and took a long slug of the heavy-duty brew.

'I think we'll take a chance and start opening again on a Sunday. We've got nothing to lose, if we can't get the takings up, Marilyn says that we might as well sell up. Danny has looked at the books and we are losing money hand over fist every day we are open, apparently. The way I feel now we might as well torch the place for the insurance money as it ain't worth a fraction of what we paid for it, ah, wishful thinking! Danny said the shop's no longer a "going concern" and we should consider selling up – but then what, Ronald?'

Marilyn was standing behind the till multitasking as usual. On this occasion she was trying to watch the two spotty locusts that had gained admission to select their bounty and at the same time listen to Mr Bowford and Trevor, while also compiling the order list for the cash and carry.

'I am reliably informed that Garwood's Convenience Stores has gone on the market as a redevelopment opportunity. You know what that means?'

Byron Bowford turned his head to the door and then back to the till, ensuring that the Rogers realised he was addressing them both. Marilyn peered over the till at a slightly overweight teenager sporting an unkempt mullet haircut who was busily placing some penny sweets into a paper bag. She felt sure with the time it was taking to spend the ten one pence coins he had left piled up on the counter that more than the odd fruit salad, black jack or flying saucer had made their way into his parka pocket. She looked up at the expectant Brigadier Bowford.

'You are now Heathview's only corner shop, the last bastion. I went to the local press about the sad demise of Mrs Garwood but they are just not interested, Salter's superstore is old news as far as they are concerned. Progress they actually called it, can you believe that? In fact, the reporter I spoke to told me that Salter's are going to start work on a petrol station next month on the site, and I would imagine that will see the end of Bruce Wyatt's garage.'

Trevor interjected, 'We've let you down, Marilyn – our protests came to nought. But worse than that, it's cards-on-the-table time, as if you don't already know this – but pretty much everyone that uses your shop also buys from Salter's, I know Leslie and I have as have you Mr Bowford. I'm so, so sorry Marilyn…' Trevor leant over the counter and placed his hand on Marilyn's arm, as Byron Bowford silently stared at the floor.

'…the only person that didn't was Granny Smith, god bless her.'

As Trevor and Marilyn welled up, the mullet-haired parka boy took the opportunity to pop a handful of white chocolate mice into his already bulging coat pocket.

*

The intercom buzzed on Suzie Kent's desk, she flicked the grey button under the flashing light. She had just arrived in the office and hadn't even had the opportunity to take her coat off.

'Morning, can you pop through I need to speak with you, it's extremely urgent – come on, chop-chop.'

Suzie thought she could hear the sound of the receiver being slammed back into its cradle, even with the thick oak door between them. She took off her coat and picked up the opened post from the white metal wicker in-tray labelled 'In' and inserted the document that she removed from her bag into the pile.

'What kept yer?' Salter barked at her. Suzie noticed that he looked unusually dishevelled, his top button was undone and his tie was at half-mast. This appearance was not uncommon after a very long lunch but an uncharacteristic look for first thing in the morning.

'I need you to clear all my meetings for today and get that halfwit to bring my car round.'

'No problem, shall I leave your post on your desk, Mr Salter?'

Colin Salter snatched the post from her hand and threw it in his top left-hand drawer.

'Well? What are you waiting for? Get to it!'

He picked up the copy of the *Financial Times* and looked again at the Salter's Supermarket share price, which had continued to rise. There should have been a downturn in the market now with the amount of stock he had been unloading, nearly three quarters of his 400,000 shares. He had been on the phone to the third-party agent that had been recommended to him by his own broker, but he hadn't been able to contact him, the phone just rang off the hook. He had the paperwork notifying him of the disposals but had checked with his banker this morning and the sale proceeds less commission had yet to reach his account. He was going to pay one Mr Albert Kenneth Wren a personal visit at the offices of Hero Sale Investments Ltd and give him both barrels; let the peasant know precisely who he is dealing with.

*

The small picturesque St Michael's church sat in the centre of Heathview. The village had grown around this beating heart, and its body now stretched for miles all around. The church and the diocese school that sat alongside had been built at the inception of the village in 1860, when vagabonds and tinkers mixed with farmers and labourers. Over the years it had held hundreds of weddings and funerals, each unique in their own right. The small graveyard overlooked the primary school playground, and funerals could sometimes be accompanied by the shrill excited screams of that playtime bought. Rector Christopher Crisp always endeavoured to schedule the funerals between the various school playtimes, and when that was not possible he always prayed to the Almighty for divine intervention in the form of heavy rain so that the children would be kept inside for a rain-day break.

Today was the second funeral in a fortnight. The first had been for Brenda Garwood who had been laid to rest next to her beloved Harry in the family plot. During his eulogy, Rector Chris Crisp had observed that only two years ago the Garwoods were happily running a thriving business that served the community, now they were laid to rest and that same business was now seen as redundant and cast aside in the so-called name of progress. When he had written the eulogy, the same thought ran through his head, as it had done when he conducted the service for the late Harry Garwood. How many people would be inwardly chuckling at the notion of a crisp conducting the funeral for a grocer? He felt immediate shame and prayed for a solid hour for forgiveness of his hubris.

The Rector Chris Crisp was also conflicted in his thoughts about the superstore. On the one hand it had practically eliminated unemployment in the village – he only knew of one person that was out of work, Mr Cloare the egg yolk-stained vest-wearing layabout with nine children who preferred the security of a couch, TV and the tidy government fortnightly cheque substantially bolstered by his ever-increasing brood. On the other hand, many of his parishioners that ran small businesses were feeling the strain, from the bakers and butchers to the local farmers, from the haberdashery and shoe shop, to the mini market and corner shop owners – and soon, from what he heard, Bruce Wyatt's garage would be losing trade too. Wasn't this the true lifeblood of the village? But in his heart lay the real truth – his biggest concern was the changing face of village life itself; more houses would follow and then more corporate businesses to service them. The seemingly inevitable new property developments would move from the grubby hands of local builders and individual landowners to the filthy claws of national property developers, purchasing larger pockets of land on a far greater scale and cramming them with small low-cost properties whose tiny gardens could be filled with a few bonsai trees. He saw Brenda Garwood's funeral as a symbolic passing of the village life once known, but recognised that he was probably no different to his predecessor who had likely mourned the coming of Heathview Manufacturing back in the 1960s which had served as a catalyst for change in its own era.

The church had been full for Granny Smith's funeral service which, much to Rector Crisp's consternation, was a rarity these days. Her daughter and family had made the trip from Newcastle and a number of distant family attended from all parts of the country, few of whom had bothered to keep in contact with Granny Smith apart from the perfunctory Christmas card. As they took their places in the reserved pews at the front of the church, Danny remembered the words that Granny Smith had once said to him when he was on his knees raking the ashes from her coal fireplace.

'Take it from one who knows – it's not what you do in memory of someone when they are dead, it's what you do for them when they are alive that counts. You're a good lad, Danny, and you'll get your reward in heaven.'

The eulogy prepared by her daughter and delivered by the rector painted a rich picture of Granny Smith's life from early education to her working life, of her family and Elvis; but there were, as with everyone, seemingly mundane details of her everyday life that would remain known only to a few. Only Marilyn knew that she would forget to include Elvis's food on her shopping list, only Eddie knew that she was Puffin' Billy from the smoking double act – and not Fag Ash Lil; only Shirley knew she loved watching Richard and Judy with a brew and a cigarette, and had started to have accidents in her bed, only Danny knew she was a classically trained pianist who loved Chopin and lost all her precious records due to the summer heat in the loft. But no one really knew the unspoken pain she had carried to the last of the loss of her beloved George, whose memory became more evocative as she felt her own time drawing to an end.

Granny Smith's daughter had asked Marilyn Rogers to gather a select few of her mother's close friends for the burial. The Rogers, Shirley, Trevor and Leslie stood together in the drizzle as the coffin was lowered into the ground; the Bowford's had earlier left the church service in a state of high dudgeon when they learned of the exclusive burial arrangements. Back in Hawtrey Way, the corner shop was in darkness from the afternoon storm clouds and all that could be heard was the scampering of Ronnie and Reggie on the kitchen floor tiles as they attempted to play with their new elderly spaniel companion who lay quietly under the kitchen table quietly observing their youthful antics.

Due to the difficulties in getting everyone seated in the church, the service had overrun and now Rector Chris Crisp was delivering the Lord's Prayer to the shrill backdrop of shrieking exuberant children having their playtime. A few children had gathered at the green wire mesh fence separating the playground and the churchyard, their fingers looped through and gripping the wire as they stared toward the far end of the graveyard at figures dressed in black staring at a hole in the ground. At the graveside, Danny brushed away a tear with the back of his hand and smiled; he had learned something very special today, her first name was Rose.

*

The Rolls Royce Silver Spirit was parked outside a large grey building in an industrial estate on the outskirts of south London.

'This can't be it! Give me the fucking map.' Colin Salter leaned through the driver's hatch and tried, unsuccessfully, to snatch the map out of Mikey Collins' hand.

'This is it boss, look 13 Meadowbank Road, City Bridge, we are here which is Meadow Bank Road City Bridge and that storage facility is number 13.'

'City Bridge? Open your eyes, it's a fucking industrial park.'

'Yes, City Bridge Industrial Park. This is the postcode and address you gave me.'

'Fuck this for a game of soldiers, wait here.'

Colin Salter climbed out of the car slamming the door behind him. He waddled over to the arrow marked 'Reception' and followed his way round to the entrance, and thumped on the sliding window. An elderly looking man came slowly to the window.

'Yes?'

'Is this 13 Meadowbank Road, City Bridge?'

'Yes.'

'I want to see a Mr Wren of Hero Sale Investments.'

'There aren't any offices here squire, just storage units and mailboxes.'

'Do you know of Hero Sale Investments?'

'Couldn't rightly tell yer, squire, all I do is let the key holders in and out.'

'Oh for fuck's sake, it's no good talking to the monkey, go and get me the organ grinder, someone who knows what is going on in this god-forsaken shithole.'

'There's only this monkey here in front of you squire, but if you don't piss off pronto rest assured I'll be out there grinding your organs fella.'

With that retort, the old man slowly slid the window shut and left a gobsmacked Colin Salter feeling a greater unease than he had done at the start of the day. He had confirmed his suspicions that something was very, very wrong.

CHAPTER 21

The Parish Council's appointed auditor was used to merely check that the income receipts from fundraising and the hiring of facilities had been appropriately banked, and the government funding had been spent with adequate supporting evidence, effectively ensuring that the Parish Council statement of accounts was materially correct. The audit would generally be very straightforward and only take a couple days to deliver. However, today the Heathview Parish Council's appointed auditor, Michelle Brewster, was meeting with one of the top brass, who was extremely high up in the food chain at the Audit Commission, to discuss a rather intriguing report that had landed on her desk two weeks ago, and the subsequent incendiary findings of her own investigations. Her line manager had quickly realised the potential ramifications and immediately decided to throw it upstairs so that he didn't have to deal with the fallout. The author of the report was a Mr Laurence Padbury and five minutes after reading his report Michelle was on the phone to Mr Padbury arranging to visit him to discuss his extremely detailed dossier. When she retold the story years later, she would always say how her heart sank as she pulled up outside Mr Padbury's decrepit bungalow with its overgrown garden, and when he finally managed to open the damp-expanded front door and she first set eyes on the mad professor figure with his wild grey hair and soup-stained straggly beard, she had to admit it did immediately cast some serious doubt on the credibility of the report. This first impression was not helped as she looked down at his attire – he was wearing a dressing gown over what she thought could be an old boiler suit or even homemade pyjamas and filthy

Green Flash tennis shoes. She stepped into the cold damp dingy hallway which was littered with all kinds of gear mechanisms and bike parts. The threadbare carpet hadn't been cleaned since Mr Padbury's late mother had still been mobile enough to push the hoover, which was at least a decade ago.

When Michelle was ushered into Mr Padbury's 'study' it was no surprise to find the converted lounge space was equally hazardous in terms of the squalid living conditions and the inadvertent man-made obstacle course which left only small pathways to carefully navigate around precarious piles of newspapers, books, correspondence and old designs filling most of the floor space. Three of the walls were covered by bookcases haphazardly filled to capacity with books of all shapes and sizes. The peeling wallpaper on the remaining wall was virtually hidden by a blanket of photographs held in place with drawing pins. She had respectfully declined the offer of a cup of tea, as she shuddered to think what state the kitchen was in and had absolutely no interest in finding out. She also felt somewhat overdressed in her grey trouser suit and cream blouse and matching high-heeled shoes, thinking that a bio-hazard suit may have been a more sensible choice of attire.

Only ten minutes into their discussion it soon became apparent to the auditor that Mr Padbury, although clearly a totally eccentric oddball, had an acute analytical mind and eye for detail; and although he was socially inept and extremely awkward on first contact, he was surprisingly articulate and passionate when discussing the matter in hand.

'So, yes Ms Brewster I am concerned at the environmental impact of the company of Councillor Gary Beaton and his flagrant disregard for appropriate waste disposal as demonstrated in the photographs in Appendix 6, and I would like that to be reviewed. But as you can see, my main bone of contention is Councillor Beaton's conduct in public office. In his councillor's public declarations of interest, he declared that his firm provided services to Salter's Supermarket PLC and agreed to sit out of any future discussions on the development, after the award of planning permission, which a review of minutes I undertook of subsequent meetings has confirmed that to be the case. However, he was involved in the Parish Council decision to recommend approval to the Town Planning Committee; again that is documented, with Councillor Beaton supporting the application. The problem is that decision was *ultra vires* – that is, it wasn't lawful – for the two reasons that I have documented on page 68. Firstly, Councillor Beaton has never signed a declaration of public office when he was appointed on the Parish Council six months earlier, secondly, the meeting wasn't quorate. The constitution states that five appointed parish councillors must be in attendance for a planning decision. Ignoring the fact that Councillor Beaton technically wasn't appointed as the correct process had not been followed, you will note that Councillor Sally Holmes is documented as in attendance. In the minutes under 'Any Other Business' there is a motion that was carried to use the Parish Council funds to send Councillor Sally Holmes some flowers during her period of recuperation following her recent operation. At the subsequent meeting in the next month the minutes welcome her back from this unexpected leave of absence. So one can generously conclude that Councillor Sally Holmes' attendance was erroneously documented, without her there they did not have the five required to make a planning decision.'

'I have to say your report seems to leave no stone unturned, it must have taken you months to put this together Mr Padbury. May I ask what your motivation is to devote what is not an inconsiderable amount of your own time to this investigation?'

'Justice and respect for democracy and our environment Ms Brewster…' The auditor's eyes briefly flicked around the squalid state of the room at Mr Padbury's last comment.

'It seems highly probable that Councillor Beaton had already received recompense from Salter's Supermarkets PLC prior to that, what I consider, unlawful decision. Whether that decision would have still been made without Councillor Beaton's interference is a moot point, it may well have been. What I do know is that it has significantly affected the livelihoods of many small businesses in Heathview. My investigation cannot extend into the financial affairs of Councillor Beaton, but you have the powers to do that Ms Brewster. I also haven't been successful in determining the beneficiaries of the estate of the late Mr Warren from whom Salter's Supermarket purchased the land at auction, but I'm sure if you do, that may well prove to be quite enlightening.'

'One more thing I wanted to ask you, Mr Padbury. Where did you get the handwritten unofficial minutes of the village meeting where Councillor Beaton was involved in a brawl at a public event? What I mean is, how can I substantiate the authenticity?'

'Of the incident? Just ask around in the village, I believe a large proportion attended. The Rogers who run The Corner Stores were particularly close to the action I am led to believe, it's how the Councillor's moniker came into being – Brown Envelope Beaton. In summary, and please excuse my language Ms Brewster, he is a right royal shithouse.'

*

This was a particularly lively brew, thought Eddie as he remained ensconced in the downstairs toilet busy killing two birds with one stone. He was sitting on the privy necking the last demijohn of tramp juice that he had been forced to rather hurriedly carry in from the storage shed as it once again wreaked havoc with his bowels. As he drained the last drop of the rocket fuel, he thought that he wouldn't even bother announcing that he'd just had an Eddie Van Halen when he went back into the shop, at ten-thirty in the morning it was unlikely with their new reduced customer base that he would even have the audience to confuse, and in any event there seemed little point as the whole purpose was to make Marilyn smile and the joy of life seemed to have left her. She had taken to cashing up three times a day and placing the cash tin into a drawer in the kitchen that she now locked. It was making Eddie's beverage tokens extremely hard to come by; his only real opportunity was if someone gave him the exact money while Marilyn was out of the shop on a break, as he could put that straight in his pocket without ringing it through the till. As a consequence, he was relying almost exclusively on Tramp Juice Ron's home brew which he purchased via their own barter system, although that was also becoming more problematic to fund as Marilyn was also keeping a tighter control on stock and now spent every Sunday afternoon undertaking a mini stocktake with Danny. This had the dual purpose of working out the profit for the week and prioritise their stock purchases at the cash and carry on the following Monday. As a result of their reduced turnover, they no longer had the cash flow to hold surplus stock and now quite often the shelves looked bare when certain stock lines ran out, and it was the ever-depleting stock of tobacco that Eddie continued to plunder with impunity and complete disregard to their perilous financial position to pay Tramp Juice Ron. He earned a nice profit too for selling the illicit brew to some of the regular customers but even those sales had dropped off as Salter's superstore ran weekly loss leader offers on beers and spirits that made Tramp Juice Ron's somewhat inconsistent and unrefined product range even less appealing.

Trevor and Leslie had been the only customers in the shop for the past half hour. They were excitedly telling Marilyn how they intended to buy Garwood's Convenience Store and set up a computer shop as Leslie had it on good authority, after he bumped into one of Caligo Blue's old corporate clients, that home computers were the next big thing. Initially they had argued as Trevor thought a video shop was the future, but Leslie had dug his heels in, mainly as he had already invested heavily in some imported Apple and Commodore Computers. Their offer had been accepted and as they were selling the bungalow they wanted the Rogers to know before the For Sale board appeared. It had given Leslie the excuse to tell Trevor that he was going to sell Caligo Blue to concentrate on the new business together; it was true, although he had only the goodwill of business to sell which wasn't worth a great deal now, and the money he had received for the sale had already been used to buy the stock for their new enterprise.

'You've been really good friends to us and we'll, no, I'll miss you.' Marilyn felt the tears again. Trevor hugged her and rubbed her back.

'Don't be daft, chicken, I'll be down here every day like old colonel silly bollocks over the road for my pint of milk and book of stamps. Don't worry, we'll be round here picking young Danny's brains as well, we don't do numbers! We're only down the road and there's no reason you can't pop in on us.'

'If we are still trading, I can't see any way out of it, Danny keeps telling me to put the place on the market while it still holds some value.'

'Is it that bad?' Leslie knew the answer to his question as the total absence of footfall in the past half hour was a far cry from the once bustling shop. He also knew that it wasn't only the appeal of Salter's superstore that had captured their clientele, it was also the steady and very noticeable decline of Eddie that curbed the appeal of the personal shopping experience to their regular clients. Leslie had noticed that his ability to use the till had gone from extremely poor to being akin to a chimp trying to split the atom, and the repeated quipping as the till bleeped his errors in protest – 'I'll name that tune in one' – was funny the first time but when you needed to get home to prepare the kids' tea it lost its lustre somewhat. It hadn't been so acute when Shirley was there, but now it was brutally apparent and laid bare for all to see. Yesterday afternoon, when Leslie had popped over to the shop, he saw Eddie on his own behind the till drinking heavily from what looked like a milk bottle, which Leslie recognised as moonshine from the Tramp Juice Ron product line. As Leslie entered the shop, Eddie thrust the bottle under the counter and placed both hands on the till for much needed support. He had wanted half a pound of ham and a quarter a pound of cheddar and a loaf of bread, but looking at Eddie's glowing face and uncontrolled nodding head, he decided that even asking would be an act of cruelty – instructing Eddie to use the meat slicer could feasibly be construed as inciting self-induced GBH – so he picked up a loaf and placed it on the counter. Eddie stared at the loaf and then ran his finger down the list of prices for fresh produce sellotaped to the till (solely for Eddie's benefit) and slowly and deliberately punched the price into the till and amazingly it didn't beep its refusal. The befuddled Eddie had then asked Leslie for '£35 for cash exactly please sir'.

'Marilyn, we need to talk about Eddie…'

*

The regional director of the Audit Commission beckoned Michelle Brewster to sit.

'This is powerful stuff,' he said, holding her report aloft in his right hand.

'One could say incendiary even, Ms Brewster. The evidence that you have uncovered on the councillor does seem to constitute Misfeasance in Public Office, which can attract a maximum penalty of life imprisonment. He was sole beneficiary of the estate of the late Mr Warren and the land was sold under sealed bid auction to which it is estimated Salter's Supermarket PLC paid 25% above market value, which they will of course argue was a business necessity for a prime site. However, none of this activity was disclosed by Councillor Beaton when he took part in the planning vote – a very serious omission. The picture becomes even murkier in terms of the award of the building works to the councillor's own company which are subcontracted back to Salter's Supermarkets own building contractors at a lower rate, leaving Councillor Beaton's company with a healthy £175,000.'

'Which didn't actually go through the company account but was a payment directly into Beaton's own personal account,' Michelle excitedly interjected.

'Indeed, and it therefore looks to all intents and purposes like an inducement or bribe. I think the evidence against Councillor Beaton is solid. However, not so for Salter's Supermarkets PLC. All of their actions can probably be legitimately explained by a top barrister who would quite easily cast reasonable doubt on criminal intent. No, they have been extremely clever to ensure that Beaton is the fall guy. The Crown Prosecution Service will certainly not recommend proceedings against Salter's Supermarkets, the case will not meet the high threshold of beyond reasonable doubt, I fear. Now we come to the really thorny issue – the one that could prove rather costly to the public purse if we get it wrong – the legitimacy of the planning consent of the Heathview superstore. Now your report states the decision to be *ultra vires*, clearly it didn't follow correct protocol as you have proved the meeting wasn't quorate. However, they only made the Parish Council recommendation for approval to the Town Planning Committee, who were the body who granted the permission and it could be argued that any objections could have been raised at that meeting, which the report does not currently recognise.'

'But it may not have even got to the Town Planning Committee had Beaton not pushed it through the Parish Council approach to serve his own corrupt agenda. If he was out of the equation, would the other councillors have voted for such radical change to the way of village life, I doubt it?'

'Quite, I do understand that Michelle, and believe me I'm on your side, but it isn't as clear cut as you think. If the planning permission was revoked and Salter's Supermarkets were required to apply again, they would either appeal the decision or go down the route of submitting the application again. Either way, they would inevitably get permission but would be unable to trade for the months it would take. They would lose hundreds of thousands of pounds as well as potentially laying off the workforce until the store re-opens. The local politicians simply couldn't allow this to happen. I take it you have ensured that correct legal process was followed in gathering the evidence, Michelle?'

'It has. The file has been subject to two separate reviews within our unit since we concluded the review, but I have been under supervision throughout the investigation. I also sought professional legal advice where I thought it necessary.'

'Fair enough, but I want you to submit all of your working papers and everything you have received on the matter to my legal team for review before any further action is taken. I would also like them to form their own independent conclusions.' He held his palm towards Michelle to stop her interjecting before he made his point.

'...and to be crystal clear, that is what will determine the next course of action.'

CHAPTER 22

The mid-morning call from Sandy Harwood, Colin Salter's stockbroker, signalled the start of a chain of seismic events for Colin Salter and the whole Salter family institution – an historic legacy that he had been entrusted to run.

'What exactly do you mean, the share price is plummeting, Harwood?'

'I mean plummeting, like an elephant carrying a piano falling off a cliff, Mr Salter. It has dropped from £4.50 to £2.00 in the hour since trading started this morning, and still on a downward trajectory. I just wanted to check it wasn't due to you offloading your whole shareholding this morning as it looks like there is a massive fire sale going on?'

'No, you know my plans for that, slow and steady – why is the price dropping like that?' Colin Salter felt a sickening feeling in his stomach, and something he had rarely experienced before – panic.

'Oh, that's good, that's perfect…' purred Harwood, '…the word in the City that is spreading like wildfire is that the profit forecasts have been massively overstated, there is a serious cash shortage and you are over-geared with your borrowing for new development and the bank is about to pull the plug. In short, you are at risk of going into liquidation.'

'That's absolute horse shit,' Salter stammered. 'There may need to be an adjustment to the profit estimates but nothing that calamitous… nothing like the picture you are painting.'

'I know that, and you know that, but when you didn't publish the trading projection after the last board meeting, Mr Salter, the shareholders became extremely uneasy and the piece in this morning's FT has sent the share price spiralling, into absolute meltdown as they try and offload their stock before the crash. I have to hand it to you, Mr Salter, you have done a very good job there indeed. Now what I was actually ringing for was to advise you to buy back the shares you offloaded now, as I think the price is bottoming out, you should be able to buy back at less than two pounds a share. What did you sell at, four-fifty, four-sixty a share?'

'What piece in the *Financial Times*?'

'The leaked report about the financial projections, and the police investigation into the sale of land for the flagship store, that was a lovely touch Mr Salter it has to be said.'

'I don't…' He was frantically thumbing through the *Financial Times* with his free hand.

'…understand this. I wanted to ask you about the share sales, I haven't seen any sight of monies from Hero Sales Investment the brokers you recommended since we started the offload a fortnight ago. I appreciate they wouldn't be quite legit but operating out of a storage facility and no sign of the sale proceeds makes me nervous.'

'Hero Sale Investments? I've never heard of them Mr Salter. The company I recommended was Caymen Holdings, they operate offshore, I gave the details to your PA a couple of weeks ago over the phone and followed it up with a fax that I sent from another building so that it couldn't be traced back to me. I've never heard of Hero Sale Investments. You have ensured the stock has been sold, haven't you?'

'What the fuck do you mean you haven't heard of Hero Sales Investments? What about this chancer Albert Kenneth Wren? Are you trying to fucking stitch me up, Harwood? You better start to offload my shares now if we are in a fire sale.' Colin Salter was now screaming down the phone as the gravity of the situation began to sink in. In the adjoining room, Suzie Kent carefully placed the telephone handset back in its cradle and hurriedly put her coat on.

*

When Jerry Bailey Johnson had first worked in her daddy's grocery business at the age of 12, it had been a Saturday morning job, although it generally extended to consume her whole day. Her daddy had been adamant that she learned all aspects of the business, and she set about it with a dedication and zeal that was something to behold. Gerald Bailey had realised his eldest daughter was never going to be much of a looker, hell that didn't matter a damn to him, he needed someone to learn and continue the business and she was certainly a quick learner, everyone remarked on it. His wife Sarah had left him and moved back to her parent's town in England with their baby daughter after she finally caught him cheating on her; Jerry had been settled in school and after much persuasion and suitable recompense, his ex-wife had agreed for her to continue her education in the States. Her daddy saw her education as learning the business and on those Saturdays she did just that, mainly working with the finance and market development teams at the headquarters of Bailey Inc. in Sarasota Florida. At the age of 19 she was leading the market development team for the Northern States and by the age of 30 she was in charge of global acquisitions. Today was a big day for Bailey Inc. they were acquiring a major foothold in the UK retail market by obtaining a majority shareholding in Salter's Supermarket PLC at a bargain basement price. The untapped UK market had such potential for growth above their own saturated market in the United States, and they saw opportunities for extending their own practices to give them major trading advantages over the competition, such as it was – this was the rise of the superstore.

*

It was 5 am in Beaton & Son's dingy office and Councillor Gary 'Brown Envelope' Beaton pushed two fingers between the venetian blinds to create a gap for him to look out at his new silver Jag parked next to the two filthy vans and flatbed lorry; the yard was poorly illuminated by the cracked and filthy security light above the window of the office. He was nursing a chipped mug containing the remnants of the bottle of Johnny Walker that usually lay under lock and key in his office drawer.

He was anxiously contemplating his next move following the call yesterday afternoon from Sally Holmes. The police had been to see Councillor Holmes and were asking about her attendance at the planning meeting where they had approved the Salter's Supermarket application. When she had asked why, they had explained that they were merely following up on lines of enquiry that had been referred to them by the Audit Commission following potentially serious irregularities that had come to light during the Parish Council audit. After he had squeezed every drop of information out of a perplexed Councillor Holmes, Gary Beaton had, without delay, called old Sybil the parish clerk, and to his horror the police had already been to see her. She had told them quite innocently, 'Oh yes I do remember, Councillor Beaton had to approve the minutes and asked me to add in Councillor Holmes as 'in attendance' to ensure that the meeting was quorate, otherwise they would have had to hold it again and that would be a waste of everyone's time. She wasn't you see, in attendance, she was having her bits seen to in hospital – women's problems – poor lamb.'

Gary Beaton knew that the police would normally make arrests at the crack of dawn and he was frantically trying to weigh up how much they knew and whether it was worth him going to ground. He had a friend that owned a villa in the south of Spain and also had means of getting him out of the country undetected – for a price. Apart from the business, he really had nothing keeping him, his wife Janice was nothing more than a front for respectability the term he had heard was a 'beard'; but even if he did an early morning flit to the sun he would make sure she was OK. If it was just the minutes, he could explain that, but what if they had more? A horrible feeling then washed over him – how old was that half-wit youth that he 'wrestled' with? Oh no the rubber trunks and secretly filmed videos – he'd left them in the toolbox at the back of the garage. Bollocks! He had already felt the wrath of the halfwit's father's club hammer fist at the village meeting, what the hell would he do if he found out about the wrestling? With a shaking hand, he downed the scotch and grabbed the faux leopard skin suitcase that he had borrowed from Janice as she lay asleep in her room earlier that morning. It was hastily packed with clothes frantically pulled from the drawers and cupboards of his separate bedroom, and the valuables of his safe at home, including Janice's jewellery. He had poured himself the mug of scotch after emptying contents of the office safe into the suitcase. He stood by the door and looked back at the paper-strewn office with the safe wide open, for what he thought was the last time. But there was something that told him not to leave, it was the same voice that had always had a grip on him – greed and the fear of his own true sexuality and of course his afternoon wrestling indiscretions being revealed.

*

The waiter looked back through the wafting tobacco-filled air at the two women seated at the rear of the little Italian coffee shop and smiled to himself as he surreptitiously pocketed the fiver tip that they had given him, rather than place it in the tip jar for distribution at the end of the shift. He had overhead them talking as he took them their coffee and pastries; he would never have placed them as sisters, they didn't bear any resemblance in physical appearance or even heritage as one spoke with an American accent, but he heard them mention their father. But then again nothing surprised him anymore and he had long since learned the frustrations of overhearing snippets of conversation. Still, they seemed extremely excited, five pounds tip excited to be precise.

'The report from the corporate private investigator had raised questions on your credentials, Jerry, and also surprisingly Brad Ellis. Apparently he has actually provided false qualifications – who would have thought it?'

'That isn't really a surprise darlin', what did they say about my credentials?' asked Jerry Bailey Johnson.

'They have found out the referees you provided don't align with your previous experience on your CV. But apparently the references weren't even taken up. It appears that task was left in the hands of Brad Ellis, so not a surprise…' Suzie Kent snorted with laughter at the same time as her sister; she tried to catch her breath to continue.

'…but they haven't yet managed to make the link to Hero Sale Investments or Mr A. K Wren. The report seems to indicate that aspect of the investigation is still ongoing.'

'Nor will they do, that's a cold, cold trail, Daddy said that the "broker" acting as our Mr Wren that called Salter is pretty much untraceable; anyway by now it's irrelevant. But I've gotta know, did they work out the names?' JBJ smirked as she dug her fork into the coffee cream pastry.

'No, come on did you think they would? Hero Sale, anagram of Arsehole and A. K Wren… Wanker!' the sisters simultaneously burst out with laughter, flecks of coffee cream spraying from JBJ's mouth over Suzie Kent's handbag, sending them both into raptures. When they had finally regained their composure, JBJ enquired to her younger sister.

'Did he read the investigator's report?'

'I very much doubt it. He put it in his locked drawer with a bundle of other correspondence that he hasn't read. He's been in a blind panic ever since the visit to the storage facility. I pulled it and shredded it. I also put the correct financial forecasts in the pile, and ensured that all of the numerous back-covering memos that Brad Ellis had sent through over the past six months were filed safely and copied, like we agreed.'

'Wonderful work, little sis, and all of his favourite journalists have a copy of that financial projection and results report, hence the share price rocking out. Daddy called to say that we have got our majority shareholding already and we are still hoovering up stock to stabilise the price. When the position finally crystallises, we will formally announce the Bailey Inc. expansion into the UK.'

'Did the family members offer up the shares then, like we thought they would?'

'They sure did. Once they saw the financial projections that I got Brad Ellis to send them ahead of this week's meeting, they tossed them like hot potatoes before the market became aware, offloading at the peak price. That is, of course, apart from the man with the largest shareholding who thought he was already offloading them! That's what fuelled the market panic and sent the share price into free fall – the family shareholders offloading their shares.'

'The outturn position is accurate though, right?'

'I have every confidence that it is. They actually have some good people who I understand have successfully unravelled Mr Bullshit's original work of fiction, but it's the numbers in the future projections that are severely undercooked; that is compared to what they will be when we implement our own supply chain management, refinancing and acquisition principles. Once the takeover is announced and our guys have had a run over the figures the market will respond as it normally does and the share price will be beyond what it was at its peak this year. After all, as Daddy always says, the stock market is just all smoke and mirrors.'

CHAPTER 23

There were a dozen thoughts racing through Brown Envelope Beaton's mind as he drove the Jag at breakneck speed back to his house. He had just ingested the last of his devil's dandruff and that feeling of invincibility had returned. Snorting the powder through his recently twice-broken nose was now a rather painful experience, but within a short time of starting to hoover up the vast quantity of Columbian marching powder, he found that it actually provided the necessary self-medicating analgesic for his throbbing snout. If Janice was still in bed – and he knew she would be as the lazy cow didn't normally get up until ten – he could stage a burglary for both home and the yard, claiming that he was the victim of some wider conspiracy. Oh yes, and as the thought percolated it came to him – he would also be able to claim on both the business and household insurances too! He knew someone who would fence her jewellery for him and that would certainly be a nice bit of folding money!

He would also have to forge some cash receipts for the business as it was pointless just claiming the actual money that he had 'stolen' – everybody else inflated their insurance claims he reasoned. He felt much calmer as the combination of the plan, the cocaine and the large mug of scotch hit him. He kicked himself for panicking like he had, but never mind, once again the cream rises to the top! He was thinking of the fictional plant and equipment for the business insurance claim, and the electrical goods and additional jewellery for the house claim – but only if he could get some moody invoices to support these fictitious purchases.

'That shouldn't be a problem to you, Councillor Beaton…' he

said out loud to himself, '…not with your network of connections!' he screamed as he manically thumped the steering wheel with both hands. He bent down to turn the volume up on the radio as T. Rex belted out the opening riff of 'Get it on'. The scotch and cocaine had kicked in nicely.

'I fucking love this track!' were Brown Envelope Beaton's last ever words. As he rose back up from adjusting the radio he felt the unforgiving impact of the tree as the Jag had left the road on a hairpin bend. 'Well you're dirty and sweet…' sang Marc Bolan as the right side of the engine, released from the shackles of its flimsy housing, forcefully made its way through the fragile frame of the stolen cut and shut Jag that Brown Envelope Beaton had bought on the cheap. It came to rest on his lap, crushing his ribcage and pelvis. His shattered ribs lacerated and deflated his lungs, splinters making their mischievous way to his heart. His feet had been pinned and flattened under the now compressed pedals with the engine forcing the driver's seat back six inches dislocating ankles, knees, hips and his left shoulder – during the post mortem the pathologist had cheerfully hummed the kids song 'heads, shoulders, knees and toes' – it was the only way she kept her sanity, and in fairness the toes could have been dislocated but in their current compressed form it was impossible to tell. His pelvis and redundant baby-making apparatus had taken the full brunt of the scalding hot engine and were crushed. That sorry area now looked like a rare steak covered in a motor oil sauce, and as the engine silently smoked the only sound was the still miraculously, operational radio, crackling, 'Well you're built like a car, you've got a hubcap star diamond star halo.'

*

The previous day the Crown Prosecution Service had privately concluded a preliminary review of the case against Councillor Gary Beaton following the receipt of the extra police evidence that they had requested. The police had advised Michelle Brewster that prosecution was unlikely as her report had highlighted that

Councillor Beaton had never signed a declaration of public office when he was appointed on the Parish Council six months earlier, which would potentially invalidate his term in office. It was a fragile and high-risk legal argument that the Crown Prosecution Service did not want to present on an expensive high profile, with all the complications that come with a charge of Misfeasance in Public Office. They concluded that even in the unlikely event that he made full admissions under caution, the case will fail in court due to the administrative error. The only strand that remained from the investigation was the legality of the planning approval, but this was a matter for the local authority to deal with within their procedures, no longer a criminal offence. As Michelle Brewster watched the local news the next evening and saw footage of the mangled car wreck, she felt a tinge of sadness to learn that she had been finally Beaton.

*

A dark-haired slack-jawed youth with a short wiry frame attired in an old garish orange Holland football tracksuit and paint-stained dealer boots, stood behind by the old oak tree situated at the back of Trevor and Leslie's bungalow opposite The Corner Stores. He cautiously peered round, although despite the glow of the nearby streetlight he was hidden in the shadow. He had heard on the news that Councillor Beaton had been killed, and he had gone down to the tree to have a look at the car but it had been cleared away by the time he could cycle there on the old refurbished BMX bike his dad had given him last Christmas. Too big for the bike, Scotty's legs protruded outwards at ten to two as he rode. When he arrived at the scene, the police were still taking measurements and photographs, and he wondered what Councillor Beaton looked like now and what would happen to his smart leather wrestling shorts – seemed such a shame to waste them. Councillor Beaton had only ever wanted to be a professional wrestler and that would never happen now. Scotty's bike was propped up against the fence running alongside the old oak tree; sometime earlier he had watched poor Mrs Rogers turning the sign to 'closed' and switching most of the lights off. He reached for the bottle beside him remembering what Mr Rogers had said – 'May as well torch the place for the insurance money as it ain't worth a fraction of what we paid for it.'

*

There was a sombre atmosphere in Salter's Supermarkets boardroom. The family members were all in their usual places, apart from the former chairman who now sat alongside board members rather than at the head of the table. This was the ultimate insult for Colin Salter, being forced to actually attend a meeting where the family business was effectively being handed over to a bunch of Septic Tanks. This was anathema to him, the once proud Leader of the Salter Dynasty – English Grocers since 1898. He looked over toward where his old throne used to reside and saw that it, like the rest of the chairs, had been replaced by the authentic ornately carved chairs that he had consigned to the basement. The period artwork had also been restored from the basement and all of the absurd egotistical photographs of Colin Salter had been unceremoniously removed and burned, unbeknownst to him, at the behest of the other family board members. The notable absentee of the previous board membership was Brad 'Bullshit' Ellis, who had been groomed as Colin Salter's unsuspecting patsy to provide false information to the board that would allow Salter to offload his shareholding and buy back at a lower price when the true financial position was revealed, a plan that had been torpedoed by Bailey Inc. That fateful day led to Colin Salter seeing his shareholding value, which when he got out of bed that morning had been worth nearly £2m, being decimated at close of business to slightly less than £1m, and that included the receipts from the sale of nearly half his shareholding. He had expected the price to continue to fall for him to buy back at a lower price but it didn't, as Bailey Inc. began to buy, the price started to gradually increase; not only had he lost nearly £1m, his shareholding had reduced from 30% to 15% in a day – in future days when someone took a severe loss on the stock market it was known as being 'Saltered'. By the next day, all trace had been removed of Brad Ellis at Salter's Supermarket HQ; by the time the shell-shocked Colin Salter had arrived, his office was deemed out of bounds as it was being searched by the police who were investigating allegations of false accounting and insider trading. He had tried to call Brad Ellis on his home number but there was no reply; it seemed he had mysteriously vanished overnight, no one had seen or heard from him. Now, less than 48 hours later, Colin Salter was sitting in his old boardroom awaiting the interim chief executive appointed by the new owners, the American retail giants Bailey Inc. The heads of the board members turned toward the opening oak doors, Colin Salter stared open-mouthed as JBJ walked through the boardroom; she placed her papers on the table and pulled out the chair at the top of the table. Before sitting she announced, 'Good morning gentleman. As you know, I'm Jerry Bailey Johnson and I have been appointed by the new owners of Salter's Supermarkets as acting chief executive. As you are no doubt aware, when the dust finally settled Bailey Inc. now have a 65% share of the company, and I do appreciate the sensitivity around this as it was as a result of you good gentlemen releasing a considerable portion of your own shareholding.'

There were silent guilty glances exchanged around the table as each had looked to save their own skin with no thought for the family heritage.

'I would emphasise that my appointment is only a temporary measure to ease the transition to the Bailey Inc. way. It will also be impossible for me to effectively fulfil both the role as chief executive and chairman, in the interim, when we have completed all the constitutional changes, as we have already discussed.'

She glanced at the family board members, clearly excluding the incredulous Colin Salter who was beginning to join the dots. He should have trusted his feral instincts which had told him at the outset that there was something amiss with this bloody woman.

'Mr Bailey, my daddy, will be acting as chairman of Salter's

Supermarkets. Mr Salter, I need a word with you now in private, please.'

A flushed-faced Colin Salter was trembling, but for the first time not with rage. He knew he had been well and truly played.

*

The flaming bottle of moonshine spun toward the storage shed. It landed on the roof and exploded.

'Bullseye!'

Scotty turned to collect his BMX bike from the fence and leave. The moonshine that Eddie had stored at the back of the shed ignited and spat flames over two gas canisters which blew the shed and Ronnie and Reggie's neighbouring sun trap to smithereens. The resultant fireball roared against the side of the brick-built property and onto the remnants of the wooden gate that once joined the storage shed to the shop. The fire then leapt from the gate to the frame of the ground-floor bay window of Danny's bedroom and quickly the front door of the Rogers' accommodation. Scotty sat motionless on the BMX, his jaw hanging even looser than its usual resting position, transfixed at the burning ruins of the storage shed and the rapidly spreading flames engulfing the last corner shop.

*

It wasn't in Colin Salter's nature to bow down to anyone, his public-school education had created a sense of privilege and arrogance which, combined with his working-class roots, had earned him a reputation as a vicious street-fighter in the world of commerce. The financial loss had shaken him to his very core, but the loss of power at the helm of the family company had seriously eroded his hubris. He now sat dumbfounded as the spectre of his future was outlined to him by the woman he had so haughtily referred to as Rick Parfitt in a frock.

'Now please listen carefully to me, Mr Salter, we intend to keep the Salter name, and normally that would extend to keeping you on the board as a figurehead with no power or say in operations or strategy, but with a healthy retainer for your troubles. However, our contact in the Metropolitan Police informs us that following the search of your office they have evidence to link you to charges of false accounting and insider trading.'

'Fuck off… what the fuck do you take me for? There's nothing that can link me to any of that. I didn't come down in the last shower sweetheart.'

JBJ threw the buff A5 envelope across the table, its contents spilling out as it reached Colin Salter. He picked up the papers, photocopies of signed memos sent to him by that imbecile Bullshit Ellis stating the illicit actions he had undertaken at his instruction. It was all there, the profit manipulation designed to deceive the board and the shareholders.

'I've never seen these before!' Colin Salter for once truthfully blustered. 'I never received these and you can't prove that I did.'

'It's not down to me to prove, Mr Salter, that's the job of the constabulary. I also know that your former colleague Brad Ellis is prepared to give written testimony against you. It will be up to the courts to decide your innocence. Whatever the outcome, you will be publicly ruined.'

The street fighter in Colin Salter wouldn't allow him to go down without trying to deliver his own knockout blow.

'Innocence! What about you, you lying bitch? You got that job under false pretences and I can pursue you through the courts; that was industrial espionage. I'll drag you and your inbred hillbilly daddy's arses through the courts.'

'I applied for the job in my own name, Mr Salter, I never hid my past employment history, you never bothered to follow it up – I think you left that task to your right-hand man. All I have ever done is carry out the board's instructions. It's all minuted, Salter.'

'Well I've got my own witnesses that will vouch that I've never received those memos and that I knew nothing about any of it. That PA of mine, she will vouch for me.'

Salter spat the words while trying to remember that damn girl's name.

'Well you can see the memos have been stamped and dated as received, that was by Suzie Kent, I believe that's the name of your PA.... unlike you, I wouldn't ever forget, because she's my sister.'

Of course she was – that was the knockout blow. A floored Colin Salter looked on as JBJ slid a sheet of paper in front of him.

'We can make all of the charges go away and legally buy Mr Ellis's discretion if you sign over your remaining shareholding to us and relinquish any claim to the Salter name. As you can see, that is a very generous offer, it's only 10% below current market value. This is a one-time offer and you have exactly 60 seconds from now to decide, at which point the offer will be withdrawn. I have my lawyer waiting outside with all of the supplementary paperwork and of course your payment in full.'

A crestfallen Colin Salter looked round at the boardroom for the last time and unscrewed the lid of his Mount Blanc fountain pen.

CHAPTER 24

The rusty Subaru van rattled its way through the Wisdom Estate on its return from the evening cash and carry run. Due to the cash flow shortage it was now necessary to make daily trips, and by the evening Eddie was unfit to drive or even successfully perambulate with the trolley around the vast expanse of the cash and carry. Danny had now settled into the daily routine of coming in from work and driving Marilyn to the cash and carry and helping loading and unloading the stock, although with each trip the volume of purchases was diminishing. It was a self-fulfilling prophecy, the less stock they held, the more lines ran out and the remaining loyal customers would have wasted journeys, so fewer customers came and takings were reduced, meaning less money to replenish the stock and so the circle decreased. It was laid bare to Danny. He could see that the business was dying and it pained him to watch his mum in denial about the business and his dad's liver condition – both were now at a critical point of failure. As they turned into the bottom end of Hawtrey Way they heard an explosion and the night sky briefly illuminated with a bright flash, succeeded by a flickering orange haze. They looked at each other.

'My god, that's an explosion – what the hell has he done!' Marilyn had experienced many occasions of the gas being left on after Eddie had used the cooker for a late-night fry-up to satiate the alcohol munchies.

Trevor and Leslie were sitting in their lounge watching *Emmerdale* when fragments of the storage shed rained against the lounge window. The force of the explosion made the door knocker lift and forcefully land sounding like an urgent request for assistance. Trevor leapt to his feet and threw the curtains open. They looked in horror at the flames rapidly engulfing The Corner Stores. Leslie was already calling the fire brigade.

'Grab the hose!' he shouted at Trevor. Normally Trevor would have responded with a quip like 'not tonight I've got a headache', so he did pause a beat before throwing open the front door to grab the garden hose that was attached to the tap at the side of the bungalow. As he stepped out, he noticed Tramp Juice Ron's son perched on a child's bike staring, as if hypnotised, at the growing flames.

'Hey, Ron's son, get over here and give me a hand.'

Scotty snapped out of his trance and threw the bike to the floor. He ran over, grabbed the hose and started to run with it across the road. As he did, it unravelled from the wire wheel that it was housed on. He got as far as the lay-by in front of the shop before it was fully extended. Trevor turned on the tap and ran across the road to direct the hose. Leslie ran across the road to join them, all three had tears rolling down their cheeks from the billowing smoke clouds.

'The fire engine's on its way, they wanted to know if anyone was inside.'

'The van's not in the driveway, surely no one could have failed to hear that explosion?' Trevor and Leslie looked at each other and simultaneously screamed.

'Eddie!'

'Look… over there!' Scotty dropped the hose and was running straight through the flames on the site of the old storage shed. Before Trevor or Leslie could say anything, he had disappeared into a smoke screen. He burst back out through the flames with Ronnie and Reggie under either arm, his once orange tracksuit now sporting a smoke-stained camouflage. He dropped them onto the pavement and headed back in. Seconds later he was back out choking as he lay a lifeless Elvis onto the pavement.

The fire station was in the centre of Heathview and only a two-minute drive from the Wisdom Estate. However, the response time would be, at best, 15 minutes as the station was manned by retained firefighters all of whom had other jobs and were not on standby at the station. Whenever there was an emergency, the station siren sounded across the village to scramble the firefighters. However, it also alerted a ghoulish band of followers that would hop into their cars and drive down to the station in order to follow the engine at high speed to the emergency scene – from a child's arm being stuck in a railing to a burning inferno started from an unattended chip pan.

As the van pulled up outside the shop, Marilyn and Danny saw the remains of the storage shed, the bags of coal that were stored inside meant the blaze still had sufficient fuel to continue unabated. They were also treated to the surreal sight of a soot-covered youth in a brown and orange tracksuit coughing and choking as he lay next to a motionless Elvis, while Reggie and Ronnie barked excitedly as Trevor and Leslie sprayed water over the blazing front door. Marilyn and Danny jumped out of the van, to the sound of the fire station siren wailing its frantic call to arms across the village.

'Eddie's in there, Eddie's in there!' screamed Marilyn. She was now hysterical. When Trevor and Leslie had said his drinking would kill him she had never envisaged this grisly end. Danny ran to the front door and tried to put his keys in the lock but the heat was too intense and started to burn his face. He dropped the keys, choking as he retreated back to the lay-by.

'We need to break the lounge window, he'll be in there!' Danny screamed. The lounge was situated at the end of the property above the shop and was as yet untouched by the flames that were rapidly engulfing the whole building.

'Have you got any ladders?' Danny shouted at Trevor and Leslie.

'Sorry, only stepladders for the Christmas decorations, it is only a little bungalow', said Leslie apologetically.

Danny pointed at the debris from the storage shed strewn across the road. 'Get some of those bits of concrete rubble and start throwing them at the window, you too Scotty, that hose is pointless.'

Tramp Juice Ron pulled up into the lay-by and jumped out of the van with the engine still running. Trevor and Leslie's first thoughts were whether the arrival of his van with its usual highly combustible load presented a greater risk to life in the near vicinity.

'Eddie's in there!' Marilyn was still screaming at a pitch that was as shrill as the continuing village fire alert siren.

Tramp Juice Ron ran at the front door and it gave way to the force of his shoulder. He fell into the hallway as and was immediately enshrouded by the smoke within. Scotty tried to follow but was beaten back by the flames that now engulfed the doorway.

Danny was throwing with all his might at the upstairs lounge window but couldn't get the necessary power while throwing the stones at such an acute upward trajectory. He then adjusted by stepping further back. He successfully landed with a couple of large stones but with insufficient force to break the pane. He could only hope it would wake Eddie from his slumber or smoke inhalation.

The fire crew were making their way to the station by various means, Bruce 'Jesse' Wyatt's garage and accommodation was directly opposite the fire station so he was already changed into his uniform and preparing the appliance. He was the driver and had picked up the radio call that it was at The Corner Stores, and he now sat behind the wheel in a state of high agitation waiting for the rest of the team to join him.

Inside the hallway, Tramp Juice Ron could barely see. Fortunately, his years of sucking on rollies 15 hours a day had given his eyes and lungs an unhealthy tolerance to smoke. He remembered the wooden frame open staircase was to his left, it was barely visible through the smoke and flames. He started the ascent. He managed the first eight stairs in two giant steps before the staircase collapsed. As he fell back towards the hall, Tramp Juice Ron made a frantic last grasp and caught the remaining top stair. With all his might, he pulled himself up onto the hall landing and lay momentarily on his back breathing heavily, his rollie still attached to his bottom lip. Still on his back, he kicked open the door to the first bedroom – it was empty. He flipped over onto his hands and knees realising that keeping low would minimise his smoke ingestion. He looked left into the open bathroom door – empty; he then continued to crawl forward along the hallway. When he stood up to open the second bedroom door, the smoke severely stung his already watering eyes. He pushed the door open, the room was empty, just a single unmade bed now rapidly engulfing in smoke. There was only the lounge ahead of him, directly above the shop. He dropped to the floor again, choking on the smoke that was increasing in density as the flames took hold in the hallway behind him. The door to the lounge was shut. Still on all fours, he reached up and turned the handle, pushed the door open and crawled in. Through the haze of smoke he could see Eddie slumped on the settee, an Irish voice rose from the speakers of the record player. 'I eat when I'm hungry and I'll drink when I'm dry…' He closed the door behind him and took the ornamental rug from the centre of the lounge carpet and wedged it under the door to reduce the amount of smoke from seeping in. '….if the moonshine don't kill me I'll live till I die.' Tramp Juice Ron opened all of the windows, two at the far end of the room overlooking the park and then the three windows above the front of the shop. As he did, he heard a cheer and applause from the gathering crowd below.

'They aren't going to get here in time.'

As Danny spoke, the bathroom window blew out, and the fractured glass rained on the screaming crowd below. The Bowfords were endeavouring to keep the growing crowd at a suitable distance as they watched in dismay at the burning building, Byron Bowford periodically turning back to look nervously at his own thatched cottage roof wondering if a stray ember carried by a gust of wind would change their life forever. One unfortunate had escaped the Bowfords' rigorous crowd management, Cloth-Eared Jack had persuaded Dot to come out to watch The Corner Stores burning, a decision he was now regretting as a shard of glass had landed on the side of his head dismembering his good ear, which now lay on the pavement in the precise locus of the trolley incident. He had a curious smile on his face as the Spacehopper dragged him by his ankles, his bleeding head wound leaving a slug-like trail in his wake. His mind had already turned to the huge potential jackpot of the insurance claim. Danny ran forward to the front of the shop and reached behind the green crates that were used to display the fruit and veg and pulled out the metal hand crank, which he inserted into the socket of the awning which he started to frantically unwind. The fire had now enveloped the shop and he could feel the heat burning his face as he watched the produce in the shop ignite and melt on the shelves.

'Go and get the mattresses off your beds, they are going to have to jump, it's their only chance,' Danny bellowed at the crowd. Trevor and Leslie looked at each other, both thinking the same thought – 'Hope they're not stained, we'd never live it down.'

'…if the ocean was whiskey and I was a duck, I'd swim to the bottom and drink my way up…'

Eddie felt a heavy blow across the side of his head, awakening him from his deep slumber. It was the substantial palm of Tramp Juice Ron's club-like hand that landed with enough force to potentially render a waking man unconscious again. However, Tramp Juice Ron had recognised the effects of his own handiwork and the milk bottle strewn next to the settee gave him the validation he required to realise that Eddie would take some rousing. Slowly, Eddie tried to lift his head as he attempted to focus on the shape in front of him. It started to reveal itself as Ronald Froggatt. He suddenly sat bolt upright, choking on the acrid smoke that was filling the room, trying to work out where he was and what the hell was going on.

'Shaps on fire boy, we gonna need to jump out of the window.' Tramp Juice Ron lifted all of the seat cushions from the settee and hurled them out of the window onto the two hastily arranged mattresses lying on the street below. They could feel the heat rising up from the shop below and the carpet had started to smoke, a point before ignition.

'…but the ocean ain't whiskey and I ain't a duck, so I'll stick to wild women and trust in my luck.'

The cheap panel door to the lounge disintegrated under the

heat and the fire immediately ignited the hi-fi speakers and the armchair positioned by the door generating clouds of toxic black acrid smoke as the flames rapidly spread towards the nearest open window. Tramp Juice Ron was really struggling to breathe as the fire greedily sucked the oxygen from the room. As he lifted Eddie so he was perched on the edge of the window, the curtains to his left caught fire and ignited the wooden curtain pole above them.

'It's an inferno, Ronald,' murmured a bemused Eddie.

'Brace yerself boy,' Tramp Juice Ron barely whispered through the fug as he pushed a heavily inebriated Eddie off the edge of the window. The crowd assembled below let out a collective gasp as Eddie fell forward out of the window, headfirst into the garish orange Happy Shopper awning below. As he landed on the awning, he did an involuntary somersault and bounced off, landing feet first onto the mattress landing area. There was a split second when the crowd were going to applaud, almost expecting a row of judges to hold up a perfect ten scorecard for his miraculous gymnastic landing. But the audible sound of his right ankle snapping like a dry autumn twig instead produced a communal wince and groan. As Tramp Juice Ron waited for a screaming Eddie to be helped off the landing pad, his back felt unusually hot. He realised he was actually on fire. As he jumped from the lounge window, flames leapt from the back of his tatty herring bone overcoat and nylon rope belt. He landed feet first on the awning, but instead of bouncing onto the mattress, his ample frame and dealer boots tore straight through the Happy Shopper logo, ripping the rollie from his lips. He landed on his back with a heavy impact, extinguishing the fire – just as the fire engine turned into Hawtrey Way.

CHAPTER 25

It was rather cosy staying in Granny Smith's bungalow. Her daughter had been insistent that the Rogers could stay there as long as they needed to get back onto their feet – which in Eddie's case was likely to be some time as he was still trying to get used to hobbling around on crutches, his leg encased in plaster. He had not only broken his ankle but also his tibia – in two places. The consultant constantly reminded him that he was extremely fortunate not to have suffered more serious injuries from a fall from that height. Eddie always maintained from that night on that alcohol had saved his life by ensuring his body was limp and unresponsive when he was pushed out of the lounge window by Tramp Juice Ron, to which Marilyn angrily pointed out that if it hadn't been for Danny's swift actions he probably wouldn't be here today spouting such utter drivel. Eddie required an operation on his broken leg and spent two weeks in traction. The hospital staff had quickly recognised the symptoms of alcohol withdrawal once the anaesthetic had worn off and provided medication to soothe his safe passage through the delirium tremens. The staff nurse had taken Danny into a private room to explain the situation as Marilyn had been too distraught to visit.

'We have had to medicate your father for alcohol withdrawal. Are you or your mother aware of your father's drinking problem? It's actually an illness…'

Danny felt his stomach turn and his mouth go dry at the phrase 'drink problem'. It was only later that afternoon as he was sitting trying to calm his father who was seeing foxes run along the end of his bed that he realised the extent of the problem. He knew that he now had to be their decision maker, and one of the first duties he would have to fulfil would be to explain this illness to Marilyn. It was something that would always live with them. The doctor had quite bluntly explained to Eddie that he had sustained significant liver damage, and that although the liver had great powers of recuperation, in his particular case he had unfortunately nearly reached 'George Best' on the damage scalo-meter and it was therefore unlikely to recover to any significant extent. He also emphasised at great length that any further ingestion on the industrial scale that Eddie had previously indulged would lead to him wearing a wooden overcoat. As the doctor started to outline the other underlying medical issues, his voice faded into background noise as Eddie tried to reconcile the enormity of his situation in his own mind, trying to calculate what a 'safe' level of drinking would look and feel like. He also wondered if he could encourage Tramp Juice Ron to expand his illicit empire to incorporate a marijuana farm, after all, his lungs were still pretty much virgin territory as he had never smoked.

The solicitor had just arrived at Granny Smith's bungalow which he had decided was an easier meeting place rather than everyone trekking to his office, especially with Eddie's somewhat limited mobility. They sat in silence in the lounge with just the sounds of the clock on the sideboard and the snuffling of Ronnie and Reggie from the kitchen as they pressed their noses to the gap at the bottom of the kitchen door to try and identify the unfamiliar occupant. They had survived the fire with just some damage to their fur which had been burned off leaving bald patches all over their bodies. They looked like two moth-ravaged fox furs. Elvis hadn't survived the smoke inhalation and his ashes had been laid to rest on Granny Smith's grave, his final resting place at her feet. At least that was the plan before a gust of wind caught the ashes as Danny was solemnly decanting them onto the grave carrying them across the graveyard, catching and lifting them into the air to be spread far and wide across Heathview.

The solicitor, Brian East, was reading the last will and testament of Granny Smith, and had asked that the Rogers and Shirley attend.

'I want to explain that due to her proximity, Rose Smith's daughter was not able to attend the reading, but as nominated executor of the will I have already advised her of its contents earlier today, and as you may expect she has been left this property and £32, 653, the majority of Rose's life savings. I will now read the rest of the will verbatim:

'To my housekeeper and friend Shirley – I'm afraid I don't know her surname – I bequeath the sum of £3,000. To Mr and Mrs Rogers, two of the kindest people I have met, I bequeath the sum of £3,000. To Danny Rogers, I bequeath the entire contents of the garage to do with as he wishes.'

Brian East handed over the two cheques to Shirley and the Rogers, both of whom were in a state of shock. He then passed an envelope containing the garage door key to Danny.

*

By the time the fire crew led by Bruce 'Jesse' Wyatt had arrived with their ghoulish entourage, the fire had really taken hold. They fought for over an hour to contain the blaze from spreading to nearby properties, with the Bowfords anxiously following any airborne ember that drifted from the inferno in the direction of their thatched cottage across the road. Eventually the fire was extinguished, with the building and its contents raised to the ground. The police and fire service investigators had concluded that an accidental explosion of a gas canister, most likely caused by an overheating freezer motor, had led to the catastrophic fire which destroyed The Corner Stores. The insurers were rather more sceptical due to the apparent financial difficulties that they had interpreted from the decreasing funds in the Rogers' business account. However, proving the downturn in business was problematic as the books had perished in the fire, and their bookkeeping son Danny Rogers had given a statement that there were significantly behind on their banking and so the considerable cash and cheque takings awaiting banking had also gone up in a puff of smoke. The insurance investigator had to accept the forensic examination of the fire service as the evidential scene had been disturbed by the time they were aware of the incident. Bruce 'Jesse' Wyatt had ensured that all incriminating evidence had been thoroughly removed even before the fire service investigators were on the scene. The insurance investigator had then gone door to door for eyewitnesses, but the only two eyewitnesses said the same thing – the storage shed exploded and Eddie Rogers was trapped in the lounge and Marilyn and Danny Rogers arrived sometime later after the explosion. All of the alibis were watertight. With great reluctance, they agreed to pay out for the building and contents.

*

The garage was situated at the end of the driveway, detached from the small semi-detached bungalow. It had two wooden doors that opened out; they had been painted lime green although the paint had peeled off in several places and the colour faded. Danny pushed the key into the Chubb lock with difficulty. He tried to turn the lock but couldn't move the key even using both thumbs and forefingers. He pulled the key out very slightly and tried again; this time the lock reluctantly opened. He pulled the unfastened door open, then unbolted the other door and pulled it open. The garage had a dank musty smell, dust particles danced in the thin shard of sunlight peeking through a small gap of uncovered window where the old bed sheet that was hung across the window was slightly too small for its intended job. It seemed immediately obvious to Danny that no one had been in there for many years. In front of him was a vehicle covered in a dust sheet. He pulled the sheet off and beneath the cloud of disturbed dust was an immaculate canary yellow 1965 E Type Jag. The car had belonged to Granny Smith's husband who had spent many hours restoring it to showroom condition. He rarely drove the car and as a result the wear and tear and the mileage on the vehicle was unbelievably low. The mileage was at the sort of level that even Bruce 'Jesse' Wyatt wouldn't have the audacity to deliver as part of his MOT time machine service. The door was unlocked, Danny climbed in and looked in the glove box where he found the keys and logbook. With trembling hands he tried to turn the engine over but the battery was dead, but in his own imagination he could already hear the throaty roar of the engine. But what truly astonished and scared him was that his only thought at that epic moment was that it could only ever be Jenny in that passenger seat, by his side.

*

The clearance of The Corner Stores site required brute force and ignorance, and so it came to pass that Scotty and Tramp Juice Ron were filling up the second skip of the day when an astonished Marilyn and Eddie drove into the lay-by. It was the first time that they had returned to the shop together.

'Ronald, what's going on? You shouldn't be doing that with your back, weren't you supposed to be on bed rest?'

'Least we can do boy, a'ter the young'en, well best ye don't know – insurance an all.'

Ronald Froggatt theatrically looked around and gave a conspiratorial flick to the side of his nose.

'The boy meant well.'

Marilyn quickly interjected.

'But Ron there really is no need, it's covered in the insurance settlement and the demolition company will clear all the debris from the site, they are scheduled to come next week.'

Eddie then slowly explained.

'The building needs to be demolished Ron, as it is structurally unsound and it's not economically viable to repair. So the whole site needs to be demolished and rebuilt.'

'Be gad to 'ave the old place back boy.'

The rollie bobbed on the man-mountain's bottom lip.

'Supermarkets nar good, nar good at all boy.'

'Well I'm afraid it won't be Ron. The plans have been put in for a pair of semi-detached houses to be built on the site. That accident, however it started…'

Marilyn paused and cast her eye across to Scotty who was just staring gormlessly at Eddie without a flicker of recognition.

'...well, it has given us a chance to start again. Times are changing, a corner shop like ours just can't compete with the likes of Salter's, we can see that now. We would have probably been bankrupt within three months if we had carried on trading.'

Tramp Juice Ron looked crestfallen as though his world had come to an end, and in truth a big part of it had. His daily visit to The Corner Stores, unbeknownst to the Rogers, was invariably one of the highlights of his day. The Rogers were in an exclusive band of four that were always pleased to see him; Scotty and Dog were the other members of that unique club. They were always there to help him decide on his tea and were often the only people he spoke to in a day (he often went days without conversing with Scotty). Out of utmost respect to their busy day he always left it to just before closing before descending on them, he also reasoned it would be unlikely that anyone else would be there. He knew that his appearance and personal hygiene wasn't to everyone's taste, but the Rogers had never judged him, and Eddie Rogers had always been a good customer and their unconventional barter system worked well for both of them.

'They even offered us a Salter's franchise to operate if we rebuilt The Corner Stores. They are now looking to open a series of mini marts they call them, apparently they are very popular in America. But what is the point of making profits for the company that put you out of business and now want to own your soul? For us, it was always more than trying to make lots of money, we quickly realised that it was about being at the heart of the community. We made deliveries to elderly customers when it actually made no business sense to do so. We allowed some of our customers to buy goods on tick, which sometimes led to them doing a runner owing us money. But I think what hurt us the most was when the community kicked us and Mrs Garwood when we were down. Most of our loyal customers deserted us for the wider choice and much cheaper prices, but, of course, we are told it is all in the name of progress. We swap price guns for electronic point-of-sales systems where the till operatives are monitored on the amount of items they scan a minute – which tells you it's about getting the customers out of the door. We might not always ring the price up correctly, but we always spare the time of day and go out of the way to know our customers. But I guess that is a microcosm of where society is heading. Napoleon is supposed to have said we are a nation of shopkeepers, as if that is an insult, but I'm proud to have been just that.'

There was a quaver in Marilyn's voice as she desperately fought back her tears at the injustice of it all. Everything they had worked for and dreamed of lay in the rubble and ashes before her, and in truth it was destroyed before the fire through evolution of commerce and technology. She had been deliberately oblivious to the changing world around her, instead choosing to focus on her steadfast belief that good would always triumph over evil. But she knew the truth of the matter all along, that a small cog is just an annoying irrelevance in an emerging digital world. There is no one to step in and save you, no guiding hand or comforting parent to protect you and make everything OK. But as her nature dictated, Marilyn tried to pull a positive outcome from the abyss of despair – her Eddie was sober for the first time in years and they had been granted this opportunity to start again, whatever form that new adventure may take.

Eddie took her hand as they stood in front of the ruins.

'Come on love, like the old Cub Scouts motto, we did our best, you me and Danny. We are part of the village history and we will always be able to say with our heads held high that we were the last corner shop.'

He felt slightly melancholy as the early morning buzz of the extremely potent home-grown ganja had started to wear off. He kicked himself for not knowing that Tramp Juice Ron had been hydroponically cultivating and selling skunk for years. He would try and have discrete word with him before they set sail as his supply was running dangerously low, after all they still had some pouches of tobacco from the last ever cash and carry run that were lying in the van doing nothing.

END

Printed in Great Britain
by Amazon

81892515R00128